The Frozen City

The Frozen City

David Arscott & David J. Marl

London
GEORGE ALLEN & UNWIN
Boston　　　　Sydney

George Allen & Unwin (Publishers) Ltd,
40 Museum Street, London WC1A 1LU, UK

George Allen & Unwin (Publishers) Ltd,
Park Lane, Hemel Hempstead, Herts HP2 4TE, UK

Allen & Unwin Inc.,
9 Winchester Terrace, Winchester, Mass 01890, USA

George Allen & Unwin Australia Pty Ltd,
8 Napier Street, North Sydney, NSW 2060, Australia

First published in 1984

British Library Cataloguing in Publication Data

Arscott, David
   The frozen city.
I. Title   II. Marl, David J.
823'.914[F]   PR6051.R/
ISBN 0-04-823258-0

Set in 11 on 12½ point Imprint by Computape (Pickering) Ltd,
North Yorkshire
and printed in Great Britain by
Billing and Sons Ltd, London and Worcester

For Aubrey Davis, who discovered the city

Contents

PART ONE

Arrival

1   Curfew

A group of men, five or six of them, their faces hidden within large hooded garments which fell over their shoulders, moved silently in the gathering dusk under the tall windowless wall. They said nothing. Tom hesitated, wanting to ask them where he should go, but there was something sinister about their silent progress and he stood still and watched them pass.

When he had entered the city through the large gateway, only minutes before, he had been seized by feelings of hope and excitement. The guard, turned from the grille to laugh at a joke shared with a girl in the room behind him, had not seen him slip inside.

It was the party following – a family pulling a handcart – which had caught the guard's attention, and even now Tom could hear the continuation of an argument, presumably about their identification papers. The voices were too distant to distinguish clearly. Nor was it possible to tell whether they spoke his own language.

Tom clutched at his coat and felt the picture safe in the pocket inside. It had been a long and a lonely journey. His shoes were battered and leaking, his trousers blotched with mud from endless hiking across fields. His skin had been flayed by the elements, so that it was brown and coarse and tough.

He felt uneasy now that he had arrived. The vision of the city had driven him on, but the reality was not as he had imagined. A thin mist swirled between the lights affixed to the high wall, and there was the sweet smell of woodsmoke adrift on the evening air. The group of man having passed on, there was a desolate emptiness in the narrow, twisting street, broken only by a distant hammering and a muttered conversation at some hidden corner.

There were two paths he could take. One followed the high wall, running round the vast bulk of the metropolis, and seeming as if it would go on for ever. The other turned inwards, sloping down to an area enclosed by tall buildings. His feet led him along this route.

How hostile the city silence seemed? In the dark nights of his journey, sheltering in a hedge bottom or in the corner of a ruined barn while the moon skimmed the ashen clouds overhead, he had suffered from cold, damp and other discomforts. He had known fear when he was lost or when unseen wild creatures came snuffling close. He had been inexpressibly lonely, far from any human habitation. But never had he experienced the feeling of rejection which came over him in these narrow streets.

A volley of bells rang, sudden and loud, somewhere above his head. They seemed to echo on and on, further and further away, until he realised that there were other bells, countless, all of them pealing at the same time throughout the city. And at once there was new movement: doors opening and closing; a sprinting figure; somewhere a horse, its hooves clattering and skidding on a hard surface, as if it were being backed into a cart.

Even as Tom stood indecisive, puzzled by the commotion, a bulky shadow materialised from the mist, passed on and then, pausing, half-turned back to him. A deep voice admonished him.

'Get along young fellow. Do you want to be stranded at curfew?'

And then he was gone into the murk.

Tom was startled as much by the man's language as by what he said. It was his own tongue, though spoken differently, with a harsh accent. After weeks of wandering alone, without the sound of a human voice, it was like a blessing.

But the curfew! The bells rang on, and they seemed to grow more urgent by the second. Where could he go? Who would take him in?

The din ceased, momentarily, to be followed by the intoning of a solitary, more sombre, bell. From the direction in which he had come there was a metallic grating, as the huge outer gates of the city were swung to and the heavy bolts thrust home. The light was failing, and the mist slipped down into the streets as if stalking any unfortunate who might still be abroad.

Tom shrank into a doorway, petrified. He wished himself

4

miles away under a thorn bush, alone but not menaced. He had not examined his tattered clothing out there in the uncharted wilderness: now he looked down at his rags and felt weak and ashamed.

At last the monotonous tolling died away. In the silence he heard himself breathing, shallowly. Along the street dark curtains were pulled across the only windows he could see. No sounds came from within. The fog, enveloping the lights on the high walls so that they broke up into dim, fuzzy circles, dampened his jacket and began to soak through his shirt.

And then, distant but growing closer, came the regular tattoo of marching feet. It rose from a light flutter to a distinct tramping, until Tom knew it was very close, behind the nearest buildings. There must be a dozen of them, the city guards. They came on and on, until – clearly no more than a few hundred yards away – on a sharp order (which Tom could hear) they halted. There was a shout, the scrabble of running feet. A man's voice called out, despairingly.

'No, no!' Tom heard. 'Misunderstanding! Lost!'

This was followed by a brief scuffle and a hideous cry. It seemed to have no ending, but to float on the dense mist, seeking him out where he cowered in the doorway.

The soldiers came on. The clack of their boots on the metalled surface grew sharper and louder, until they turned the corner – there were in two files, arms lightly swinging – and advanced towards him. They were so close that he could make out the design of their uniform, blue and green with gold epaulettes. The leader wore a large drooping moustache.

Tom was lifting his hands as if, impossibly, to hide himself from their view, when the door behind him swung open and, stumbling backwards, he collapsed in a heap on the floor.

2 The White Room

A hand dragged him inside and the door slammed shut. For several seconds his numbed senses were aware only of the closed door, its heavy metal knob. And then, slowly, he stood and turned round.

He was in a room, that was the fact of it, but the feel of it was very different. Green lights seemed to turn the warm air to liquid, and the faces that gazed upon him appeared to be fixed to bodies that swayed like seaweed in a gently swirling current. Indeed, the whole room began to sway, and Tom found himself unable to breathe. The green, underwater world faded until the faces became pale globes floating in darkness, these too ebbing, dissolving. He fell to the floor once more.

Sunlight flooding his senses. He was alone again, and in a different room, large but sparsely furnished. There was a bed, upon which he lay, two chairs and a writing desk. Opposite there was a large window, but the glass was frosted and it was set in a simple frame with no obvious means of opening it. The walls were white and interrupted by just one small painting, the subject of which was hard to determine under its cracked layers of darkened varnish.

Tom tried to move but his legs felt weak. The harshness of the light hurt his eyes and he rested his hand across his face, trying all the while to remember the events that had brought him here. There was a tangle of confusing images, but as he recalled the soldiers, the scream and the green room full of faces, his confusion turned to fear. What was he doing here? Who had brought him to this bed? Why did his legs refuse to move? Was the door to this room locked, and had he become a prisoner?

The last question was answered almost immediately, for the

door in question swung open and a girl stepped inside carrying a tray. She smiled at him.

'Mother thought you would like some breakfast.'

She put the tray down beside Tom, who only stared silently at her.

'Fancy you being out after the curfew bell. Whatever possessed you?'

He remained silent. His mouth was dry, and the words which kept racing around his mind refused to fit themselves together to form a sentence. The girl sat on the end of the bed.

'You don't say much, do you? You really are ill, perhaps. We thought it was fright that made you faint.'

Now she spoke coaxingly.

'Have some of the breakfast, won't you? You're ever so thin.'

Tom looked at the tray upon which rested a small jug of milk and a plate with bread and cold meat. He reached for the milk, drank a mouthful, and felt himself able to speak.

'You're very kind. . . .'

But once more he lapsed into silence, this time because the urgency of his hunger had suddenly taken control of him. He broke pieces from the bread and pushed them into his mouth. It was delicious bread, coarse and nutty, and the meat was salty and satisfying.

'Been here two days and nights, you have. Lying there shivering and muttering. Mother says you've churned up the elements for us: that misty weather lifted the night you came here and we're into the clear skies and frosts of the first winter.'

The girl, who must be about his own age, sat and watched him eat. What did she think of him? His clothes were worn and dirty. His hair was unkempt. He smelled a bit, he was sure.

'Would you like some more?'

Meeting his dazed expression she shook her head lightly and was gone again, downstairs.

For much of that day he slept, his slumber interrupted at intervals by the girl with his meals. He would try to rouse himself, allow her to push food between his lips, tilt a cup so that he could drink. Then he would fall back again, faint and indescribably drowsy. He felt, in the fitful moments when his brain cleared, that hour upon hour was passing. Only gradually did consciousness steal back.

7

Daylight was fading. As he lay still, staring at the darkened ceiling, he seemed to hear a sound rising from beneath him, an eery sound as of distant voices raised in song. In was indistinct, yet when he shook his head from side to side the singing did not go away.

Then, from much closer, female voices rose on the air, one of them anxious and admonishing.

'He can't stay, you know that, don't you? He might endanger us.'

'He's too weak to go anywhere at present, mother. Give him a little time.'

'Why did it have to be our door – and during the meeting, too? Do you think he recognised anyone?'

'It was too dark, and he fainted almost straightaway.'

'He can't stay. He'll have to go.'

Then the voices ceased, leaving on the air only the faint singing which lulled him once more into a deep sleep.

By the middle of the next day he was feeling much stronger, and with his strength came curiosity. What was the meaning of the green room and its occupants? Who was this mysterious girl who bent over him with such tenderness?

'Are you able to walk now?' she asked.

He levered himself to his feet. His legs were still weak but a few hesitant steps answered the girl's question. She looked at him, her eyes large and dark blue, and smiled sadly. It came upon him quite suddenly that she was very pretty.

'I've brought you fresh clothes,' she said. 'There's a washroom next door. Soon you must go from here.'

He sat on the bed, heavily. Tears began to fill his eyes.

'But where can I go?'

'That I can't answer.'

'Who are you?'

But she ignored the question, busying herself with the tray.

'Why do you care for me and then turn me away?'

'It has to be,' she said. 'I know nothing of you and you nothing of me.'

He reached forward and clutched at her arm.

'I remember a green room. When I arrived. You know what I am speaking of.'

8

'We can't talk of such things.'

'And last evening I heard singing – voices like a choir.'

She pulled herself away.

'If you have any regard for me,' she said in a strained voice, 'you will never ask me such questions or ever mention this house to another soul.'

Tom could only nod miserably.

For a while, after she had gone, he wandered around the room exercising his legs. Closer inspection of the picture revealed nothing: it was, perhaps, a portrait, as there seemed a paler oval at the centre. Was he imagining a strange resemblance to the picture he carried in his pocket? At the thought of it Tom looked anxiously for his coat and found it draped over a chair. The picture was still there.

The frosted glass of the window prevented a view of the street below, although he judged that he was a long way up. The sky itself had turned from pale blue to sombre grey, and fluttering blurred white shapes beyond the glass suggested that it was snowing.

On the wall, below the window, he saw something scratched into the white plaster. It was a tiny inscription, and he peered closely to read it:

> Wear me as your helmet
> falling masonry will break
> across my back.
> Wear me as your spiked heel
> I will bite into ice for you.
> T.W.

He did not fully understand the words, but the initials seemed to spring at him from the wall.

At first light next morning the girl appeared, carrying a black overcoat. Her eyes were red, as if she had been crying.

'You'll need this.'

It buttoned tightly across and reached down to his ankles. The buttons themselves were of a peculiar oval design, like a human eye.

The girl led the way down to the street, down to the door he had fallen through. Was this, then, the green room? Now it was not green or remarkable in any way. Confused, he stepped into the snowy street and, as he turned to say goodbye, she leaned forward and kissed his cheek. Then swiftly she was gone and the door was shut.

Tom stood in the gently falling snow, desolate and perplexed. The disappearance of the green room was one mystery: but there was another. As he had followed the girl down the stairs they had passed a partly open door. There had been stairs that led down and down, and far in the distance he could see lights and, he fancied, movement. But most startling of all he could hear a distant sound, a sound that was lacking in these empty streets – the sound of a city going about its business!

3 Scarlet Daggers

Tracks in the snow revealed that he was not the first abroad in the early morning. Animal footprints passed close to the house, one of each set lighter than the rest as if the creature were limping on its way. And fainter, because now almost silted up, there were the marks of large boots, the strides between them impressively lengthy.

The sky was heavily muffled with drifts of snow yet to fall, so that the light was murky although the sun had been above the horizon for more than an hour. Was that why the city seemed so desolate?

No, there was another reason. The buildings against the street had turned their backs upon it. As he started on his way Tom observed not only curtains still drawn against the day, but doors sealed up or obliterated. In many cases coarse rubble had been piled in the opening and roughly cemented, as if the task had been carried out in haste. In others the old unused door remained, but was heavily barred, with great sharp spikes driven into the ground before it. And where there was no side entrance, so that the front door was necessary, it was always immensely strong and pierced, at eye-level, by a Judas hole so that visitors could be closely scrutinised.

On his coat the flakes fell fat and white, lingering a moment before dissolving into a twinkling wetness. On the road the white carpet was already half an inch thick, and the roofs of houses – some lightly covered, others patched with dark areas of melted snow – revealed which parts of the buildings were inhabited. Always they were the parts furthest from the street.

And then he noticed a peculiar decoration. On each house, usually so high up as to be almost hidden under the eaves, there was a square black tablet. Painted on it was a single emblem – a scarlet dagger.

It was while he paused before one of these curious devices

11

which was rather lower than most (so that he could make out the ornate hilt of the weapon and its wickedly sharp point) that Tom's attention was caught by a movement further along the street.

Turning, he saw on the other side, half-hidden by the massive porch which screened the doorway of one of the larger houses, the figure of a boy. He was staring intently at Tom, and the marks in the snow behind him suggested that he had been trailing behind for some distance. He was a fair-haired lad, slightly built, and about his own age. He wore a long, dull brown jacket and a pair of black boots which reached almost to his knees, the sombre effect of this offset by a scarf the colour of fresh leaves wound several times around his neck.

Tom raised an arm in greeting, but there was no reply. The other youth continued to stare. When Tom called out, his voice echoed strangely in the empty snow-blanketed street.

'Can you help me? Do you live here?'

Still the other gazed impassively ahead, almost as if he were blind and deaf. But blind he certainly was not, for when Tom began to cross the street the young lad turned and ran.

Tom gave chase keenly, stronger than for many weeks after the food and rest he had recently enjoyed. But the long coat hampered him. He felt himself losing ground to his quarry, who seemed to sprint across the slithery surface with never a slip or check.

After they had run back along the street for a few hundred yards, the boy turned into a narrow alleyway Tom had not noticed before. It ran between the sides of houses – drawn curtains again, guarded doors – and into another street similar to the first. Tom saw the lad rounding a bend some way ahead, and then he was following footprints as his only guide.

Now there were sounds in the city, though muted and distant, but still there were no signs of any other living creature. He trod unbroken snow, always running alongside the tracks of the boy with the green scarf. These turned off the street to cross an area of wasteland, where an immense pile of rubble was the only testimony to what must once have been an imposing building. He picked his way over the ruin, wondering at such a complete destruction. The footprints plunged into a series of alleys.

The sounds were louder now: hammer-blows and what seemed to his ear to be the creaking of a winch and the scraping of metal on metal. And once (though he could not be sure, since the blood pounded in his ears from the running) he thought he heard a shout. And now there were other footprints entering this maze of closed-in passages – at first the tracks of individuals and then those of pairs and groups of three and four. It became increasingly difficult to follow the footprints of the boy who had been watching him with such interest.

And then – still before he had seen a single person – he came to a meeting of ways where the snow had been trampled to a dirty pulp. The clues disappeared. Five paths radiated from the spot, each running between poor, ugly buildings as grey and closed as any he had passed. One of them had had all its snow pounded to water and was obviously used as the main thoroughfare of this district, and Tom followed it, now slowed to a walk and apprehensive of what he might discover.

Smoke, swirling into his eyes and open mouth, was his first introduction to the hidden life of the place. It billowed over a wall which protruded half across the path. On the other side of the wall was a courtyard and to the rear of it a large furnace glimmered deep red with burning coals, and the smoke lifted off it in great dusty clouds alive with sparks.

'Who's this, then? Who's our visitor?'

The words were spoken from the shadowed recess of the workshop by a man who emerged slowly into the dull light of day. He was a tall thickset man, immensely broad across the shoulders. Despite the weather, he wore nothing above his trousers but a stained leather waistcoat. He beckoned with a large and muscular hand.

'Come on then. Let's be taking a look at you.'

Tom obeyed, meekly. Scared though he was, he thought the man's rough speech not necessarily hostile.

As he entered the workshop he saw a vast amount of equipment hanging on the walls – metalworking tools, hoops of iron, ornate grillwork and a host of other objects whose purpose he could not guess at. The heat of the great furnace swept across his face and he flinched from it.

'I was passing by,' Tom said.

The blacksmith (for such, clearly, he was) looked down on

13

him from his considerable height and folded his arms, as if contemplating what he should do. His shaggy black eyebrows drew together in concentration.

'Passing by,' he repeated, slowly.

And another voice, a lighter and a sneering voice rising from somewhere low down, joined in.

'Passing by was he? Bad luck for him, I'd say. Doesn't do to pass by when workers are needed.'

Tom stepped back to look behind the furnace and discovered a thin, shabbily dressed man sitting on the floor with his legs splayed out in an unnatural position. In his fists he held the handles of a pair of stout bellows and, keeping his eyes fixed upon Tom, he now jerked himself into action, pumping air into the coals.

'Apprentice material, I should say.'

The remarks of this wizened creature seemed to galvanise the blacksmith into action. He strode forward and grasped Tom by the shoulders.

'How strong are your arms?' he demanded. 'What work have you done?'

'Very little,' Tom stammered. 'I don't want to be a blacksmith.'

'Neither did I, but I had no choice. Nobody has any choice.'

Miraculously, there was a reprieve at that moment as two men entered the workshop. Tom noticed that, before speaking, they both half-turned towards one corner and gave a slight nod of the head, with a clenched hand against the forehead. It was done in a second, and as if from habit, and the men immediately engaged the smith in a conversation about iron gates. On the wall in the corner to which they had gestured was another plaque bearing the scarlet dagger emblem.

As the three men began to talk earnestly about prices Tom saw his chance of escape and began to edge gingerly towards the street. But he had moved only a few yards when the bellows-pumper sang out.

'Someone's trying to leave without permission.'

At this the blacksmith looked across, muttered something to his companions and grabbed Tom by the arm. Without a word he thrust him to the rear of the workshop, the force of it

14

hurling Tom against the wall. He fancied he heard a snigger from behind the furnace.

No sooner had the two men left than the singsong voice began again.

'Some people have to be shown the way. Some people don't make things easy for themselves.'

And again this appeared to stir the smith to anger. He seized hold of Tom by the arm and dragged him close to the furnace.

'Off with that coat!' he demanded. 'Let's see what you're made of!'

Trembling, Tom did as he was ordered. He watched the coat hurled across the room, to land in a heap on a wooden bench. Beneath the new coat he still wore the old thin garment with which he had arrived in the city, for it held his precious picture, and, anxious that this should not be damaged, he quickly slipped it off and ran over to the bench with it.

'What eagerness!' mocked the bellowsman, pumping vigorously, and Tom – in his desperation – was almost glad that he had run so that they might be lenient with him.

'But a little encouragement might make him more eager yet.'

The smith advanced with a heavy hammer in his hand. He was a fearful sight, his muscles picked out in the glare of the flames, his face gathered in a scowl.

'Get the rest off!' he commanded. 'It's a man's work you'll be doing.'

Stripped to the waist, Tom felt slight and puny against the blacksmith. The hammer that was pushed into his hand was heavy and unwieldy. The gases from the blazing coals choked him.

The blacksmith handed him a narrow bar of iron which immediately tilted away from him and hit the edge of the furnace with a sharp clang.

'Control the thing!' boomed the smith, putting a huge, muscular hand around Tom's. 'Lift it here.'

He manipulated the iron into position over the red coals and lifted the hand in which Tom held the hammer. He hurled the hammer down upon the iron so that pain shot up

15

Tom's arm, and he would have released his hold had not his hand been trapped inside the other's far stronger one.

'We're making hinges,' the smith explained, less harshly. 'Like these.'

He picked a piece of shaped and flattened metal from the floor. Tom had seen many like it on doors he had passed – large and heavy like the doors themselves. It was difficult to believe that they were created from such thick bars of solid iron. He liften the hammer and dropped it upon the metal. It seemed to make no impression.

'Someone isn't trying,' taunted the voice from the floor. 'Someone needs coaxing.'

Tom raised the hammer again, his shoulder aching with the mere lifting of it, and brought it down on the iron bar once more. Again there seemed no result.

'You come and do it, then!' he cried, in a sudden temper. 'If you're so clever, you can do it!'

A giggling laughter, which yet seemed totally without humour, was the only response.

'He can't,' muttered the blacksmith. 'His legs don't work.'

He pushed his thick fingers into the top of Tom's arms as if feeling for the sinews, causing him to cry out in pain.

'Someone isn't trying,' repeated the creature on the floor. 'Someone's being defiant.'

Now the blacksmith seemed to lose all patience. He shoved Tom violently in the back and again lifted his arm and dealt the metal a resounding blow. Tom's whole body shook with the force of it. The smith repeated the action, roughly and violently, and again and again. Sobs rose through Tom's tortured body, his breath escaping in short gasps between the blows. He could not cry for mercy. It felt as if he himself were being beaten against the metal on the furnace. His head swam and his eyes closed.

And then it stopped. A woman of middle-age had entered the workshop. Despite a clumsiness of gait and a dowdiness of clothing, which emphasised the shapelessness of her body, she clearly commanded respect. She seemed to pay no particular attention to the scene by the furnace, nor did she utter a single word of greeting. The smith released his grip on Tom to watch the newcomer cross the room towards a door in the far wall.

16

Before she reached it, however, she swung round to the bench on which Tom's clothes lay. Something had evidently caught her attention. She lifted the new overcoat and took one of the buttons between her fingers. After examining it closely she looked at Tom for the first time.

'Where did you get this?' she asked urgently.

Tom was unable to speak. The shock of his ill-treatment by the blacksmith seemed to have affected his vocal chords. And he was unsure of what he should say. He treasured the memory of his time in the white room as the one pleasant interlude in months of hardship and fear.

The woman signalled towards the pile of clothing.

'Fetch these and follow me,' she ordered.

The blacksmith stood passively by as Tom left his side, gathered his clothing and passed through the doorway. Even the bellows-pumper remained silent, as if overawed.

Beyond the door was a wood-panelled hallway, where the roar of the furnace was already dulled, and then a lighted corridor along which Tom followed the ungainly figure of his rescuer.

He was taken into a small room, with warm-coloured wainscoting and large and deep armchairs. Tom dressed himself while the woman busied herself in a cabinet, at last laying her hands upon a pair of spectacles. She put them on.

'Come now,' she said, recognising Tom's nervousness. 'Sit in that chair and stop your teeth chattering.'

'I'm sorry,' Tom replied, wondering what he should say. 'The blacksmith was forcing me to work in the forge.'

'That doesn't surprise me at all,' said his host in a matter-of-fact tone. 'You're easy prey, young lad. What are you doing here?'

'I was passing by.'

'And that is no answer at all, if I may say so.'

She pulled out a handkerchief to wipe her glasses. The room was warm and cosy. Tom's gaze passed from the oil paintings on the wall, to the large stone fireplace and to the heavy black curtains which reached to the floor. And then, with a start, he noticed, high on the wall to his left, the plaque with the scarlet dagger design. He was sure the woman had not nodded towards it.

17

'Passing by in order to end up where?'

Was it the release from the pain in the forge and the comfort of this lived-in room, or did this frumpy woman really have a kindly look about her? Tom had been looking for someone he could trust, and apart from the girl with blue eyes (who would not allow questions) he had found nobody.

'I don't know.'

'Don't know? Come now' – it was clearly a mannerism – 'Come now, young man. Let us not have mysteries. You speak with a stranger's accent; you visit the dangerous parts of the city. What is your purpose?'

Tom hesitated for a moment, wavering. And then he decided to trust his intuition that she was honest. He reached into his inner pocket for the picture he had carried for countless miles and thrust it under her bespectacled eyes.

'Have you seen this man?' he pleaded.

4 Above the City

His hope faded almost as it was born. The woman frowned and pushed the picture back at him.

'What are you asking of me?' she demanded. 'Why do you show this to *me*?'

'But you don't understand,' began Tom. 'I'm ...'

He stopped. He had meant to explain that he was alone, that the picture was of his father, that he was searching for his father. But she frowned at him uncomfortably. If she discovered that he belonged to no group, that the buttons on his coat signified nothing more than the kindness of a girl, would she then deliver him back to the smith? She averted her eyes from the picture.

'I can't help you, I'm sorry.'

It was then that Tom detected something different in the woman's voice – could it be an element of fear? Could she possible be a little frightened of him or, rather, of whom she supposed him to be? Sensing an advantage Tom addressed her with as much authority as he could muster.

'Who can help me then? There must be somebody.'

The woman hesitated.

'I know of someone who might help you.'

Her voice was reluctant, but Tom's was eager.

'Where does he live? Is he near?'

'Not far. The smith will take you. But why did they send such a young boy?' (This last question was to herself and demanded no reply.) 'You'd better stay here till nightfall. You can go then.'

Tom wanted to ask about the curfew and soldiers, but he felt his ignorance might expose him. Instead, an inspiration prompted him to feel each of his pockets and then to say: 'I've lost my papers. They must be in the smithy.'

The woman looked worried.

'I'll see,' she replied – and was gone.

Nightfall, and Tom stood ready, his coat buttoned tightly and, in his pocket, in addition to his precious picture, a complete set of newly forged papers. The smith entered dressed as in the morning, but now with the addition of a roughly woven cloak thrown about his huge shoulders. Tom could not suppress a shudder at the arrival of his former tormentor, but the smith's face showed no hostility, and his voice was friendly.

'It's a cold night little man, and icy underfoot. You must tread careful.'

He led the way through a door that opened onto an upward flight of stairs. Tom felt both dwarfed and comforted by the huge bulk of the man and followed readily, though puzzled that they should be climbing stairs when they were already on the ground floor. At the end of the first flight they turned a corner and were facing yet more stairs. Up and up they walked until Tom's legs ached, but he dared not pause for fear of being left behind by his giant companion.

Eventually they arrived at a steel door, and as the smith opened it Tom was forced back by a gust of cold air. The door had opened onto a narrow parapet which ran between a slanting roof and a low wall. On the other side of the wall the sheer drop was eventually swallowed by the blackness of the night. The air was full of fine snow, carried in eddies around the walls and chimneys by the wind.

The first part of this journey high above the city streets took them along the parapet for several hundred yards. Tom dared not look to his left for the wall was no higher than knee level, and where the parapet was blown free of snow the surface was hard and slippery. But his fears were multiplied a hundredfold when he reached the end of the parapet, for there was a door in the wall of the next building which could be reached only by crossing a narrow bridge, a mere plank's width (though it seemed to be of metal) and for support a single handrail.

Tom hesitated before following the smith onto the bridge, but he knew that he must follow, and so forced himself forward. Looking down to his feet he saw the thin strip made pale by a dusting of snow and below that a vast black chasm. He held the rail with both hands and eased himself along passing

20

one hand over the other, but never letting go. The sensation was made more sickening by the vibrations that were created by the smith's heavy footfall, and the thin crust of ice that coated the bridge.

If my feet slip, thought Tom, I shall plunge into that blackness – and he shut his eyes.

'Hop across, little fellow.'

A giant hand lifted him inside the door. Another swung the door shut on the icy air. Once inside, Tom had to sit down: he was shaking and sobbing quietly. The smith stood patiently for a minute or two then, with a voice of amazing gentleness, encouraged him: 'It's all right little man. You'll be all right. But it's best we were going in case they start the flares.'

Tom climbed to his feet and numbly followed. Who 'they' were and what 'the flares' were seemed of no consequence.

Back in his home village Tom had once seen a play performed. The director, one of the few educated men in the area, could find no actors of talent among the villagers. He had, therefore, devised a play with a large cast, none of whom said more than a few lines. The play was interesting enough, but the plot was impossibly obscure. Tom's life, since he had entered the city, was beginning to feel very much like that play.

They walked along a corridor, roughly plastered and without doors, and then down several flights of stairs. The corridor and stairs were lit at intervals by lights set into the ceiling, but there was no sign of habitation in the building. Eventually they came to another door and this led once more to the roofs, but now at a much lower level. The streets below them were visible, though dimly lit, small puddles of yellow light forming around street lamps.

'We must be careful now: we can be seen. We follow this ledge along to those chimneys. After that we have to edge our way along the ridge. It's a bit grim, but you'll be all right if you take care.'

After the bridge this prospect held little fear for Tom. True, if he fell from the roof he would probably be killed, but at least the ground was there, clearly visible. He followed the smith to the chimneys, which were a curious complex of brick stacks, arranged to afford steps to the ridge of the roof. Here they sat astride and edged their bodies along with their hands. As they neared the end of the ridge where the roof sloped down to meet another building, the smith turned to Tom and grinned.

'Nearly there, little man.'

Tom's relief was short-lived, for suddenly the darkness became as brilliant as midday; a white ball hung glowing in the sky above them and there were shouting voices: 'There – up there!'

Shots rang out, thin sharp barks in the cold air. The smith grunted, his huge body sagged forward, and then slowly keeled over and slid down the slope of the roof and into the space beyond. Tom lay flat along the ridge. He heard a heavy thud as the smith hit the street, and then the flare faded and he was in darkness once more. With as much speed as he could manage he pulled himself along to the end of the ridge, slid down the roof to an adjoining wall, and easing himself along it felt for a door. All the while there were voices from below, and one louder than the others.

'You've got one of them, but it's the other you want, the other. Try another flare.'

But before the instruction could be followed Tom had found his door, scuffled desperately with the catch and was inside. Pressed against the inside of the door in total darkness he gasped for breath, dizzy with fear. The shouting voice was one that he had recognised: it was, without doubt, the voice of the bellows-pumper.

He stood, hunched, inside the room, totally ignorant of his surroundings – whether he was in a confined space or a vast hall. He reached out with his arms, but met nothing. Pressed against the door, he fancied he heard faint sounds from the street below, but it might have been his fevered, his terrified imagination.

Minutes passed until, with a suddenness which caused him to jerk himself upright, a dim shaft of light appeared before him. It grew, escaping from behind a door which was slowly being pushed open. Two figures entered the darkness and, silently, came to him and grasped his arms. He offered no resistance. He was half dragged, half carried into a dimly lit corridor. Rough hands turned him to the wall, jostled his arms out of his coat and explored his inner clothing.

Presumably (his head reeled) it was the same hands which

22

swung open an iron door and thrust him into a small window-less room, furnished with a low bed and a single hardbacked chair. In one corner there was a washbasin, on one wall there was a shelf of books, and stretched on the bed there was a gaunt man of about thirty with closely cropped hair and a lined and agitated face.

5   The Prisoner

'Hey ho!' the man crooned in what at first seemed a jovial tone. 'A *lamb* to the slaughter this time, is it? Well, I never!'

It was when he cackled and his eyes remained frozen and hard that Tom realised this was no good-natured welcome. The door slammed shut.

'What have they got you for?' the other asked him, sitting up and swinging his legs to the floor. 'I hope you did a good deal of damage.'

'No,' Tom replied. 'I've done nothing.'

'Caught in the act, were you?'

Tom avoided replying by crossing the room to the wooden chair and dropping onto it. He felt close to collapse.

'No, you're quite right to say nothing,' said the thin man. 'That's the wise policy. They'll be listening to every word. If you've secrets, keep them to yourself.'

On an impulse he leapt to his feet and swung a kick at the wall. He then raised his fists and hammered on the plaster.

'I know you're there!' he yelled, his face screwed up in fury. 'I can feel you through the wall. Scum! Cockroaches!'

The fit passed, he sank onto the bed and turned once more to Tom.

'They'll torture you,' he said confidingly. 'Bastinado. You know what that is? They'll bare your feet and beat them like drums. Bruises first and then the bones crack.'

Tom covered his face with his hands and felt himself shiver.

'Perhaps they'll torture me, too,' the prisoner said in a matter-of-fact voice, 'but that will only be for the sport. They know everything about me already. I've got no secrets.'

He lay back on the bed.

'Then they'll kill me,' he added lazily. 'That's all they can do. They've no choice whatsoever.'

Tom was shocked into speech by the man's casual attitude to his own death.

'Why must they kill you?' he asked.

This brought on a burst of mirthless laughter.

'Because if they don't, dear young fellow, I will most certainly wipe *them* out, every last one of them. I'll squash them into the ground.'

Here he sat up again and his body tautened. Although he looked in Tom's direction, his eyes never seemed to focus on Tom's but on some distant horizon. He stood up and began to pace the small room, restlessly.

'Only when every last one of them had been eliminated,' he declaimed, pounding one fist into the air, 'will the city be purified.'

Although the man spoke with great anger and bitterness, Tom strangely felt no fear of him. For all his hammering on the wall it seemed that his fury was expressed chiefly in the continual flow of words. And though he spoke confidingly to Tom, he never seemed to desire an answer. It was as if he were talking to himself *through* Tom.

'It's an evil world,' he proclaimed fervently, still stalking up and down the room, turning every few paces because of its smallness. 'And this is an evil city, overrun by vermin. We've got to stamp them out!'

He paused, and leant down towards Tom.

'Are you with us?' he demanded in a hoarse whisper. 'Are you one of us?'

Since Tom had no knowledge of the conflict referred to by the prisoner he could not give an answer.

'Aren't you afraid to die?' he asked, simply.

At this the man flung his arms in the air with a gesture of contempt.

'Afraid? It's an honour! To die for the cause.'

He pushed up the sleeve of his tunic to reveal his upper arm. Vividly pricked into it – the outline a rich blue, the centre vermilion – was the large tattoo of a dagger.

'Listen.' He moved closer to Tom and spoke in a low voice. 'If you ever get out of here, tell them that you met me. Tell them I won't let them down.'

'But who ...'

25

'Marcus. That's my name. Just say Marcus. They'll know.'

He sat on the edge of the bed.

'That's if they let you go, which isn't likely. You'd know too much.'

'I know nothing,' protested Tom.

'Yes you do. You know me. You know my name. Perhaps you even know where we are.'

'I've no idea.'

'How did you get here?'

'I was led here,' said Tom. 'It was dark. I don't know the city.'

The prisoner shrugged.

'I was brought here unconscious,' he said. 'They know that once we discover any of their hideouts we'll find them all. Then there'll be some blood spilt.'

This was too much for Tom to stomach. In a blind panic he stood up and – to occupy himself – took down a large book from the shelf. It shook in his grasp.

'Why must there be blood?' he asked numbly.

'Because there'll be no rest until the matter is finished,' his companion replied. 'We're too deep into the struggle to turn back. It's them or us.'

It was a book of maps, which fell open in his hands. His eyes, not focusing properly, were aware of towns and rivers and forests.

'You and I,' said the prisoner, 'we don't matter. Let them do what they like to us. It's the cause which matters.'

He lay back on the bed with his arms behind his head.

'I've been tortured before,' he said baldly.

There was an awful silence.

'What happened?' asked Tom, dreading the answer.

'Burns. They ran the flames over me. It was in the open and they lit a large fire. Of course, I knew it was for me, long before they told me. What a glorious blaze it was, red hot in the centre. Then they asked me for information which I had, and I refused. I'll always refuse.'

Tom returned to the chair, feeling sick. He could see the fire, and the men gathered round it, and the other one lying pinned to the ground.

'And then they brought the flames to me – at first not very

26

close, but gradually nearer and nearer. You have to think of something else – there's a tip for you, young lad. Absent yourself mentally when it happens. It eases the pain.'

He gazed calmly at the ceiling.

'But I could smell the burning.'

Tom leafed through the book, wildly fumbling the pages. They were thick and old, with broad margins. The maps were extremely detailed.

'I told them nothing,' the prisoner said proudly.

There was a map of an area he knew and, comforted by the discovery, Tom turned another page, and another, following a route he roughly recognised. Finally, and gratefully, he came to the map of his own home area. His fingers traced the familiar mountain range, moved in a curve along the road which ran along the foothills to the village.

To his amazement, he found that the page had been marked. The village – one among so many, among hundreds in these pages – had been ringed by two thick circles of ink.

'Stand by!'

The call, from the prisoner on the bed, was followed immediately by the opening of the heavy door and two large men entered. They signalled to Tom, and he put down the book and let them take his arms.

'Don't cry out,' urged the prisoner. 'Whatever they do. Don't give them that pleasure.'

He heard the voice calling to him even as they took him outside and swung the door back into place.

'For the cause, remember. Don't cry out!'

Tom was aware of nothing but the dreadful image in his mind of the torture chamber, with a fire and irons and heavy objects to beat his feet, and the thought that they would never let him go.

6 Eagle's View

'Child, you seem ill!'

The man to whom he had been taken – a tall, silver-haired, grave man – was certainly no torturer. He looked down on him with a tender concern.

'Are you troubled?'

Tom was indeed troubled, the relief and the confusion issuing in hot tears which flooded his eyes and filled his throat. He bowed his head, ashamed.

'Come, be seated.'

It was another room without windows, but much larger and of a curious shape. On the wall facing him there was pinned a large map of the city, with green markers dotted about it. Through his tears they glowed like small beacons. The floor was thickly carpeted, and there were comfortable chairs grouped together facing the map as if the room were used for meetings. Turning his head, Tom counted eight walls, one of them largely obscured by thick draped curtains of a mustard colour.

There was a silence, during which his questioner studied him thoughtfully. He seemed to Tom a man of great dignity. He moved slowly, but easily – now he sat in a chair close to Tom – and when he spoke it was in slow, measured tones.

'I think perhaps apologies are called for. I am sorry you were treated rather roughly. We have to be a little cautious, you know.'

On a table to one side of them Tom saw his new coat, with the old and tattered one half-hidden beneath. Lying next to them was his picture and the forged papers. He found himself stammering.

'You're not going to, to . . . ' He could not say the word. 'You don't intend to harm me?'

A puzzled expression crossed the man's face.

'Harm you, child? Why, no indeed. And why should I?'

Tom felt that he should not explain his fear. He felt a queer loyalty to the prisoner in the small room. But at the same time – perhaps as a reaction from his terror – he found himself angry with the tall suave gentleman who remained so calm while other people suffered.

'You hurt the prisoner,' he accused pugnaciously. 'You tortured him.'

The words hung outrageously in the air.

'Poor child.' He turned away from Tom for a moment as if reflecting on what he should say. 'That man is a great danger to us, but we have not injured him in any way. Quite the reverse.'

'He said terrible things had been done to him.'

'And so they probably have. He is a man who is attracted by violence, and violence is doubtless sometimes done to him. But not by us.'

'What will you do with him?'

'That I cannot tell you. It is true that we cannot simply let him go.'

'Then you will not let me go!'

'Child, you do not understand.' Again he turned away. 'How could you? This man is evil. He would bring danger to a great many good people.'

It was true that Tom did not understand. When the prisoner had warned him of his captors he had believed they were wicked men. Now this man told him that the wickedness belonged to the prisoner.

'But enough of that,' the man continued, as if suddenly impatient of Tom's questions. 'I have some things to ask of *you*. These papers I recognise as being drawn up by us. By what name are you really known?'

After some hesitation Tom yielded up his first name, unwilling while he remained undecided about the man to reveal more than necessary.

'Well Tom, you must tell me a few things about yourself. You have come far?'

'I have travelled for weeks on end.'

'Alone?'

'Yes, quite alone.'

The man seemed, for some reason, embarrassed – or was it

moved? – by this simple statement. He put his two hands against his cheeks as if for greater control.

'And where have you come from?'

Tom named his village and began to describe his journey – the cold nights, the hunger, the kindnesses and the rejections of the people he occasionally met. But he had not told the tenth of it when he was silenced by a wave of the hand.

'This picture,' the man asked, turning to the table. 'Why do you carry it?'

'It is of my father.'

His questioner stood up, abruptly for one who moved in so dignified a fashion, and turned to the map on the wall. But he did not seem to be studying it. Although his fingers toyed with the green markers there seemed no method in what he did. Tom thought it was as if he were fidgeting, which clearly could not be so.

'I am looking for my father,' he continued. 'I believe he may be in this city.'

'Ah.' It was almost a sigh. 'That's it, child.'

He turned.

'And why here?'

'I don't know. My mother believed it very strongly.'

Thoughts of home, not for the first time, began to infiltrate Tom's consciousness but, as before, he repelled them. He knew that if he remembered the sights and sounds of his village, pictured the people going about their business, he could not face the hardships which he had borne for so long and which he must continue to bear while his father remained lost to him.

'Tom, I will show you something. Fetch your coat.'

He followed, through the thick mustard curtains and a door beyond and up a narrow flight of winding stone stairs. The air struck suddenly chill. They emerged in a small, low, circular room which had openings at regular intervals all around it. Approaching one, Tom discovered that they were at the top of a high tower, with views across the city. The moon shone fiercely in a sky of dark velvet, the heavy clouds having retreated to the east where they gathered densely, a menacing dingy grey. The roofs stretched away below them, sparkling white under the triumphant moon. How vast the city was, how immeasurable!

'You come at a time of anguish for us all,' his guide explained

30

in a tired voice. 'Although some things must remain hidden, there are matters you must understand. If only' – he added quietly, almost to himself – 'so that you are to survive.'

So high above the city, Tom felt for a moment jubilantly free, as if he had only to open wide his arms and soar like an eagle, up and up towards the burning moon. He had a desire to fling himself through the opening, but when he put his hand against the stonework the coldness of it somehow reminded him of how earthbound he truly was and how, if he leapt for the inviting space beyond, he would plummet like a dead weight. This, in turn, reminded him of the terrible fate of the blacksmith, and he withdrew from the gap with a shudder.

'Here, Tom – look from this side. There below you, see? Do you recognise that tower and the great gate?'

It was the gate by which he had entered the city, and he was surprised to discover that he had not come very far. His eyes followed the narrow road round by the wall until he found the place at which he had turned off, down the slope, before he heard the guards marching. Where, then, was the house with the green and the white rooms, and the gentle girl with the blue eyes? It must surely be the tall white building with shutters across its windows. Except for one high window, where a light shone behind a curtain. Who was in that room? he wondered. What was she doing? Did she remember his brief stay in the room with the white walls and the faded painting and the cryptic lines scratched into the plaster?

'All this area here,' the tall man explained, sweeping the flat of his hand in a broad arc, 'from that tower by the east gate, to that other tower you see on the wall in the distance, then back by that massive fortification you see through this window' – they moved round as he spoke – 'all this is under my command.'

He allowed himself a weary smile.

'Or it would be if we had control over the city,' he added. 'In fact I command a number of loyal people who hope that one day we shall live in happier times.'

'And then you will be in charge?'

'And then, for a while, I shall perhaps be the eastern commander in fact as well as in name. But we may have to wait for a long time yet.'

It was not late, and lights shone in the city below them, in some parts dimly and sparsely, in others in thick bright clusters. In many buildings the lighted rooms were the high ones, leaving the lower areas along the street in darkness.

'Tom, I can help you find your father.'

His heart lurched. The hope rose up in him like a physical thing, lifting him.

'You know where he is?'

He had to restrain himself from seizing hold of the man's coat and shaking information from him.

'*Where is he?*'

'I do not know myself but, if you are prepared to put yourself in our hands, I shall make every effort so that you are guided towards him.'

Tom, overcome, did not know how to reply.

'You are right to hesitate,' said the commander, misinterpreting his silence. 'You know nothing of us, and you will be putting yourself in danger. Understand that we shall be using you for our own ends. I am not acting simply from kindness.'

They stood together, elbows on the stone, gazing out over the city.

'You are too young, Tom, to judge easily whom you may trust and whom you should fear. Later you will read the signs more expertly. But you must believe me when I tell you that this city is in the hands of a malevolent power. Men are forced to obey what they know is a manifestation of evil.

'It cannot last for ever, because there is more goodness than evil in ordinary men. Already we find that although the people will submit to force their spirit remains free. When the call comes, they will respond.'

Tom saw that the man's hands shook against the stone sill as he spoke, and his eyes were bright with tears. A chill breeze stirred the grey hair at his temples.

'My father,' Tom broke into the silence. 'How far away. . . .'

'I cannot say. I imagine, very far. You see how the city stretches, beyond the eye. You may have all that way to go.'

'And is it all as it is here?'

'There are places less troubled, Tom, others even more cruelly suppressed. Weigh that in your mind before you decide.'

32

He turned, and they made their way to the staircase, Tom following the commander down.

'I shall not force you,' the slow, tired voice rose to him. 'If you wish, you may leave unharmed. The mission I would propose to you is not an easy one.'

'I am ready,' Tom replied.

7 The Mission

Lost in the depths of a huge armchair, roasted by a fire almost the equal of that at the blacksmith's forge and fed beyond his measure, Tom sat and waited for the commander's return. His life had never known such total comfort and he drifted into a deep sleep.

He felt himself to be a snow crystal gently falling from the black heavens, through the sky's midnight blue, turning and turning, caught by the light of the moon and the gentlest of breezes and wrapped in complete silence. He fell past roofs, he fell past windows, past faces he fell – the girl in the room, the blacksmith, the bellows-pumper, the prisoner, the commander, and finally the face of his long lost father, now alive and smiling unlike the frozen image of the picture that he carried.

And then, through the silence, a voice calling his name. The voice grew louder and more insistent until Tom wakened, shaking his head and opening his eyes. He was awake and the voice continued, but appeared to have no source. Opposite was an armchair identical to that in which he sat, but it was unoccupied. Tom looked round the room, which was of no great size, but that also seemed empty. The voice continued: 'Wake up, wake up! You've slept well, but there's work to be done!'

Tom turned to where he imagined the voice came from and there in the shadows by the fire and lit only by its flickering red light stood a man. At least, the face was that of a man: the body was more that of a small boy. He was the most complete dwarf that Tom had ever seen, and Tom's startled expression and the stare that followed it prompted the little man to further speech.

'Yes, I'm small, and I've reason enough to be glad of it, so stop gawping. We'll be seeing plenty of each other, you and I, so you might as well get used to me.'

He moved to the empty armchair, stood before it facing Tom

and suddenly bounced upwards and backwards into it, seeming momentarily to disappear into the folds of leather. Re-emerging, he continued to speak.

'I understand from our commander that you've agreed to undertake a certain mission for us. Is that correct? A nod will do.'

Tom nodded.

'I also understand that you know very little of our situation here. Correct? A nod will do.'

Again, he nodded.

'It is advisable, therefore, for you to appreciate something of the background before I explain this mission that you've undertaken.'

Tom nodded vigorously as if to prove that an invitation to do so was unnecessary. The dwarf scowled.

'Stop moving your head like that. It's unsettling. Now listen carefully' – and he sat back in the armchair, looked at the ceiling and began what seemed to be a carefully prepared speech.

'For many centuries our city was ruled over by a dynasty of city lords: princes, you might call them. At first these city lords ruled alone, having total power over the people, but as the centuries passed a system evolved in which the city lord shared power with an elected group of citizens, known as the citizens' council. These citizens were chosen carefully to represent each group within the city. The rich, the poor, the tradesmen, the artisans, the professions – all were represented.

'It was a system that seemed ideal. The citizens could not assume too much power because there was always the city lord to answer to, and the city lord was restrained by the need to consult the citizens' council. There were times when members argued for the interests of individual groups with such fervour and at such great length that things did not get done, or were done too late.'

He paused and sat forward.

'You hear me, I trust. You're not falling asleep?'

'No, no,' answered Tom urgently. In truth the strangeness of the dwarf and the fascination of his story were keeping him wide awake.

'Well then, this is how it was. There were times when corruption entered the council chambers, but generally they ruled fairly and with the interests of the city at heart. For a long time, indeed, the people were satisfied and the city flourished.

'But satisfaction is never permanent in human affairs. Groups began to murmur – "They are weak ... we need stronger government ... we need people who will get things done ... there must be more discipline ... "

'So the murmurings grew, and from them there emerged a movement whose aim was to destroy the city lord and the citizens' council and seize power by violence.' (Here the dwarf's voice dropped and was tinged with a mixture of sadness and anger.) 'And they succeeded. Their emblem is a blood-stained dagger; they call themselves the Red Blade and they rule from a grim fortress call the Citadel.

'Entering the chambers, they cruelly murdered the council members and, it was thought, the city lord himself. The people were stunned by the viciousness of their rule, and people began to disappear.

'You might think there was nothing surprising about that – I daresay the prisons were full enough, the graveyards too. But some people disappeared so completely that it became clear that even the Red Blade didn't know where they were.

'It also emerged that the city lord had escaped the bloodshed in the chambers and that the Red Blade still sought him. Rumours spread that he ruled in secret in another city.'

The dwarf looked closely at Tom, and added quietly: 'A city below this one.'

Yes, he looked closely. Did Tom's face betray anything? He could not be sure.

'But the rule of the Red Blade had anchored itself firmly and bloodily, and people forgot.'

As the story unfolded Tom found himself gripped by a strange and feverish excitement. Frightened he certainly was at the prospect of being thrust once again into the dangerous streets of the city. Terrified. But the mysteries of the vanished lord and the fabled underground city enthralled him.

'There are many of us who wish to restore the rightful government. We have control of the rooftops, but the streets are still under the tyranny of the Blade.'

'But why should you trust me?'

The dwarf shrugged.

36

'Why should you trust *us*? Let us call it intuition, Tom.'

Now he struggled out of the depths of the large chair.

'Your mission is nothing less than to find the underground city – if it exists. There is a room for you in the House of the Star: you will find it in the old quarter. You must leave tomorrow.

'We shall meet every so often, but you must not know me in public. If you make a mistake in that direction I shall not hesitate to betray you.'

He reached into a deep pocket and held his hand out towards Tom with the palm upturned.

'Take this,' he said.

Tom had to bend to make out the flat metal object that was presented to him. It was oval in shape and, peering closer, he saw that it was a representation of a human eye with a bright blue iris.

'Anyone who carries this,' explained the dwarf, 'is a friend. But remember that there will be more enemies than friends.'

'But why do you have faith in me,' Tom asked, 'if you yourselves have failed?'

'You are not known in the city and you are a child. It's a protection of sorts. When you leave here your only contact with the commander will be through me. It is safer for us all that way.'

Still Tom persisted.

'There is something you have not told me,' he said. 'The commander mentioned my father. He said. . . .'

'Very well. A few years ago a man came on a long journey looking for the underground city. He contacted us but we could not help him. He disappeared. It is possible that if you find the city you will find the man.'

'The man. . . .' interrupted Tom wildly.

'We believe that man is the man in your picture.'

PART TWO

Quest

8   At the House of the Star

Ignoring the wild tumult of talking, laughing, backslapping, leaping up and down, singing and whistling in the large and crowded room behind him, Tom rubbed his hand against the window-glass and peered into the frosted world beyond. The snow lay deep and crisp. The buildings across the street were distorted by the thick ice clamped to the outside of the pane.

For almost two weeks he had been a prisoner in the House of the Star, trapped by the bitter howling gales of what the people called the second winter. At night, in his small room on the floor above, he heard the wind career along the canyon of the street, dislodging loose tiles and wooden boards, jangling chains at the doors like a madman set loose in an ironmonger's shop. By day, as the snow silently swirled in fierce eddies, he sat reading in his room or came downstairs to where the lodgers were joined by local people and passing travellers in search of warmth and company.

It was the afternoon and the light was fading. The snow, at last, had stopped falling. An old lady, so heavily wrapped against the weather as to appear scarcely human, struggled through a drift which reached to her knees.

'Dreaming of building a snowman, young Tom?'

The question, half-shouted in a jovial, attention-seeking manner, was put by a man whom, a fortnight ago, he would have shrunk from looking in the eye. He wore the blue tunic with green sash and gold epaulettes of the city guard. Half a dozen of them had taken to calling in at the hostelry for a drink and noisy conviviality, and as the weather worsened their visits had become longer and more frequent. They had almost adopted Tom as their mascot.

He smiled awkwardly. A few months ago he might, indeed,

have played in the thick snow, but now it seemed a childishness.

'Here's a nose for it,' called another of the platoon, fishing a large cigar butt from an ashtray and laughing to show all his teeth.

His companions joined in the merriment. A shabbily dressed white-haired old man sitting alone on the fringe of their group and puffing on an ancient pipe had his hat lifted from his head for a moment and waved in the air.

'Got to keep a fellow warm!' chirped one of the young men, almost beside himself. 'He's already got the hair to match!'

The old man seemed unruffled by the attack and the hat was replaced. Smoke drifted from the battered bowl of his pipe and the aroma struck keenly at Tom's nostrils. The guards turned to a game of cards which, however, seemed to demand much the same volume of shouts and laughter.

There were some twenty tables dotted about the room, all of them occupied. A few were grouped round the large fire by the far wall, and at one of these was the man they called Old Weasel, an emaciated figure whose fingers plucked at the strings of an instrument Tom had never seen before, rather like a large mandolin. On his head was a black beret, pulled down hard to his ears. Occasionally he raised a thin voice to accompany the tune, but he received little attention from the people around him.

Above them, on the wall, was the grim insignia of the Red Blade. Tom had at first watched closely as visitors entered, thinking he could test the strength of their allegiance by their reaction to it, but this was not possible. Nobody more than nodded towards the plaque, and the guards, who were obviously loyal, sometimes swaggered in so full of themselves that they appeared to overlook it altogether. Good humoured as they seemed, however, Tom could not forget his arrival in the city and the chilling cries of the unseen man seized by the guards after curfew.

The glass had misted over again and he rubbed at it impatiently. He meant to go out. Day after day he had waited for a break in the weather so that now – although darkness was gathering and the snow was deep – he could not contain himself. And yet if he rose immediately he would be noticed and might be asked difficult questions. All eyes would be upon him. He remained seated and gazed around the room. Who was friend and who was foe? Who, if anyone, was entrusted with his secret? His room was paid for, but who knew why?

He had invented a story, should anyone ask what one so young was doing at such a place alone. He had come from a distant region following the death of both his parents, and thrown himself on the mercy of a relative. This man, being none too eager to help and having no room for him at his own house, paid for his lodging at this hostelry until a more permanent solution could be found. It was an alibi which would allow him to remain here for months, if necessary.

Somewhere out there – to the east it must be – lay the house with the white room which he must visit once again. Surely that glimpse of a subterranean world had been no dream. Surely it must be connected with the legend he was entrusted with exploring. Tom clung to this hope as fervently as he had believed, on his travels, that once inside the city gates he would immediately find his father.

'Can I persuade you to a hot toddy, whippersnapper?'

It was Clem, the man who ran the house, with a tray of steaming drinks. But Tom did not want to delay himself.

'I'm warm already, thank you,' he replied.

'Is there no draught from that window?'

'None whatsoever. I'd be too warm by the fire.'

Clem smiled down upon him with a knowing expression Tom had noticed before but did not understand. It was impossible to fathom whether it meant that he knew of Tom's mission or that he was of the other side and suspected him. Perhaps it was only his peculiar manner.

'A fine luxury, that window,' he added, shaking his head and continuing on his rounds.

It was indeed a rarity in this city, the ground-floor window, but this was a strange building. It was tall, and yet Tom had never been able to find a way of climbing higher than the first floor where his own room was. The stairs mounted to a long corridor with bedrooms leading from it, but there seemed to be no way up. His own room somehow seemed larger outside than inside, so that he was always surprised by the snugness of it.

Clem had a large wife – both taller and broader than himself –

who seldom mixed with the clientele but whose occasional weighty presence diminished the volume of their babble in an instant. She always wore black and she walked with menacing strides. Tom could not believe that Clem owned the hostelry: he had too much the air of the superior servant. But his wife, whom everyone called the Sphynx (when she was away) could have led an army.

'Holloa! Forfeit! Forfeit!'

The guards had finished their game of cards and were determined to have a little sport with their less exuberant neighbours. One of these, a man with large expressive eyes and a fearful stammer, was about to leave, and two of the guards, grinning hugely but rather menacingly, were blocking his way.

'Nobody leaves without a forfeit!' cried one of them.

'But wh-wh-what can I do?' pleaded the poor man, whom Tom knew well by sight. He was staying in the very next room to his. 'I c-c-can't recite anyth-th-thing.'

'Can't recite,' exclaimed another of the guards. 'What's he to do?'

'Play an instrument!'

'N-no. C-c-can't.'

In a desperate urge to make himself understood and to escape he flung his arms about in a ludicrous fashion.

'Let him dance.'

'N-n-no.'

'Dance! Dance! Dance!'

The call was taken up by others of the group and the victim had his hands and elbows manipulated by the strapping guardsmen, who began to jig him along on a tour of the tables.

Tom, embarrassed and dismayed, looked for someone to help, but no assistance was forthcoming. Some people looked away, others obviously enjoyed the spectacle. Old Weasel, on an order from one of the platoon, struck up a rhythm on his instrument. The guards began to clap, and this was picked up at other tables, the pathetic man being shuffled through the crowd, his eyes wide with fear and humiliation.

The mad procession came closer and Tom wanted to signal to the man how sorry he felt for him, but, tugged this way and that by his tormentors, he only looked wildly around the room and failed to notice Tom at all. Would this cruel baiting stop if

Tom leapt to his feet and protested? He could not, however. The idea flashed across his brain but his feet did not move.

One of the spectators was watching the scene closely, but with no show of emotion at all. Tom had often seen him drinking alone in a corner: he would be there when Tom went to bed, which suggested that he, too, was a lodger here. He was a man of about forty with closely cropped grizzly hair and a pair of gold-framed spectacles. He always dressed immaculately, the colours carefully matched. He spoke very little. Now his eyes followed the unhappy business, first resting on the stammerer, next on one of the guards, but it was impossible to judge what he made of it. His gaze met Tom's for a moment and quickly moved away.

'Enough! Enough!'

A member of the platoon, presumably of a gentler disposition than his comrades, let go of the unwilling dancer's arm and prevented the little troupe from advancing further. They stood back, laughing harshly.

'You've entertained us splendidly, sir. You're free to go.'

The group broke up and the released prisoner stumbled forward, blindly.

'Bravo!'

'A born dancer!'

'What energy!'

And now the unfortunate man, his large eyes watery with mingled relief and anguish, had to undergo a volley of backslapping and false bonhomie.

How Tom hated the city in that moment! He hated the commander every bit as much as he hated the odious Red Blade. He hated himself for being drawn into the struggle. He had no certain friends. It was not at all clear why he had been led to the House of the Star. Perhaps it was because there were people here who were loyal to the commander. But possibly – and just as likely – it was because here the enemy were at their strongest. He would be used in order to learn what he could about their organisation, and – if he were discovered – he would be simply another failed spy executed by the Blade.

In a spirit of wretched disillusionment Tom rose to his feet and collected his coat and his boots from where he had left them under the window. He had no choice but to continue with the mission. It provided the one opportunity of finding his father, although that hope rested only on a vague legend. His feet sank into the fur-lined boots. He would seek out the house with the white room – and perhaps run his head straight into a noose.

The white room! A pathway cleared through his depression at the thought of it. In his mind he was outside already, standing on the threshold, and the girl with blue eyes was greeting him. There was hope in her kindness. She understood.

He struggled with the catch of the large door, aware of an icy draught on his forehead from the narrow gap between door and wall. The second winter, they said, would persist for weeks to come. He had never known it so cold.

'Whither to, young Tom?'

A hand grasped his arm and tugged him back into the room. The guard with pearly teeth smiled down on him with a playfulness that failed to disguise the viciousness underneath.

'You haven't paid your forfeit yet, my lad.'

Perhaps if he had waited a few minutes more they would have been settled in their chairs intent on other business, but the excitement of their sport with the stammerer was still alive in them. They clustered around him, grinning unpleasantly. They would not be denied their fun with him.

'I was coming back,' he said helplessly.

'You'll be coming back,' said another, 'after you've gone. And you can't go until you've paid your forfeit.'

Tom looked around him desperately. He heard muted sympathetic noises, but nobody dared to outface the city guards.

'This is no time for venturing out,' said the tallest of the platoon, putting huge hands around Tom's ribs and lifting him in a swinging motion towards the centre of the room. He landed lightly. 'It's less than two hours to curfew.'

'He wants to make a snowman. That's it, eh Tom?'

They were being cheery with him, but to satisfy themselves rather than Tom. He knew they would not allow him to leave without a show.

'I don't care about going out,' he said.

'Oh, too late, too late,' he was told. 'You meant to go out and there's no changing your mind now. A forfeit's what's required, your worship.'

46

There was no enthusiasm for it outside the small circle of guardsmen, but they had worked themselves up to it. Off came his outdoor clothes. They cleared a space for him, backing away to give him room to perform while they struck ridiculous poses as if waiting for an artiste to appear.

'What's it to be?' demanded one of the platoon. 'Another dance?'

'No, no,' his companions protested. 'Let's have something different. Give us something stirring. We're bored fellows with great imaginations. Come on, come on!'

Standing helpless among them, Tom became suddenly defiant. He knew he could not escape, but the anger he had felt when the stammerer was made to dance surged up in him again.

'I'll give you a song from the country,' he said aggressively. 'They're better than city songs.'

It was a foolish remark, no doubt. It was meant to be insulting to the city. But the guards clapped their hands and hooted their approval.

'A country song, eh? And it has a decent chorus, we hope?'

'Of course it has.'

The guardsmen seemed relieved not to have to bully him into submission. They sat on their chairs or lounged back against the tables.

'The chorus then, Tom. Let's learn the chorus.'

Even as he began singing, in the raucous fashion common in his own district, part of Tom slid away back along the tracks he had followed, through wilderness and forest, to the places his family had known for generations.

> You reckless moon
> Mare with no rider
> Leaping the billows
> You reckless moon!

He sang with eyes half-closed, but he was aware of a strange reaction from the white-haired old man who sat close by. As the first two lines came to a close his eyes took on a startled expression and the pipe fell from his lips. It was over in a moment – his hands fumbled for the pipe and trapped it on his chest – but Tom knew that he had not mistaken it. The man

47

pushed his hat more firmly onto his head and looked at the floor.

'Bravo, Tom!' enthused pearly-teeth. 'An earthy peasant song. Haunting, wouldn't you say fellows?'

'A fine chorus. Let's have it again!'

And again he sang it, and gradually more voices joined in. Old Weasel began to pick out the tune. There was a relaxation throughout the room because the guards were appeased; they would not humiliate him.

> You reckless moon
> Mare with no rider . . .

One face remained frozen as the volume of singing increased around him. The gentleman with gold-rimmed spectacles fixed a stare upon Tom, as he had earlier upon the dancing stammerer. His lips did not move with the others.

'It goes well, Tom. But what of the story? What's the song about?'

He spoke up enthusiastically now.

'It's a story of what the moon sees as she sails across the night sky. She looks down on the countryside and the people in their houses.'

'A pretty idea. Let's have it then. Some applause for the maestro, please.'

And, to his confusion, there was a hurraying and a banging on the tables that must have been heard a street away. The forfeit was forgotten. They wanted the song.

He had not sung it – had not even thought of it – for years, and yet the words arrived in his mouth spontaneously. They spoke of the labourers home from the fields, women with children, animals in the barns.

> Bats leave the oak tree, flit in the darkness
> Low past the alders gurgles the brook

He saw, at once, a particular oak tree, in a field corner where a path crossed and under it – for it was a fine day in summer – a family party with friends. It was so finely pictured that a large fly hummed close, threatening his sandwich, and he flapped it away, protesting.

And all the while that he saw it so vividly the words continued to flow from him, as if they were coins he tipped effortlessly from his pocket:

A light at the window, the flicker of flames
Heads by the fireside, a leatherbound book

— a scene which he knew as if the song were written precisely for him, although never before had he thought of it in relationship to himself. The family shared the large volume, the father reading a page, slowly and with great dignity as the children stared into the coals and weaved additional thoughts around the words. And, at the conclusion of the page, the book was passed to the mother who took her turn — her reading of it faster and lighter, but suddenly dramatic where the text required it. He heard the voice, and he saw a head turn from the fireside to smile up at the mother, and he knew it was himself he saw turning.

When the chorus was repeated they all took it up, hands clapping out the rhythm, Old Weasel animatedly plucking his strings, the guardsmen thumping the table tops with their fists in time with the beat. But Tom, a sob in his throat and tears welling up in his eyes, only mouthed the words without a sound escaping, his hands held out before him as if conducting an orchestra.

Under the hedgerow the vagrant is sleeping
The leaves for his pillow, his feet in the mire

He found voice to continue and he saw the vagrant (a tinker who had called at the house one day when he was feeding the hens and who had startled him by rapping on the slatted henhouse roof with a pot), and he saw the hedges that ran by the lane that led from his house towards the flatlands that gave way, gradually, to the lower mountain slopes in the distance. And he was by the river again, floating boats (what were they: twigs from the alders?) and splashing his sisters. And with him always, although he could not now see her, was the presence of his mother and the echo of her voice, gentle and coaxing. And so as the music played and he blurted forth the song he was home again and no city existed and he had not lost his father.

49

At the end of the song and the last chorus they all struck up again, unwilling to bring it to a close. Large hands hoisted him onto a table top and he stood above them, in an ecstasy, blinded with tears.

> Mare with no rider
> Leaping the billows
> You reckless moon!

Then what a commotion of yells and applause. They lifted him down — not aware of his emotion; too full of their own pleasure — and tousled his hair. The guardsmen loved him again. They called him Tomkin and Mr Tom and Tom-tiddledum. And then up again onto shoulders and he was borne towards the door.

'The best of the evening to you, young peasant swain!'

'Go forth under your reckless moon!'

Large hands fumbled with buttons as they helped him on with his coat, his boots, even with his gloves.

'And your hat. Where's your hat?'

'No, I don't need one.'

'You'll freeze your ears off, young Tomtit!'

And at last the door closing on their quips and their chuckles, their self-important noises.

A blank whiteness in the street. The silence made his head swim. The surface of the snow curled like the gentle waves of a flowing river, and as high. It had a thin frozen crust.

The cold burned his ears. His cheeks felt as if they bled. He blew gently and watched the plume of his breath disperse.

There was little time: he must return by curfew. He could not hope to do more than find his way to the house and then trudge back again. Nevertheless, fascinated by the dense beauty of the snow, he could not resist pausing to scoop the airy whiteness into his gloved hands. When he pressed upon it he heard it creak and shrivel into a tight ball.

Above the doorways the drifts hung, massively poised. He flung his missile and there was a silent explosion. Dislodged, a thick wedge of snow sliced in two and plummeted into the softness beneath.

He was playing after all. How peculiar it had been, the

50

singing in the House of the Star. He had not meant to amuse them. When he thought of the poor man with large damp eyes being tugged between the tables in a mock dance it seemed brutal and unfair.

But, although he had only to open the door and enter, it was a world away. Here in the snow he could see and hear no one. The high walls of the buildings climbed towards a pitch sky in which a few stars glinted, frostily, and the new moon was a radiant sliver. The cold had already penetrated his thick coat, and he began to walk down the street, lifting his feet high over the piled snow.

Brighter than any star in the sky was the planet Venus. As a country lad, Tom knew the heavens: he had used the constellations to guide him towards the city, and now he took his bearings by them once again. Further to the east Jupiter was high above the horizon and near it, smaller and smudgily red, was Mars, bringer of war.

He turned at the first corner. Against the wall an ancient waterpump had an enormous white hat, precariously balanced upon it. Unable to resist the temptation he bent once again to gather the freezing flakes into a ball. It was then that a flash of colour caught his eye.

Standing at the corner, half-screened by the enormous building which reared up towards the evening sky, was the lad with the long green scarf. He was gazing intently at Tom, who stood upright, feeling the snow melt into his glove. Surely he was rather younger than Tom. He had no expression on his face, not even curiosity.

When Tom moved, however, he showed himself to be extremely alert. He had disappeared from view before Tom had taken two paces forward.

'Wait!' called Tom. 'I want to talk to you!'

But the other hurried away, scuffing the snow in a thousand directions.

51

9   The Monument

Tom floundered through the drifts in despair. He could not catch the boy with the green scarf. For a few minutes he struggled to keep up, but he knew that, as before, he would not succeed. They were, in any case, heading in the wrong direction. Although he had first seen the boy outside the house with the white room there was no reason to think that he was going there now.

Did he hear a distant laugh of triumph? He could not be sure. But, giving up the chase, he felt downcast and humiliated. Inside the hostelry he had been eager to begin his quest: now he felt the hopelessness of it.

Passing through a small square, he noticed what appeared to be the remains of a monument, half-buried in the snow. It was obvious from its breadth that it had once been impressively large. All that had survived some crude act of destruction was the fractured stump of the base.

Tom was puzzled by these signs of neglect in a city crowded with sturdy buildings, and he trod a laborious path across to it, his feet breaking through the crust of the snow and leaving a trail like pockmarked skin. Had there once been a statue here, perhaps? The dark stone now seemed to represent nothing more grand than a jagged, broken tooth.

He kicked a boot against it and thin shards of snow slid from the top. He stooped to look more closely. The stone was very hard and smooth. For a reason he did not understand Tom looked round him, almost furtively, before squatting on his haunches by the wrecked monument.

There was no one. Only the pure white vistas of snow along the streets and capping the roofs; only the monstrous closed-in buildings reaching towards a sky sprinkled with faint stars.

Bending to the stone again he rubbed at it with his gloved hand. He did not comprehend his own actions, what he hoped to find, but he felt a sudden unevenness beneath his fingers. Scrabbling in the snow he uncovered what seemed to be an inscription at the base. In fact, it could only be the end of an inscription, for as he swept the last of the powdery covering away he discovered the jagged remnant of another line at the very top of the broken masonry. He crouched to one side, allowing the pale light of the moon to pick out the words which remained.

He could not believe what he read. He looked round once more into the silent streets, empty and white, and felt his scalp tingle with a strange fear that had no name.

> Wear me as your spiked heel
> I will bite into ice for you

There was nothing under the lines, but Tom could not forget how shaken he had been when he had first met these words on the wall of the white room. For the initials beneath had been those of his father. The weirdness of finding the inscription repeated on this fragment discovered by chance in a city square filled him with an unease he could not explain to himself. He rose from his crouched position and felt horribly threatened, as if forces which he could not fathom were creeping up on him, ready to pounce.

And now these vague but potent fears became mixed with the horror of being caught in the streets after curfew and, although the first bells had not yet sounded, he began in a panic to career through the piled snow towards the House of the Star. His legs would not move quickly enough. With each pace he felt as if his boots were being tugged back, preventing him.

His heart hammering, his breath catching and rasping, he reached the sanctuary of the inn at last and leant trembling and faint against the stout outer door.

10 Old Weasel

'Mind you don't say no word to a soul. That's my advice to you, my laddie.'

'I haven't. I won't.'

'Nor a signal of no kind. There's many a body who's been undone through a careless moment.'

They sat in the tiny room Old Weasel called his home, sipping strong tea from heavy mugs. It was the afternoon of another bitterly cold day, through the length of which the wind had swept the snow in shafts through the streets, preventing any journeying out. After lunch, when they were the only people left at the large wooden table downstairs, the old man had surprised him by a swift beckoning movement and his invitation.

'I've lost more friends through loose tongues than for every other reason put together.'

His old black beret hung on a hook over his bed. It was half an hour since he had taken it off, but Tom found his eyes still fixing themselves on the curious contours of the wizened old head that normally hid beneath it. It was a completely hairless head, blotched with a dozen shades of red, pink, blue and grey. The bones were thin but prominent. They enclosed hollows and formed brittle ridges. It was a landscape, an immensely varied landscape that invited detailed exploration. When he spoke there were tiny movements here and there, fascinating to behold.

'These are troubled times, but nobody my age has ever known anything else. I'm a survivor. I don't live well, as you see – but I live.'

The room was clean, but there was very little in it. If it contained all of Old Weasel's possessions then they were no more bulky than could be squeezed into the sturdy cupboard attached to the wall in one corner. His strange musical instrument leant against it and Tom, never having had a chance to study it before, noticed that endless loving polishings had given the wood a soft and glowing quality.

'Been with me fifty years,' said the old man, observing Tom's interest. He put down his mug and took the neck of the instrument in one hand. The fingers of the other hand alighted on the strings with the unconscious deftness of birds on a wire. The tune he plucked from it made Tom start.

'Let's say I wasn't kindly disposed towards you.' The music ceased abruptly. 'Let's say I was suspicious of this young wisp who'd arrived from nowhere. I'd listen very carefully to that song, now wouldn't I?'

'I don't understand,' said Tom fearfully. 'It's just a song from the country.'

'It is indeed. A song about the reckless moon and the gurgling brook. A fine tune I hadn't heard before.'

Tom stood in alarm, but the old man waved him down again.

'No laddie, I'm not that suspicious chap myself. Don't fret over that. But I see things and I'm giving you a timely warning.'

The instrument was returned to its place by the wall.

'Don't give yourself away, that's what I say to you.'

'But I haven't,' protested Tom. 'I've hardly talked to anyone since I arrived here.'

'Ha!'

He wagged a finger towards Tom, accusingly.

'Lesson one, which you'd do well to heed. We give ourselves away as much by what we *don't* do as by what we do. Similarly by what we don't say. Speak by all means, my sparrow, but take care the tongue doesn't slip. That's what I mean to say.

'Why – I might ask, if I were suspicious – does this young lad arrive out of the blue at the House of the Star, a hostelry notorious for attracting the strangest clientele in this part of the city?'

'For a very good reason,' Tom spoke up boldly, his alibi well prepared. 'Because when my parents died. . . .'

But Old Weasel waved him into silence.

'That you've a story, I don't doubt, and it may be true or otherwise. But every rogue has proof of his innocence. In fact he usually has better proof than the virtuous man, which is another warning for you. The story doesn't matter.

55

'What our suspicious character asks himself is first, what wind has blown this young leaf into his path. He then asks himself where he might have come from. The accent tells him something, but perhaps not quite enough. And then – what luck! – the young chap sings a native song of his home village and the job's done for him.

'Now he examines this infant's behaviour. Look – he speaks to few people. Why's that? Is he shy? He doesn't appear particularly so. Has he something to hide? A possibility at the very least.'

Here Old Weasel paused and cocked his head on one side.

'Why does our young friend look so wistfully from the window of an evening? Has he an errand he badly wishes to undertake?'

Tom did not know how to reply. The frail old man seemed to be offering advice, but might be taunting him, hoping to find out more. He felt chill with fear. He felt that everything he said would be analysed: even things he did *not* say.

'Countless years,' said Old Weasel, changing tack suddenly, 'I was a messenger. That was my profession. There's no part of the whole country my feet haven't trod at one time of my life. A job for cunning is a messenger's.'

He rose and lifted the large teapot.

'Another, while it's still warm?'

'No thank you.'

'You're wise, no doubt. There's more tea than blood in these old veins.'

He lifted the lid, stirred the contents with a spoon and poured himself another mug of the thick brown liquid.

'There's many who think "messenger" is another word for "spy". Of all my colleagues from over the years in the service of a dozen different factions I don't know more than two or three who escaped with their lives. That's the mark of the troubles we've known. Leaders have been overthrown and the new rulers themselves toppled within a week.

'I tell you, my laddie, there were times when I carried a message to a distant town not knowing whether it would be friend or foe who greeted me at the gates. Now you imagine dealing with a perplexity like that!'

'How did you?' asked Tom, forgetting his fear.

56

'Caution, deception. A wise head. Kept my own council, made my own rules. There were times for delivering messages and times for quietly destroying them.'

'But how did you know what the messages said?'

'Lord bless you, there's no man would take the job who couldn't unseal a note and reseal it without a trace. A very necessary skill. I remember one time I read a letter through – highly confidential it was – and, at the foot, it said "Dispose of the messenger". Dispose of me!

'As you can see, they didn't. And why not? Well, I knew a fellow who was desperately anxious to make himself known to the ruler of the town I'd been sent to. He had a favour to ask. I let drop a few hints and before you could say "gullible" he was *bribing* me to let him deliver the message.'

'But then,' Tom broke in, horrified, 'he was killed instead.'

'Instead. I survived. Messengers have to be good survivors. That's the first virtue.'

Old Weasel bent forward.

'Don't be squeamish, laddie. These decisions are forced upon you. If the message hadn't been delivered I'd have been a hunted man for life. As it was, they thought me dead and I found myself a new employer.'

He took deep gulps from his mug of tea.

'Other times, when they trusted you, they'd send a message by word of mouth. It was for you to put it across the best way you could. Then you were like an ambassador, but with no protection whatsoever. There are vicious rulers who'll put the bearer of bad news to death as though he's responsible for it himself.

'You learn to watch people closely so that you can react in time – dodge the knife before it's thrown.'

Tom found his own reaction completely confused: he was excited by the story but disturbed by the cynical moral that accompanied it.

'Ha!'

Now the old man laughed at a memory, and the skin tautened on the frail cheek bones and quavered along the gaunt neck.

'On one occasion when I was working in the far west of the country I had to deliver a word-of-mouth message to the ruler of a nearby town. My task was to ask for military aid, men and arms. I was within five miles of the town when I met a long straggling line of people, all of them exhausted, some of them wounded. The garrison, had been overthrown. The town had been seized by a band of brigands.

'Now, it was impossible to judge how powerful these brigands were. If I returned home with the news I stood a fair-to-middling chance of being run through with a sharp sword. What to do, eh? Well, I waited a couple of days and then I strolled up to the main gate of the town, saying I had a message for the chieftain.

'A fearsome man he was, I can tell you. Crude and strong, and not well washed. But you have to keep your head as a messenger. I told him that my master congratulated him on his victory and wished an alliance with him. I know the words for that kind of thing.

'The next few days were uncomfortable. First I had to convince him that there was any reason my master should wish to make peace with him: if you can't talk fast and smart you're no good as a messenger. Then I had to hope he wouldn't send an envoy of his own so that I would seem, to my master, to be untrustworthy. And then I had to wait upon events.

'It was a bloody time. Most of our times have been bloody. Within a few days an army was at the gates seeking to regain the town. I paced up and down, ready to turn either way. A wave of attacks surged right up to the walls and was then repulsed. The brigand chieftain sensed victory and then had it snatched away. A renewed attack breached the walls. Men poured through.

'Still I waited. The battle was open. But towards evening it became apparent that the brigands were losing. They retreated to the innermost tower. Now I acted. I raced to the dungeon, which had a solitary guard.'

Tom, caught up with the story, sat forward.

'You were armed?'

'No, no. Wouldn't know how to use a knife, save to cut up my meat. Wit is my only weapon, my laddie. No, I went down to the dungeon and I approached the guard drunk as a lord. I was swaying everywhere, falling down and slowly climbing to my feet, pushing and shoving him, singing in a slurred voice. Poor chap didn't know how to handle me.

'He pushed me away a few times, but when I tried to dance

with him that really touched his temper. He buffeted me against the wall, unlocked the door and kicked me inside the dank hole where they put the prisoners. Very nasty it was, too.'

'But why?'

Old Weasel frowned disapprovingly.

'Come, come now. Can't you see it? You want a good deal more of cunning, my laddie. Consider what happens when the victorious army breaks in. The brigands are hanged or decapitated or whatever seems best for them. The prisoners are released.

'And there am I, the enemy of the brigands, cruelly mistreated, released to give my master's original message. All is well. Military aid is granted – and I survive.'

Well pleased with the memory he took his mug once more to the teapot, but found it too far cooled.

'Survival has nothing to do with strength, Tom. It's all up here.'

And he tapped the top of his head with a bony finger.

'I ended my working life in this city,' he added, 'and there's no more testing place than this. It's vicious and brutish. It's treacherous. And what applies to the city as a whole applies to any one part of it and any one hostelry within it.'

Tom felt that he should be grateful for the warning, but it seemed that he had been told very little at all. He spoke quietly, though urgently.

'But who,' he asked, 'who should I fear?'

'Oh dear me, no. It won't do, laddie.' Old Weasel appeared offended by the question. 'Tell me, if I were a suspicious character, how would I react to your eagerness? Wouldn't I wonder why the young chappie was so anxious? It seems to me that you've learnt nothing at all.'

But he relented a little, and sat down next to Tom.

'No secrets, that's the rule. There's never a secret that can't be broken. Whisper a word and you'll find it painted six feet high on the wall when you turn the corner in the morning.

'Old Weasel's taken a liking to you and that's the beginning and the end of it. He's given you the warning. He watches and he listens and he knows what he sees and hears. But he doesn't tell.

'And why? Old Weasel's a survivor.'

11 Mazes

The next morning was serene and beautiful. The last grey clouds were gone, replaced by a sky of limpid blue whose brightness fell onto the snow and transformed it, the reflection lighting the city from below as the sun lit it from above. The buildings seemed almost to evaporate in this light. Tom stood at his window. The past few weeks became unreal, a dark dream peopled with shadows. The soldiers, their hapless victim, the boy with the scarf: had they really existed?

He was eager to be out to begin his search. He breakfasted in the parlour downstairs, alone save for the landlady, whose brooding presence confirmed the reality of his situation. Compared with the food of his native village the breakfast seemed tasteless and was quickly finished. The woman in black – brusque and silent – gathered his empty plates. Tom put on his overcoat and stepped out into the morning.

For the first time since his arrival in the city he felt relaxed and happy walking these strange streets. Workers had been out early, clearing passages through the snow which now, discoloured and lumpy, rose even higher at the sides. The House of the Star was in an old quarter and the buildings here – now that he saw them in the light of day – seemed less threatening despite rare touches of the grotesque: a grimacing face carved onto a door lintel and painted with violent and unlikely colours, red eyes, blue protruding tongue; a wall with a large painting of a burning man, his face defying the flames that enveloped his body by wearing a malevolent grin; a wall studded with the skulls of dead animals, each partly embedded in the roughcast surface. Tom could barely suppress a shudder when he passed these things. They were not so very unpleasant in themselves, but what sort of people would have created them?

The streets were narrow, the houses at times almost touching above his head, but to his surprise he came to one open space the size of several houses and filled with small trees. He gazed on them with a feeling of shock. It was, he realised, the first time he had seen growing things since he had entered the city gate. Leafless now, they nevertheless reminded him of the countryside that had hitherto seemed firmly locked out by the city walls. And there (he looked upon it in wonder) moving briskly between the bare branches was a small brown bird.

People moved along the streets wrapped in heavy winter coats, their faces muffled and difficult to see, for despite the bright sunshine it was still achingly cold. Tom travelled in the direction that he imagined the house with the white room to be. The streets grew broader and the buildings larger until they opened onto a large market square. This provided Tom with his first sight of a large number of people engaged in normal activity. They pushed, argued, struck bargains in the way of all markets. He threaded his way between the crowded stalls, his eye taken by one which seemed devoted to displaying cult objects of the Red Blade: brooches and badges bearing the emblem, belts with dagger buckles, and plaster hands holding aloft imitation daggers painted with dripping blood. There were also various printed texts designed to be hung on walls, one of them bearing the legend 'Only one city – and that for the Blade' and another 'There is only corruption beneath the surface'. Tom wondered at the meaning of this.

At a stall selling fruit he bought a bag of large mottled apples. Biting into the juicy flesh brought back a flood of memories of orchards and late summer and sunshine. In my heart, he thought, I belong to the country and not to this strange city. But this thought could not displace an odd feeling that had been growing within him ever since his first entry through the city gate, and that feeling was that he did in some way belong here in these streets; that this was somehow real, and the village that he had grown up in was part of a dream that he was now waking from, even though the waking was, in part, dreamlike itself.

'Never have I seen someone so thoughtful about eating an apple. A very special apple, perhaps – or a very special someone.'

Tom dropped what was left of the fruit in surprise and turned to face the speaker. He was surrounded by people, yet none appeared to be the owner of the voice that had addressed itself to him, and which he half-recognised, until, looking down, he found close by his side the dwarf. He motioned Tom to follow him and began to move through the crowd towards the edge of the market. Tom found it difficult to keep pace with the little man, whose size gave him an advantage of movement and also made it easy for him to disappear behind people.

Before they were clear of the crowd Tom had lost him. Unsure of what to do, he decided to wait by the corner of an alley that climbed in steps from the market square. The dark silence of the alley behind him contrasted oddly with the activity before him, and Tom was musing on this fact when he was disturbed by an object which came rattling down the steps and lay at his feet. It was a smooth round stone. Picking it up, Tom found on it the words: 'To remind you that I'm here'.

He turned and ran up the steps; the alley beyond was deserted, as he had known it would be. He returned to the message. What could it mean? Was it to encourage him, to reassure him, or did he detect a slightly menacing tone, a threat even?

For lack of any better plan he decided to carry on along the alley, believing it to lead in the general direction that the house with the white room lay. But it led him nowhere; or rather, it led him into a maze of tight alleyways that eventually deposited him, thwarted, in the market square once again.

This became the pattern through the long hours of the morning. Roads which seemed wide and inviting would become narrower and twist back upon themselves so that Tom made no progress and was continually being led back to places that he recognised as having already passed – the market, the small plantation of trees and, eventually, even the back of the House of the Star.

His legs ached, his stomach was pinched with hunger. Tom went to his room and wept, exhausted and dispirited.

Lunching on another apple, Tom decided that the city must have actually been designed to confound. A street plan would have simplified the task, but no street plan existed. Instead, he must attack the problem in a more systematic way.

Sallying forth once more, he devised a new method. He would turn right at one junction, left at the next, right at the next, and so on until he reached the city walls, and then he would follow those round to the gate he had first entered by; from there it should be easy to retrace his steps to the house with the white room.

But this, too, was unsuccessful. He never reached the city walls. Instead he found himself back at the market which now, in the early afternoon, was almost deserted, with only a few stalls in evidence. He began again, starting with a left turn. It again led him in an enormous circle.

The frustration gripped his throat. His forehead burned, his temples throbbed. Tears were not far from his eyes. Should he stop someone and ask directions? But he was terrified of giving himself away. He averted his eyes from the faces of passers-by.

Once more he found himself in the square with the trees and the solitary bird. There were four streets leading from it: surely he had tried them all? There was no point in going further. Yet there must be a way. He set off again.

This time, by finding an alleyway he had not noticed before, he emerged at the square with the ruined monument. As if to emphasise its degradation, this was now hidden from view beneath a dirty pile of cleared snow. Heartened by the discovery, he struck out along a broad thoroughfare, only to be led, as ever, into narrow streets which – resist it as he might – forced him back to the market square.

He would not give up. In a delirium almost, he trudged the city streets. He lost consciousness of time. He passed and re-passed the familiar landmarks. His feet took him on, with a will of their own.

'Hey! Boy!'

He stopped. He looked behind him. It was several seconds before he realised that the woman who spoke to him was gazing at him with an expression of concern.

'Aren't you well?'

'Yes. Yes.' The sound of his own voice seemed to wake him up. 'I'm lost.'

'Oh, lost are you? Where are you heading?'

It was too late for second thoughts.

'I want to get to the city gate,' Tom said. 'The one to the east.'

He pointed, but the woman took no notice. She shouted across the street in an urgent voice.

'Dirk! Come now, quick! There's a boy asking his way to the east gate!'

Tom heard movement in the house across the way.

'I'm coming,' called a voice

'I'll keep him!' yelled the woman. 'But you hurry, Dirk!'

Even now they could hear running footsteps from the side of the building, and it sounded as if there were at least two pairs of feet in motion.

'What's the matter?' asked Tom, fearfully. 'Why did you call?'

The woman grasped his forearm by way of reply.

'The east gate you want, is it?' she said through her teeth.

Tom did not wait to hear more. Tugging his arm free – and even as three burly men came running into the street – he held his coat tight about him and sprinted towards the entrance of an alley. He heard their heavy footsteps hammering along the paving and he looked desperately for a place to hide.

He turned off the alley into another once, twice, three times, but still they pursued him. At first they had called after him but now, saving their breath no doubt, they chased him in silence, save for the sound of their boots on the ground. He could hear them, but he did not dare look round. Were they close? Were they tiring?

Now he came to the market square once more. There was a large open space containing nothing but a few stalls and the odd pile of rubbish. One of the stalls was draped with hessian and he flung himself beneath it, shrinking back from the sides, his body shaking.

His pursuers pounded into the square. He heard them talking urgently among themselves. They split up. He heard the footsteps in three directions. One man came towards the stall, but he was running and clearly had not considered that Tom might be hiding there. He passed so close that Tom saw one of his boots.

He remained there for a long time. When he emerged the sun was falling behind the buildings, rapidly sinking the streets into their former darkness. All the day's promise had vanished. He returned to his room, limp and bewildered.

Over supper Tom found his spirits reviving. He had slept for an hour after his return and now he sat in the warmth of the downstairs room, drinking thick soup and biting into grainy bread. The life of the inn ebbed and flowed around him. The city guard were in again, swaggering and roistering before the fire, and Tom sat alone in a pocket of silence.

Perplexed he was, but he began to be fascinated by a sense of intellectual challenge. Here was a puzzle to be solved. Two facts had emerged from his endless walking: one was that it was difficult to find that which he sought; and the other was that it was difficult, if not impossible, to lose himself, for he was continually turning back on himself.

The house, he knew, could not be far; he had seen it from the tower. Was it possible that this part of the city was somehow sealed off from the surrounding area? Perhaps the whole city was divided into sections shut off by rings of buildings: that would certainly explain his circuitous routes. If that were the case then he would have actually to travel through a building in order to arrive at another part of the city. But which building? And how, with most doors firmly closed or blocked up?

The alternative was, of course, the rooftops. Once more Tom found himself wrapped in confusion, faced with so many unanswered questions. How could he find his way to the roof of the House of the Star? Could the dwarf help him? If so, why had he not offered advice before? How, in any case, was it possible to find the dwarf?

Another question concerned the terrifying events of the afternoon, when he had been hunted by the three hefty men. Why had it been wrong to ask for the east gate? Was any travel outside this sector forbidden? And then a more disturbing thought entered his brain. Perhaps the woman had been so quick to seize him because she had been warned. Was someone perhaps looking for him? Could he have been betrayed already?

He looked around the large room. Who would suspect him? Clearly not the city guards. They regarded him almost as a pet, to be cosseted and occasionally mistreated. The one with pearly teeth sat at a table playing a board game with the white-haired old gentleman, and he waved at Tom cheerily. The ancient pipe sat, dribbling smoke, on a corner of the table as its shabby owner leaned forward to study the game. The board was coloured green and red and the pieces, of blue stone, were representations of weapons – knives, clubs, crossbows.

65

Each evening there were new faces, but Tom felt that the danger, if it existed, must come from one of the regular guests. Had he really divined something strange in the look of the proprietor, Clem? And why – he met his gaze now – did the man with gold-framed spectacles and crinkly hair pay such close attention to the people around him without ever betraying any emotion?

'M-m-may I sit here?'

Tom's thoughts were broken by the new arrival at the table.

'I'm a little l-l-late for s-supper.'

'Of course,' Tom said, pushing the large board piled with bread to his companion. 'The soup's very good this evening.'

He thought with embarrassment of the incident two nights before when the poor man had been paraded around the room by the guards. His large eyes, though no longer filled with tears, seemed to express a deep inner sadness, even when his conversation belied this.

'G-good, good! I've w-w-worked up an appetite!'

He ladled the soup into his dish and bent his head to scoop the liquid into his mouth, greedily. Although he and Tom had adjoining rooms they rarely met. When they did run into each other, however, he noticed that the man's stammer improved as the conversation continued. He seemed to relax.

'You're right,' he said. 'It's excellent s-soup.'

He wiped his mouth on a clean white handkerchief and, the sharpest pangs subdued, proceeded to drink in a more leisurely manner.

'Well, young man,' he began after an interval, 'and wh-what have you found to amuse you today?'

Tom picked at a piece of bread. The moment the question was asked he caught a glimpse of Old Weasel, plucking a tune by the fireside, and an answer dried in his throat.

'Have you b-been outs-side?'

'A short walk.'

He felt wretched. He felt sympathy for the man after his recent humiliation and therefore condemned himself the more strongly for his evasion. The remark was, surely, an innocent one.

'But it's been a f-fine day.'

'Still a little cold, though.'

Tom was surprised by his own resolution. It was as though the weeks of uncertainty and danger, the warnings of Old Weasel and the frustrations of the day had bred in him a new determination not to be downtrodden. His conscience told him that it was unfair: that the man was trying to be pleasant. But Tom knew that he would not give anything away.

'D-d-did you g-go to the market square?'

'Not today,' Tom said.

'That's a l-lively place to v-v-visit. You can b-buy yourself a cheap l-lunch there. Fruit, for instance. Very good a-a-apples.'

'I'll remember that.'

The man smiled at him and wiped his mouth once more with the handkerchief. He had suffering eyes.

'But watch out for r-r-rogues,' he said.

Climbing the stairs to his room after the meal, Tom again found himself wondering about the puzzle of the city streets, which seemed to form mazes within mazes. He passed along the thickly carpeted corridor, with doors to right and left. If there was a way out of this sector he was determined to find it. A way up, perhaps.

As if in answer to his thoughts there suddenly came the clatter of footsteps from somewhere above his head. It ceased momentarily and then started again, but more faintly. Surely it was further along the passage. Running lightly forward, Tom strained his ears to hear the sound again.

12 The Great Invisible One

And then the footsteps were gone.

But Tom's determination to discover the way up was quickened. On this floor there were three connected corridors leading to seven doors. Tom's room lay behind one door, and he had once seen into his neighbour's room as the stammerer had entered: it was a small one similar to his own, similar to Old Weasel's. That left four doors, and behind one of these must be the flight of stairs leading upwards.

Most of the guests were downstairs. What he had to do involved a risk, but Tom knew that he would have to take this risk if he was to succeed. His own door could not be locked and he now hoped that this was true of the others. In quick succession, his breath stopped in his throat, he tried each one of them. Each swung open easily. Each was unoccupied and similar in size and furnishings to the three that he already knew.

The operation was completed within minutes and he was back in his room, shaking from the excitement of anticipating the welcome that might have greeted him had any of the rooms not been empty. And yet, how easy it had been. Why had it taken him so long to decide? A flatness overcame him: now that he had acted, it was in vain. He had discovered nothing.

Or perhaps he had: something was wrong. He looked round his own room and tried to estimate the size. Seven rooms the size of his could fit comfortably into the bar downstairs, and the corridors were not so very wide either. But the bar downstairs was only one of a whole complex of rooms. The outside of the building suggested that the first floor had the same area as the ground floor, so what had happened to the missing space? The walls could surely not be so very thick, and nor was this just one wing, for windows from the corridors looked out on all four sides of the building.

Pieces of the puzzle were beginning to fall into place; ideas were beginning to form. Each of the small rooms had a window like his own, and there were four windows in the corridors – eleven windows in all. And outside? Strangely agitated, he hurried down the stairs and through the crowded bar. His progress was slowed by the greetings that were called to him, by hands lightly touching his arms and shoulders, but – on the pretext of needing a breath of fresh air – he at last reached the door and stepped outside.

Even in the dark it was easy to count the windows on the first floor: four on the side immediately above the main door, four on the side facing onto the alley, five at the back and five on the remaining side. He was right! As with the city itself, the house comprised sealed-off units interlocking in such a way that only the closest scrutiny would ever suggest the existence of anything more than was immediately apparent.

How, then, was he to get to the rooms between the rooms? Did two staircases lead up from the ground floor? He had only ever seen one, but surely another must exist. There must be a way, if only someone or something would show him. He felt totally helpless, and it must have been this sense of helplessness which now made him think of his mother and her faith in the old beliefs. How he envied her those certainties. He gazed up at the rooftops, white with frozen snow. She believed in a power beyond this mortal world.

And then an idea, a fine piece of trickery, stung his mind and brought a smile to his lips. It was just possible that it would work. He lifted the catch and re-entered the House of the Star.

The fire-flung shadows of a large semi-circle of men played on the furthest walls of the bar. They were in good humour this night, toasting themselves before the flames, the chill misery of another working day driven away by warmth, beer and entertainment. Tom smiled with them, laughed with them, nodded with them and shook his head with them, all the while waiting his chance.

There was, it soon emerged, a special reason for the guards to carouse, for one of the group – the tall, burly one who had hoisted him onto the table to sing – had been promoted to the rank of captain. His face was ruddy in the firelight and the glass in his hand seemed always to be full, although he drank from it continually. He touched it against those of his companions, waved it above the heads of the assembled company when he told a joke, raised it up and down to the rhythm of a tune played by Old Weasel.

He was, it appeared, a popular choice. The atmosphere was pleasant, relaxed. The guards mingled easily with the other guests. Even the immaculately dressed gentleman with the grizzled hair could be seen exchanging a word with his uniformed neighbour. Clem appeared from time to time, to proffer trays of drinks or to hurl huge logs into the fire, and always he was detained with some story or joke before picking his way through the throng back to the kitchens.

The evening grew long with their talk. The guards became light-headed, loose-tongued. One tipped his glass, laughing to watch the amber fluid pour into the lap of his companion. But the man with the drenched lap, who on another night might have flared into anger, himself laughed and sympathised with the other's loss. One of the platoon even pretended to engage the landlord's wife in a dance, only to be driven back by a scowl as the company hooted and cheered. And still Tom waited.

His chance came at last during a rare pause in the conversation, one of those moments when all fall silent and appear to drift into their own private musings, gazing vacantly at the fire or into their glasses. He spoke quietly and without emphasis, almost as if to himself.

'It's on nights like this one would thank the Great Invisible One for being alive.'

There was a silence, broken by the sound of one of the guards choking on his beer. They looked at him in amazement. The one with pearly teeth seemed to speak for the others.

'Who is this Great Invisible One you would like to thank?' he asked, quickly glancing up at the dagger emblem on the wall. 'I'm sure I know nothing of him.'

'Sounds treasonable to me,' put in another.

'Why, my mother told me of him when I was a child,' Tom answered. 'It was he who made us, and who watches us.'

'Watches us?' demanded a third man, looking around

apprehensively for a hidden pair of eyes. 'What do you mean, watches us?'

Before Tom could reply to this second question he was interrupted by the captain, who stood close to the fire and who now decided to give the congregation the benefit of his wisdom.

'Religion, that's what he's talking about.'

The captain's face was hot and flushed. He was rather drunk and his mood had become ponderous.

'Let me tell you a story and then you'll understand.'

He leaned heavily against the wall with his eyes closed and began to tell his story slowly and deliberately, as if it were something he had once learned by heart and could now produce effortlessly, just as Tom had sung his song of the country without conscious thought. The story at first appeared to have little to do with their conversation, but his hearers were too polite, or too befuddled or, perhaps, some of them, too afraid to interrupt, and they listened intently.

'In the gathering dusk of an autumn evening a young man stood outside a city wall. The gates were closed and he was too late to enter; in any case, he had no permit and it was doubtful that he would be allowed in. The city rose from a coastal flat and there was no shelter for the young man from the wind that had begun to gust in from the sea. On his back he carried a knapsack. He walked to a freshly ploughed field, took the knapsack from his back and with his hands began to scoop a hollow in the ground large enough for him to lie in.

'Then from the knapsack he took two sheets of oilskin and carefully laid them in the hollow, one on top of the other. A low drystone wall provided large stones to anchor the edges and, that done, he crawled between the two sheets, wedging his knapsack near the edge to allow the access of air. The night's darkness was now complete and the space between the oilskins was utterly black, but warm and secure; for the young man knew that on this moonless night his shelter could be seen by no one. His day had been long and he was tired; within minutes he was asleep.

'But this sleep was soon disturbed. The wind catching the edges of the oilskin caused it to flap and crack like a whip. As he lay cursing the noise above him he became aware of noise beneath him. He pressed his ear to the ground. He could hear

71

hammering and, yes, voices far away. But surely they could not be beneath him; it must be an illusion. He lifted his head and listened: nothing!

'Pressing his ear once more to the ground, he again heard the faraway voices and the hammering. It was definitely coming from beneath him. Memories stirred of stories he had been told as a child, of the earth spirits, of the gods of the harvest and spring growth, stories that were laughed at and ignored by his friends as the mere pratings of ignorant peasants.

'The young man grew afraid; had he not also scoffed at these spirits, and would they not wish revenge? He quaked with fear and, pressing his mouth close to the ground, he begged forgiveness of the spirits, and vowed to serve them for as long as they gave him life.

'The next day he refolded his sheets of oilskin, packed them into his knapsack once more and, without attempting to enter the city, set off home. Once back in his village he set about convincing people of the reality of the old earth spirits. At first they laughed at him and called him crazy. But as he repeated his story over and over they began to listen. He set up a shrine in the fields and each day performed strange rituals before it. These rituals attracted followers.'

Here the captain paused, and his eyes opened a crack, swiftly surveying his audience.

'On the following Midsummer day two events occurred: the young man recruited his hundredth follower and believer' – and now the captain grinned hugely – 'while beneath the northern city plain underground sewers that had been under excavation for the previous two years were finally completed.'

He pushed himself from the wall triumphantly. Had he not told his story well? Stooping forward, he patted Tom on the knee.

'That's religion, my boy, that's religion. A nonsense. No disrespect to your mother, mind you.'

Some of the other listeners, having been slow to understand the story, were beginning to laugh.

'Ha, that's a good one! He thought the sewer-builders were spirits! That's rich, that is!'

But Tom frowned.

'No,' he said loudly, and with great determination. 'That's not true. It's not like that.'

The Captain stilled the others with a wave and addressed Tom in a fatherly tone.

'You tell us then, Tom. How is it?'

Tom left his chair and joined the captain at the fireside.

'At night,' he said, 'when you stand in the fields under the stars, you can feel him watching – not always, but sometimes. He's completely invisible, and completely good, and he completely surrounds you, and he's definitely there. Or sometimes, by the seashore, when the light of the sun bounces off the sea and seems to wrap you in itself, then he's there in that light.'

As he spoke these words Tom pictured his mother's face, for the words had been hers, and he knew that he had been just as uncomprehending as these people who watched him now.

'It's not superstition, or – ' (he grinned at the captain here) 'or underground sewer-workers. It's real, and if you wished you could feel it for yourselves.'

But the captain shook his head.

'No lad. I've lived for many years – some would say *too* many – and I've trudged the streets many a night after the curfew beneath the stars. I've felt nothing such as you describe. Imagination is what it is. Imagination, coupled with your mother's teaching.'

Tom, refusing to be put off, leaned forward and fixed the captain with his eye.

'But how could you expect to feel the Great Invisible One, here in the streets, surrounded by houses and people . . . ?' (Here Tom threw up his hands and turned to the whole company.) 'No, it's no use. You'll never understand. Perhaps if you were to stand up on the rooftops, above everything, and look up at the stars, perhaps then you would feel him, perhaps he would come to you then, perhaps. . . . '

The speed with which the subsequent events occurred amazed him. The captain spoke abruptly.

'Right, men! We have a duty to this lad: on your feet!'

The guards stood up. One or two of them, unsure of their ability to do so, held onto chair backs or to the wall. The captain examined them quickly and singled out two of the steadiest.

'You and you,' he ordered. 'You too, Tom – come on.'

73

And Tom found himself being marched out of the bar into a smaller room behind it, through another door, down a flight of steps into the cellars, between a row of barrels, grey and cobwebbed and standing one on top of another, beneath a low stone arch with a carved keystone, through a narrow passage to a spiral staircase which wound its way up and up. They climbed silently, the evening's celebrations now telling on the legs of the three guardsmen. Their pace grew slower and slower as they climbed higher and higher. At last they reached a door. Through the door, and Tom was there, on the roof, on a small railed platform, standing beneath the stars between the three tall men.

He stood trembling, partly from excitement and partly from the coldness of the night after the warmth of the downstairs bar. The captain looked down at him, smiling.

'What now lad, eh?'

They stood there, a little cluster of human beings, high above the streets of the city, silhouetted against a moon which had escaped from behind a cloud and now flooded them with sudden light.

'You must be very still and wait for him,' said Tom in a hushed voice.

For several minutes they stood still and silent. Along the snow-capped roofs they could see for miles in each direction. Nothing stirred. Finally the captain spoke.

'Well, my lads – do you feel anything?'

They shook their heads, impatient to be done with the business.

'And you, Tom? Do you feel anything?'

Tom shook his head dumbly and hung his head in the universal gesture of dejection.

'No. No, this time I don't. I can't explain it.'

The captain put his hand on Tom's shoulder and spoke almost tenderly.

'Don't take it so badly,' he said. 'You'll get over it. These fancies are just part of growing up. Better to face facts, especially here in the city: no time for country ways here. Come, I'll buy you a drink and we'll warm ourselves up again, eh?'

This suggestion noticeably cheered the guards, who had

grown very cold standing on the exposed roof for no reason that they could well understand. They led the way down.

'I'm not meaning to be cruel, now,' the captain continued, following close behind him. 'You understand that.'

Tom was relieved that he did not have to show his face. His heart sang with elation within him. Not only did he now know a way to the roof, albeit without yet having solved the mystery of the other floors, but also – while he had been standing out there in the cold air and the moonlight had poured itself over him – he had felt it, for the first time in his life, the presence of the Great Invisible One, and he had been enveloped in the feeling of complete power and complete goodness that his mother had spoken of. And at that moment he had looked towards the east and seen, clearly under the moon, the house with the longed-for white room.

'Nothing on the roof, young Tom? Better try putting your ear to the ground!'

'Give the boy a stiff drink, Clem. We can all of us see things after a few jugs of good ale!'

Of course he had to endure a round of bluff, though good-natured joking when they returned. He did not mind it at all, but he tried nevertheless to play the part of disillusion and dejection slowly cheered by good company. It was a difficult part to play, for he felt jubilant and full of new hope. The evil that manifested itself everywhere that he looked in the city no longer seemed so overwhelming.

He glanced at Old Weasel who sat, eyes averted, plucking a sonorous melody from his burnished instrument. The firelight flickered on the glowing wood. Surely, if he knew, the old messenger would be proud of him, the cunning he had used. But, then – he probably understood everything already. There was nothing that escaped him.

The company had never been so contented. A few of the guards were actually nodding in their chairs and the white-haired old gentleman was snoring throatily, his pipe happily keeping itself going for a while on a table. His belly heaved and fell under a stained and buttonless shirt. The old slippers on his feet had holes in the toes.

'A toast! I give you a toast!'

The captain, whose night it was, had not finished yet. He carried a jug among the guests, topping up their glasses.

'Let's salute a *future* captain of the city guard – the Great Invisible Tom!'

And tonight he did not mind their nonsense in the least, not even the tipsy heads thrust close to his own as they bumped glasses and yelled his name.

There was a way to the roof. There must be a route across the city skyline. His fears, his memories of the blacksmith, were submerged for the moment beneath his newfound hope. He must find his way to the railed platform once again and pick his way across the buildings by night.

Not this night, however. Even as he mused about the task before him his eyes began to close, and he had to force himself awake, shaking the encroaching sleep from his head as he prised himself from his chair. It had been a long and eventful day – the hours of walking through the city, the pursuit by the three men and the adventure of the evening – and his body ached for rest.

It was not to be granted immediately. When he reached his room and swung open the door he found that someone was there before him.

13 Angry Words

'That was a foolish mistake, to ask for the east gate.'

The rebuke, uttered in a harsh, high voice, was delivered even before he had shut the door behind him.

'It might have been the end of you – and it would have served you right!'

The dwarf sat perched on a chair, his knees drawn up to his chin. He had flung his coat on the bed and helped himself to one of Tom's books.

'I didn't mean to,' Tom said, lamely.

'Ho! That's a fine one! He didn't mean to. But he did. That's the inescapable fact. He did!'

Tom dropped into another chair. He was about to explain, to say that he had been tramping the streets for hours when the woman had surprised him, but he felt suddenly angry. It was not only his tiredness: he felt the injustice of the dwarf's attack.

'And he might have undone us all in the process.'

There was a silence, which seemed to surprise the dwarf. Perhaps he had been expecting an apology. He jumped down from the chair and stood before Tom with his arms folded in a challenging manner.

'I wouldn't have needed to ask,' Tom said, 'if I had been told in the first place.'

'Oh! He wanted to be told!'

'If someone had explained the city to me,' Tom persisted, 'I might have been on my way to accomplishing the mission by now.'

'Or on your way home!'

The dwarf stood immobile before him.

'Why, might I ask, did you want the east gate? Why do you need to leave this sector at all? A trifle suspicious, wouldn't you agree?'

Tom considered before replying. It seemed to him that the

commander, and so the dwarf, was fighting against an evil force. He knew enough of the Red Blade and its cruelty to sympathise with their cause. But he remembered the words of Old Weasel and reflected that no good could come from telling what little he knew.

'I have investigations to make.'

'A-hah!' The dwarf cackled, mirthlessly. 'He has investigations to make. He's a sleuth!'

Tom could abide this treatment no longer. He leapt to his feet and found himself shaking his fist in the little man's face.

'That's what you want me to do, isn't it! I'm supposed to be doing your dirty work for you, discovering things you haven't the wit to find out for yourself! And what help do you give me? You tell me nothing that I need to know, but come strutting in here as if I'm your servant!'

The outburst shook them both. They both sat down. The walls, fortunately, were thick.

'I'm not your servant,' Tom added, emphasising the point.

The atmosphere was uncomfortable, but fatigue and his anger had dulled his sensitivity. He did not care what the dwarf thought of his behaviour. As for the dwarf, he sat fidgeting his fingers, composing himself.

'Well now,' he said after some minutes. 'I think that perhaps we should start again, don't you?'

'If you like,' Tom replied.

'I do like. We both should like. Because, unless we work together we can't possibly succeed.'

Tom said nothing.

'I will agree that you were told very little. There was a reason. We could not be sure of you: we had to watch. You might have betrayed us at the first opportunity.'

'I didn't.'

'So we find. But, had you done so, you would have had few secrets to give away.'

'You could have explained about the city streets.'

Here the dwarf seemed to make a concession.

'Perhaps we should have done so,' he said. 'But – I'll be frank with you – we had no reason to imagine you would need to leave this sector. We believe that the answers are to be found at the House of the Star.'

Tom's temper began to rise again.

'And you have therefore risked my life by setting me down in the most dangerous area!'

'Of course.'

This time the dwarf was clearly in no mood to compromise.

'Don't you want to find your father?'

'You know that's why I am in the city.'

'Then the dangerous way is the only way.' He perched forward in his chair. 'What have you discovered so far?'

'It's too soon,' Tom replied. 'I've nothing to tell you yet.'

'But weeks have passed!'

'The weather kept me in,' Tom countered.

'But "in" is where you need to be. Have you learned nothing of the people?'

'Nothing that helps.'

The dwarf frowned, but seemed to be making an effort to control his irritation.

'And the eastern gate,' he said. 'Why do you wish to go there?'

'It's not the gate itself.'

'The sector, then. Why does it interest you?'

'I can't say.'

'Ho!'

'No, I can't say. Not yet.'

The dwarf hopped from his chair again and began to pace the room.

'There is a five-letter word called Trust. There's a rune we learned at school – I wonder if you know it?' (He paused for a reply which never came.) 'The first T stands for truthfulness, the R for reliability, the U for unselfishness, the S for stability and the final T for tolerance.'

Still Tom said nothing.

'We need that trust between ourselves.'

The dwarf continued his progress around the room until it brought him to Tom, who looked him steadily in the eye.

'How do I reach the east gate?' he demanded.

The question deflated the little man in an instant. He turned his back on Tom and occupied himself for a while at the shelf of books above the bed.

'Of course there are routes through the buildings,' he said

79

eventually, 'but they are very well guarded. You need passes. It's almost impossible.'

'But not quite impossible,' Tom insisted. 'We came here ourselves.'

'We have our own route, but it is open to very few. The risk is too great. I may come and go.'

'But I may not.'

'No – not at present.'

'At present?'

'It would need special sanction. From the very top. Perhaps it might be arranged.'

Tom spoke urgently.

'How long would it take to arrange?'

'I don't know. A week or two, perhaps. But perhaps not at all.'

'And the rooftops? There's a way across the roofs?'

The dwarf seemed to shudder. He shut his eyes and shook his head.

'It's perilous. Our people sometimes use that method, but only in an emergency. I can't' – the very thought seemed to injure him – 'I can't cope with those heights myself. I once. . . . '

But he did not finish. The memory was obviously too dreadful.

'I'll try,' he said. 'I'll do what I can to get you the sanction.'

The hostility had passed. They spoke more quietly now.

'I will show my trust in you,' the dwarf went on, 'by letting you further into my confidence. Your work is more vital than you were aware. We face nothing less than the extinction of our organisation – the extinction of all hope.'

He began to dress himself for the bitter cold outside.

'We are weakening. Every day another of our leaders is seized. If we make no fight now the cause is lost – we have to make one great effort. Yet many of our comrades have lost heart. They lack the courage to take up arms and challenge the Blade on the streets. We need to inspire these people.'

'Is that possible?'

'There is one way,' replied the dwarf. 'The myth of the underground city is well known. If it exists, and if we can find it, our faint-hearts will be persuaded to stand firm – to fight alongside those good people underground.

'That is why your mission is of the greatest urgency.'

He paused, with his hand on the doorknob.

'Unless we risk everything now we shall all be destroyed – and the Blade will rule for a thousand years!'

14 Vertigo

Along the spine of the roof the thin snow had frozen to white ice. His fingers would not grip. Leaning forward, straddling the ridge, he was aware of his thighs slipping, twisting him over, however gingerly he edged forward. The roof fell away, glistening under the moon, with dark patches of slate where parcels of snow had shot down the steep slope and plummeted into the black abyss.

He could not look down the hundreds of feet to the ground. He saw only the pitch of the roof, inviting him to plunge into the spaces beyond. When he raised his eyes he found himself alone in a gaunt silhouetted world of gables, parapets and chimneys.

Six more feet and there was nothing that he could see. The roof ended there. A breeze buffeted him, pushed him off balance, but the more tightly he grasped the masonry the more his fingers skidded on the polished snow.

Taut with fear, he inched forward. At the end there was a projecting strip of metal: a lightning conductor, perhaps. He reached out – carefully, tremblingly – and clutched it. He pulled himself close to it and shut his eyes.

There was no sound. The city was asleep. If he fell, nobody would know. His frozen body might lie, lost among the high roofs, never to be found.

He opened his eyes. Beneath him an icy slope gave access to a long flat area. Behind him – he turned, cautiously – crumpled snow revealed the route he had taken from the House of the Star, down a steel ladder, along a stone walkway to the precarious ridge on which he sat. If he slid down the incline, a distance of perhaps ten feet, he could not possibly climb up again. Yet he knew that his nerves would not allow him to return the way he had come. Gripping the metal so tightly that it cut into his flesh, he manoeuvred himself to the top of the slope, cradled his knees in his free arm, and let go.

The impetus sent him slithering along the roof on his back, his feet ploughing through thick snow. His hair was flecked with it. He stood up and beat the flakes from his coat with stinging hands. The roof was wide, with no balustrade or ornamentation of any kind. To right and left the nearest buildings stood well back: he feared even to approach the edge and gaze across.

Ahead of him there was an adjoining roof, but much lower down. He knelt as near the brink as he dared and looked over. The wall fell sheer for twenty feet: there was no foothold of any kind.

Sick with desolation, he raised himself to his feet. The breeze mocked him. The moon sailed on, pitilessly. He was trapped, with no chance of being discovered. All around him the buildings rose dark and forbidding against the sky. Heavy grey clouds were building up in the west – clouds that his companions at the hostelry had told him marked the onset of further storms.

He retraced his steps, knowing that it was hopeless. The slope could not be scaled unless it was dry. If only – it was a childish thought – if only he could leap from one building to another he could cross to the eastern sector in twenty bounds. He could not be sure where one sector gave way to another, and he was now too low to see the building with the white room, but he had studied the cityscape carefully before leaving the railed platform and he was sure that he knew how far to go and in which direction.

In a panic he returned to the edge where the wall dropped smoothly to the lower roof. Was there really no way down? Had he perhaps overlooked a snow-covered ladder that led to the safety of the next level? But it was mere foolishness. The wall was flat and steep. A mountaineer would have shuddered at the prospect.

Now he cursed his own conceit. To have thought it would be so easy! To have congratulated himself on his trickery, without considering the consequences! Where was the Great Invisible One now? In his moment of triumph he had told himself that he felt the goodness and the power, but now he could not bring that feeling back. He stood stiff and straight, as if challenging the spirit to appear, but he was unable to receive it. He watched the clouds lifting out of the west, bringing more onslaughts of driving snow, and he shivered.

What of the sides of the building? It was in desperation rather than hope that he crouched to peer over. Here the drop was immense, broken hundreds of feet down by a narrow ledge which was itself high above the ground. There was no window to call at, no sign of human habitation at all. He kicked his way through the snow to the other side. The view was identical, the wall as sheer.

And then he noticed what at first seemed to be thin shadows at the corner nearest the lower roof. But they were not shadows. Hurrying across, he discovered that iron stakes had been hammered into the wall, descending. They were set irregularly and were spaced well apart, but it was obvious that they had been designed for people scaling the wall because, further down, they changed direction and took a lateral route towards the next building.

Tom flattened himself on the roof and edged himself into position. Once he was satisfied that his feet would find the first bar he gripped the stonework as firmly as he could and swung himself over. For a second he hung in the air, his fingers trembling with the effort, and then his boots touched the metal and he struggled into a standing position. He had to turn half sideways in order to keep his footing, since the stakes came straight out of the wall. Steadying himself, he craned his neck to look for a handhold. There was another iron bar to his left just above knee height, but when he stooped to reach it with his left hand he felt his right slipping away from the roof. Twice more he tried it. The iron way had been designed for men.

He flattened his body against the wall, his arms aching with the effort of supporting him. There was only one solution, and it horrified him. He must position himself as close to the stake as possible, skewed round with his left hand hovering, and then, for a brief moment, let go completely, falling onto the iron support.

He prepared himself and counted slowly to ten, but at the last his nerve gave way. He had to stand upright again. The second time he was sure he would go, but his right hand seemed frozen to the roof. Always he let his eyes look no further down than the section of wall he had to cross.

84

Something pressed uncomfortably against his chest. It was the picture that he always carried safe inside his coat. If his father could see him now! He thought of his father, perhaps – or was it a wild dream? – perhaps deep underneath the city while he was far above it. And, in the moment of reflection, he dropped and clutched the metal bar, bracing himself hard against the wall.

Now it was possible to lower his legs onto another support. He moved hands and feet alternately, picking his way down the face of the wall, which was smooth and glistening with tiny crystals of ice. The sky above the hard line of the roof was dark, invaded by the first of the dense snowclouds. Below – he looked for the first time and was almost undone. Unreal in the deep distance, a miniature street glimmered white through the shadows. He would fall and fall and roll and float before he ever reached it. His body felt as though it pulled him away from the wall, eager to plunge into space. His brain somersaulted. His hands gripped the stake violently. Their hold was too rigid: the iron would slip through. He would surely topple.

He could only press himself against the wall until the worst of the fit had passed. There was so little space between life and death, so great a divide between hope and achievement. He started down again, but clumsily, stiffly. His heart raced, his brow was covered in sweat, his hands ached with the strain of holding onto the iron.

After a while there were no more stakes beneath him. He stood on the last support above the chasm. A double row of spikes ran to his left, towards the low roof, the higher ones only just within his reach. He had to stretch his arms to hold on as his left leg swung in the air for a footing. Here, where the iron ladder changed direction, he discovered a marking on the wall. Leaning back a little to examine it, he found it to be the sign of the eye which the dwarf had shown him at their first meeting. He carried the metal disc in a safe pocket. There was no colouring on this etching, but it was unmistakeably the same device.

Spurred on by this finding, Tom moved more easily across the face of the wall. He was able to reach the lower roof and haul himself onto a wide shelf which ran between two steep slopes. He sat for a while, his head in his arms, panting, his eyes closed. He had never imagined such terrors.

Now the way was easier for a time. He climbed a ladder, wickedly iced along the rungs but secure to the wall, and found himself on the first of a series of flat roofs. He could see for some distance ahead, and between the roofs there were wooden plank-bridges with rope supports for the hands on either side. Taking care to look only ahead, he began to cross the first of these bridges. The ropes swung a little as he held them, but he was able to keep his balance without difficulty. He breathed more freely.

He was on the fourth plank, crossing a gulf of some thirty yards between grim grey buildings, when he found that a section of rope to his right had broken away. He approached the spot nervously. The rope was strung on metal posts driven into the planking at intervals of about ten feet, and he saw that it had snapped in the centre. The two ends hung uselessly in the void. He wondered, with a shudder, whether the weight of a man had broken it.

He started across, holding the remaining rope with both hands. It was wet and in poor condition: the strands had begun to fray and separate. He was just beyond halfway, and leaning as heavily as he dared, when it snapped and he was flung forward. His fingers grappled furiously for a hold. His body slid across the planking, his head already out over the edge. He felt one leg lose its contact with the wood and his body turning over. His fingers found a crack in the worn surface of the bridge and he dug them in, frantically, but the other leg began to slip away. He could not prevent it. He was out over the edge, tugging at the one anchoring arm. There was not enough strength in it. He swayed, all but gone, his body twisting away from the plank and then returning.

Slowly, not to disturb the tenuous hold he had, he raised his free arm and groped to locate another purchase in the wood. His fingers dug into frozen snow, scrabbled wildly, and found, at last, what appeared to be the head of a large nail. He dangled, feeling his strength ebb.

He knew that his aching frame could manage only one mighty effort. If it failed he would hang suspended for a few seconds more before spinning off into the void below. He tensed his body for the attempt, took a quick deep breath and hauled upwards, his muscles feeling as if they would tear out of his arms, his neck straining, his legs kicking fiercely. Halfway, and the agony was unbearable. He came up and forward; he reached a knee onto the planking; he rolled himself over; and he lay hunched and heaving and safe.

It was impossible for him to stand again. He dare not trust the rope. His feet might slip. Once his breath was back, he crawled forwards on all fours like an injured animal, his hands raw and numb. He crossed onto the next roof and collapsed in a heap.

The worst was over. Soon he came to a properly constructed thoroughfare. Where there were steeply pitched roofs this pathway was built into the side, with a parapet on the open side. He stumbled gratefully onward, his eyes clouded with tiredness.

When the route climbed to a high point he paused to take his bearings. At first he could not see the house with the white room. He looked into the middle distance with a growing despair. But when he turned towards the buildings nearer at hand he discovered with joy that the house he sought was now almost within reach. It was not accessible by the route he was taking – it lay at an acute angle from it – but it was clear that he must have already crossed into the eastern sector. He had only to find a way down.

The first door that he discovered would not open. It was under the eaves and approached by an iron staircase. He threw himself against it, but made no impression whatsoever. Soon afterwards, however, he came across another, this time let into the pitch of the roof. The handle turned and the door swung open. Steps led down steeply, and the turning of a corner plunged him into complete blackness. His boots thumped heavily on the stone. He steadied himself against the wall with one hand, descending slowly.

After some minutes he began to feel uneasy. He was not lost, since it was possible to climb back again to the door in the roof, but the darkness was oppressive. Every so often the stairway changed direction, but always it led steeply down. He began to touch the walls to both right and left for fear that he might pass a door unawares.

The door, when he found it, was in front of him. He collided with it. He fumbled for the handle and stepped into a murky light. High to his left there were small windows in the wall. The steps led straight down now, with not the slightest turn. Tom began to count them, reached five hundred, and tired of the exercise.

Some minutes later he was surprised to find, to his right, an archway leading to a corridor. It was deeply shadowed, but he imagined that it must lead to rooms. The air was chill, even so far from the roof, and the area clearly was unused. Another twenty steps down and he came upon an identical passage. There was an eeriness about the darkened entrance and he hurried on. He passed another three archways, all deserted, and then came up against a stout wooden door. This time the handle would not turn. He tried it this way and that. He leaned on it, pulled it and pushed it. The door was so heavy that when he tried to shake it there was no movement and no sound. It was only after some considerable time wrestling with it that he stood back and noticed a large square section in the centre. He touched it and immediately felt it yield. His fingers pushed against the top and it tilted away from him to reveal a sizeable opening.

On the other side, once he had swung the flap to, the opening was completely invisible. The door was panelled and decorated, giving no hint of its secret.

The windows were a little larger now and the air was warmer. And when he came upon another passage he was surprised to find a plant hanging in a pot from the arch. There was no sound, but he felt that there were people along the passage. He moved more stealthily, descending past several more corridors, until he reached a point at which the stairs made a sudden turn. At this moment, around the corner he heard footsteps and he drew himself up against the wall.

There was something he recognised about those steps – the steps of several people at a time, in unison. He had heard them before, and the memory was not pleasant. It was the sound of marching. The steps drew near, very near, and passed on, tramping.

The city guards! The crunching of their feet faded away. What were they doing here? He turned the corner and found

88

the answer. He faced a door, the final door. Cold air swept through the cracks around it. He had reached his destination: the street lay beyond. Tearful with relief and tiredness, he sat propped against the wall and fell asleep.

He was awoken by new sounds from the street. There were the muted conversations of people up earlier than their neighbours, a man and a woman he thought. And then came the clatter and creak of a horse and cart, passing at an easy pace.

From inside the building there was nothing. Tom rose, rubbed the sleep from his eyes, and quietly opened the door. A light wind was blowing large white flakes along the street. He stepped outside, his boots making fresh marks in the snow.

15   In the Night Cafe

'Where are you going, boy?'

The man seemed to have appeared from nowhere. He looked frail and slightly mad, with his intense eyes and his wild grey hair and knotted beard. The firmness of his grip on Tom's arm disposed of any lasting belief in his frailty, but his sanity remained open to question.

'Where are you going, I say?'

Tom flinched. Was the man some sort of official set to question strangers in these empty streets? He certainly looked nothing like one. His clothes barely held together, their raggedness was so complete, and the way that he shifted his staring eyes, looking first one way down the street and then the other, suggested that he was as fugitive as Tom himself.

'You look a bright sort of lad; the sort of lad who wants to know things, to understand things. You come with me, boy, and I'll show you wonders that will make your mind dance, that will set the constellation of your thoughts into movement. You come with me!'

Tom found himself tugged across the street, into an alley, and from there through the door of a low building. It was a night cafe, so well hidden that its custom must of necessity be drawn from those intimate with the area. The door swung to behind them. It was like entering a forest, the light of the streets giving way to a strangely greenish gloom. The only light came from a window which faced the narrow alley between tall buildings, and it was muted even before it fought its way through the grimy glass.

Tables stood in clusters, scrubbed and bare. At two or three of these breakfasters sat, silent, their heads remaining down even when Tom and his companion entered. There was a stench of stale wine and smoke, mixed with the smell of food. But, despite the gloom and the unwelcome odours, Tom was attracted by the warmth and privacy of the place.

By the door was a small bar, and there stood the waiter, a cloth slung over his shoulder and a cup in his hand. He surveyed the two new arrivals carefully as they made their way to the furthest and darkest corner of the cafe, Tom in tow. Sitting down, the older man waved to the waiter who, until this moment, had scarcely moved – even the hand with the cup seemingly frozen into immobility. Now he set down the cup and approached the table.

'My young friend and I would each like a breakfast, if you please.'

The waiter turned to Tom to verify the order and there was a sympathetic look in his eye. Tom nodded his head uncertainly, and the waiter shrugged and disappeared towards the kitchen. Once he was gone the old man leaned forward, speaking in a hoarse whisper.

'I know the secrets of the city, my boy: would you like me to reveal them?'

The man's eyes had begun to burn with a sudden intensity that frightened him, and the tone of his voice was changed, too; the voice that had coaxed Tom into this cafe and ordered food from the waiter had become higher, faster and edged with malevolence.

'I was the keeper of the archives, all the archives. Before they burned them, that was. I had access to all of those documents before the flames snatched them away – those ignorant pigs of soldiers, what wouldn't I pay to see them and their brutish faces vanish in the flames instead? Ha! They grinned, you know: they grinned! I escaped them, though. You can't fool a city archivist so easily. Oh no, I had the beating of them.'

He spoke with a dreadful fevered seriousness, his lips flecked with spittle. Tom felt himself mesmerised as the river of speech rolled on and on relentlessly.

'They thought they were dealing with a madman, you see. Can you believe that? They thought I was mad. The poor fools! Do I look it, eh? I had the beating of them, all right, the beating of them.'

This monologue was cut short by the arrival of the breakfasts

91

which, though short of being delightful, were at least more easily digested than the bearded man's speech, which left Tom completely mystified. The waiter again gave him a sympathetic look and made his way back to the bar. The old fellow pushed his food aside with a gesture of contempt and carried on talking as animatedly as before.

'Thought they'd captured everything, they did. But they hadn't. Oh no, they certainly hadn't! Ah, the archives – what a treasure house they were! My father kept them before me, you know. You knew that, did you? Yes, it's a family tradition – thirteen generations of city archivists. I'm the thirteenth, and the last, thanks to *them*!'

At this point his eyes welled with tears, and he took a fork and crudely thrust a mouthful of food between his lips as if in order to control himself. He consumed it messily, noisily. This done, he leaned forward and, prodding Tom with the end of his knife, he said softly:

'But they didn't burn all of them, you see. This hand snatched some from the flames.'

Tom looked down at the hand and noticed, for the first time, the dreadful swollen scar tissue that covered one side. The man grinned, horribly, but the expression changed in a moment as he looked over Tom's shoulder towards the door.

Tom turned and witnessed the dramatic entry of a patrol of city guards. The man leapt to his feet, whimpering, but within seconds the soldiers had pushed their way across the cafe, scattering tables and chairs. The terrified creature threw his arms around the still seated Tom, as if to anchor himself and prevent arrest. The movement thrust Tom backwards and the chair overturned, throwing them both in a tangled heap on the floor. The poor wretch, meanwhile, was screaming and clutching at table legs, chairs, anything, in a futile attempt to prevent their carrying him off. The soldiers waded in roughly and yanked them to their feet, bundling them off towards the door. Tom, confused and afraid, made no effort to resist and his sudden exit from the cafe was prevented only by the waiter, who stepped forward and held up a hand.

'It's not the boy's fault; don't take him. This old fool is always grabbing people and dragging them in here. He's mad if you ask me, quite off his head, but the boy here's done nothing.'

The captain looked down at Tom, who was near to tears, and shoved him towards the waiter contemptuously.

'Take him, then. We've got our man.'

For several minutes the screams of the old man could be heard fading into the distance. The other breakfasters, who had observed the violent scuffling in silence, returned to their eating, each alone with his thoughts. Tom was badly shaken and sat with his head in his hands for some minutes. When at last he regained his composure and opened his eyes he found the scene unchanged – the customers chewing dumbly, the waiter with his cloth by the bar. The incident, which had been so short-lived, seemed never to have really happened, so unreal was it.

The waiter, who until now had said so little, came over and sat next to him.

'Have you somewhere to go, lad?' he asked.

Tom, surprised by the question, said nothing.

'You're a stranger round here, I know that, and strangers are rare in this sector.

'It's a guess, then, that you're running from someone. No, no – I'm merely thinking aloud. You needn't say anything. "No prying" is the motto of this place.'

Tom spoke slowly.

'I'm looking for someone,' he said.

At this the waiter glanced rapidly around the room. He stood up and cleared his throat.

'No names,' he said. 'It's our second motto. Now, you wait here a moment, lad. Do you promise.'

'I promise.'

'I've a little idea. You just hang on.'

16   Strange Papers

As he sat waiting, Tom became aware of an unfamiliar weight in the pocket of his coat. Plunging his hand inside, he discovered a bundle of papers held by a knotted cord. They looked old and were charred at the edges. He stared at the bundle, remembering the shrill screams of the mad archivist.

The cord was difficult to untie, but his struggle with it seemed to go unnoticed in the darkened cafe. Eventually he was able to slip the papers out. He unrolled them, straining to make out the faded writing.

Document I (fragment: the edges charred)

> . . . the forest and facing the plain.
> Who could say that he had no fear?
> The sun pinning my shadow to the ground by day,
> scraping a hollow in the earth at night
> to escape from the wind,
> my mouth moistened by torn fingers.
> Who could say that I had . . .
>
> . . . plentiful as the stars
> that fill the night sky
> lie the graves upon the hillside
> now that the excavations are finished.
> A hundred years – men born to carry earth
> have died still carrying earth
> and men born to masonry have sat and waited,
> their hair turning white, their bodies wasting
> and they have died, still waiting.
> A mountain range has grown . . .
>
> . . . and a boy will enter the city.
> Through the gate, unwelcome he will creep
> like a tick entering the wool of the sheep

he will come, and like a tick he will
drink the blood of the city.
But another will follow seeking a father.
Secretly he will enter the city –
like a steel comb he will enter the sheep's wool ...

Document II (full sheet – hand written – tiny blocks of writing
seemingly scattered at random across the page)

I sing of a city with no night –
do you remember the stars?
I sing of a city with no clouds –
do you remember rain?
I sing of a city with no warrior –
do you remember his wounds?

No birds sing beneath
the city's vaults;
the eagle's wing cracks
against stone.
There are stairs
into the snow;
we will climb into
the freezing air of winter
and watch gulls engrave
white arcs onto a grey sky.

An eye of blue,
vivid blue,
that stares and never closes.

Document III (clearly a section from an official document
relating to payment of functionaries)

City keeper – 30 pieces
Street watcher – 20 pieces
Lampman – 20 pieces
Sanctuary guardian – 15 pieces
Watcher in the Tower – 40 pieces (plus associated rooms and
    robes)
Keeper of the Stairs – 50 pieces
Executioner – (post removed)

City poet – 10 pieces (plus associated room and pen allowance)
Keeper of the artificial birds – 15 pieces
Keeper of plants (city/real) – 15 pieces
Keeper of plants (city/artificial) – 15 pieces
Transporter of plants – 15 pieces
Garden maker – 25 pieces
Painter of stars – 25 pieces (plus 30 pieces for other maintenance of sky vault)
Moonmaker – honorary (unpaid)

Document IV (handwritten, the script becoming increasingly loose and erratic, as if written in a fevered state)

An account of the birth and death of the star machine

I Olegial in my 37th year decided to replace the peeling stars of the sky ceiling with an illusion more convincing to my fellow citizens, and I set about the construction of the star machine whose clockwork mechanism unwound in such a way as to allow a beam of light pass through an everchanging grid, thus casting a multitude of small stars in movement across the ceiling. At its first trial the machine was received well and I was complimented for the birth of a new heaven. Astrologers once more turned their heads upward at a sky no longer static, and astronomers began to map my lights and plot their movements, commenting with excitement at any new light caused by a flaw in my machine. For two years I basked in the praise of the whole community. Sad the fate of man. Short the reign of praise. My machine developed a fault that sped the mechanism to destruction, first flinging the stars in wild confusion across the sky and then freezing them, hauntingly. Astrologers predicted the end of the city, causing great fear among the population. Astronomers tore up their carefully calculated charts in anger. Praise turned to abuse and my machine was smashed. I have lived these last thirty years shaven-headed among the remains of my machine. People have forgotten my moving sky, and each night I am rebuked by the golden stars that remain fixed and staring. Recently I have constructed a rainbow machine. Dare I test it? Dare I . . .

17 An Old Acquaintance

There was a movement in the shadows. He hurriedly thrust the papers into his pocket as the waiter returned to the table.

'Have you got work, lad?'

'No.'

'Would you like a job with us here, then? My Lucy says it's all right. There's not much money in it, I grant you, but there's a small room going with the job.'

'Thank you,' Tom replied, 'but . . .'

'It's not hard work. Mostly nights, but not every night. Not much money, but we can offer a room and food – and when you've got a roof above you and food inside you money counts for little enough.'

Tom was moved by the man's kindness.

'You're very generous,' he said, 'but I can't stay. I have to find the person I mentioned. It's important.'

The waiter stood back.

'You must choose,' he said. 'You're old enough to know your mind – though you're young enough to find trouble, in all conscience. Will you make me another promise?'

'What is it?'

'That you'll think about what I've said and not forget it. You'd find it a safe place here, lad. Not many outsiders get in here.'

'I won't forget,' Tom said, rising. 'I would stay. . . .'

'I know, I know,' conceded the waiter, opening the door. 'Business is business, lad. Good luck to you.'

He escaped from the stifling fug of the cafe and the crisp air seemed to buoy him up. He strode forward, feeling an elation which quite overcame his tiredness. Even the strange affair of the archivist's papers was for the moment forgotten. He knew he could not be far from the house by the east gate, with its longed-for white room in which he had been protected and nursed through his first days in the city. And as he passed along the silent streets, the walls of the buildings etched with hard dry snow, he was sure that already he recognised certain features – a doorway here, up there high on a wall an especially vicious example of the red blade insignia.

Then he came upon a huge pile of rubble which he instantly knew. He had scrambled frantically over the fallen stones on the morning he had left the house and the tearful girl. It was as mysterious now as it was then: a large building which had been utterly demolished. He remembered his despair on that cold early morning. He had been pursuing the boy with the green scarf. . . .

Now there was a movement beyond the ruined building and, as in a dream, he caught sight yet again of the slender lad, one arm pulling the scarf tight across his throat. It was no dream. On catching Tom's eye he turned swiftly and skipped along a nearby passage, soon completely lost to view.

But Tom had not given chase. He was surprised to find that he had no impulse to catch the youngster. Was it that he felt the task beyond him? No: this morning he felt alert and full of enthusiasm. He fancied himself the taller and stronger of the two. Nevertheless, he was not drawn to follow.

Instead, he hurried along the now familiar streets. The snow had been cleared in the centre and he was able to make good progress, his cheeks and his forehead smarting from the smack of the chill early morning wind.

Somewhere he miscalculated and took the wrong path, but almost immediately he found himself under the high wall, close by the eastern entrance to the city. He stole close. A dim light flickered in the guardroom. There was a murmur of voices. The huge iron gates were heavily bolted, impenetrable.

Keeping to the shadows, he hurried down the hill just as he had done on his arrival in the city. The tall buildings were sullen, closed and dark. A little further along he saw where the road disappeared into a bend: from round that turn the city guards had marched that terrifying evening. On his left was the building he had looked for so anxiously – that he had gazed down upon from the tower when he talked with the commander; that he had seen like a distant beacon as he picked his treacherous way across the rooftops. He approached nervously and touched the wall with a hand. It was cold, but massive and real. And here (he reached his fingers into the gloom) here was the door through which he had tumbled into the room which swam with liquid green.

But there was no door!

He groped, disbelievingly, for the handle, but there was none. His eyes, becoming accustomed to the halflight, discovered nothing but flat wall. It was not even possible to see a join where a door had once been.

Smitten by despair and an unnameable fear, Tom crossed the street to look back at the building. He had not mistaken it. This was clearly the house with the white room. But now there seemed to be no way in at all.

He looked up at the windows. It was not credible. A whole line of them had disappeared, leaving no trace. The white room, so far as any observer could tell, had been entirely obliterated.

A harsh cough alerted him to the presence of another early morning frequenter of the city streets. A gaunt man with close-cropped hair, hunching himself against the cold, appeared from around the corner. He had not yet seen Tom, for he seemed intensely interested in the buildings on the far side of the street. He carried what appeared to be a notebook, and he paused to consult it – running a finger over the contents – before coming on again, his head still turned away.

After hesitating a second time, he advanced to the very spot Tom had been standing only moments before. It was as if he, too, were seeking a way into the building. He looked in the book again and then up towards the rows of windows, all in darkness.

At that moment Tom recognised him. It was, without doubt, the prisoner Marcus whom he had last seen in the small cell before he met the commander. How well he remembered his chilling tales of torture! Tom's insides melted with fear. The man was a paid killer for the Red Blade – one, moreover, who enjoyed his foul profession.

The notebook was pushed into an inside pocket. Tom began to edge away, his heart racing. He dare not run. He walked silently towards the bend in the street, his feet gathering pace. Another twenty strides. . . .

'Wait! Hello!'

The sounds echoed through the empty streets. Oh say they were not meant for him! He hurried on, not looking back. But he heard the running footsteps behind him and even as he reached the corner a hand grasped him by the shoulder.

'Hey, wait young fellow! Don't we know one another?'

18 Dog-fight

'It's my little fellow-prisoner, is it not? And all in one piece!'

He took Tom's chin roughly between thumb and forefinger and titled his head this way and that as if looking for scars and bruises.

'You escaped the swine, did you? How did you manage that?'

His lined face seemed always in motion, the eyes darting, the tongue playing along the lips. Tom remembered his restlessness in the cell, how he had flung himself against the wall.

'They've paid for meddling with me, they have!'

He set off down the street with a gesture to Tom he could not disobey. They turned into a narrow alley, flanked by high walls.

'Paid?' Tom asked nervously.

'The fools! They took the weapons from me and imagined that was enough. They forgot these!'

He paused for a moment and held his hands in the air, the fingers curled and grasping, the muscles straining. They were like talons.

'Amateurs!' he muttered scornfully, leading Tom into a network of mean passages. 'The ones I strangled were fortunate. The others have been hunted and destroyed like vermin.'

They came at last to a neglected house of two storeys. The paint had long since flaked from the woodwork and the sills were feathery with decay. Patches of plaster had broken away from the wall, which was stained with deep-seated damp. The door was rotten and yielded to a push.

Inside, the house had a matching sense of degeneration. Low down on the walls Tom noticed an evil-looking black and green fungus, and there was a moist, earthy smell that was not pleasant. They passed through a kitchen area to a cavernous room containing two large and shabby chairs. He was motioned into one of them.

101

'Will you drink?'

'No. No, thank you.'

'*I* will.'

Marcus produced a bottle containing a colourless fluid and filled a large tumbler. He gulped a mouthful, coughed violently, and took another swig. The glass, Tom noticed, was long unwashed.

'That's where warmth comes from,' he said, putting the bottle by his feet as he sat down. 'There's no fire in here.'

There was a pause, during which he stared closely at Tom as if he were making up his mind about something.

'You escaped,' he said eventually. 'Tell me how.'

'How?'

'What happened when they took you away?'

Tom began to think quickly. It was suddenly clear to him that the gaunt man who sat so menacingly close to him perhaps regarded him as a sympathiser, a friend of the Blade. Of course he knew nothing. How, Tom wondered, would Old Weasel have dealt with such a situation?

'I was taken to a man they call the commander,' he said. 'A tall man. He asked me questions and threatened to kill me if I didn't answer them. I refused.'

'Ah – there's my cocksparrow! Refuse, did you?'

'I told him he would never wring a word from me.'

He was saved from becoming ridiculously dramatic by a tremendous growling sound which seemed to come from the other side of the wall. Marcus leapt to his feet.

'Silence, Fang!' he shouted, throwing open the door and disappearing into the room beyond.

The growling gave way to a series of ferocious barks. There was a metallic sound, as of a chain being taken from the wall, then a dull thud and a horrific yelping.

'Quiet, I say!'

Tom, who had covered his ears to shut out the noise, could not remain in his chair, but rushed through the door. He saw first Marcus, swinging a length of heavy chain, and then, cowering in a corner, a huge black dog, its teeth bared, its yellow eyes wild. Its unkempt hair stood out in an unruly shock, save for a strange area across the chest where it was flattened and sparse.

'A handsome brute,' said Marcus, with a thin smile, waving the chain so that the poor creature pressed itself even more firmly back against the wall. 'But he must save his anger for when it's needed.'

Without explaining this remark he led the way back into the other room. Tom heard a continuous low growling from the dog, a prolonged grating sound from deep in its throat. They sat down again.

'So you told them nothing?'

'Nothing at all.'

'And you escaped.' He laughed loudly and practised once more the grip with his fingers. 'No broken necks, I suppose?'

'He took me up to a tower. There was a view across the city. While he was gazing down below and threatening me with vile tortures I crept down the stairs. I reached the bottom before he raised the alarm.'

'And you found a way out?'

'It was easy. I'm small enough to hide in tight spaces. I'd seen a coil of rope in the tower and, when they'd gone, I climbed the steps again, tied it to the balustrade and let myself down.'

'You lowered yourself from the top of the tower?'

'Yes. I nearly let go the rope more than once, but it reached all the way down.'

'You've a head for heights, youngster?'

'They don't bother me,' Tom lied. 'It was better than remaining their prisoner.'

Marcus shook the liquid in his glass and sipped noisily.

'It wouldn't have mattered. Once I escaped they were doomed. You wouldn't recognise that commander today.'

He swirled the liquid again, enjoying the revelation, revelling in it.

'Not recognise?'

'Pieces are missing. An ear, for instance.'

Tom shrank into the worn back of his armchair.

'He'll talk eventually. They all do. We're about to rid the city of these scum once and for all.'

The low grumbling sound from the other room faltered and resumed more urgently.

'You're a likely lad, there's no mistake. Like to do some work for me, would you?'

Tom had no voice.

'Oh, you needn't be afraid I shall ask your business. Silence is the keyword, my mannikin. One unguarded word and you're a dead duck in this game. But we're on the one side, whatever your particular duties have been. We serve the same masters.'

Still clutching his glass, he stood and moved closer.

'Well?'

'Of course,' said Tom quickly. 'Tell me what I should do.'

Now the other's manner became manic. He paced the room with his fists clenched in front of him, his face twitching.

'Search and destroy!' he declaimed. 'That's what we'll do. Search and destroy. Until there's not a single one of them drawing breath!'

He crossed the room once and twice more and then flung himself into the chair, spilling the remains of his drink onto the floor. He closed his eyes and took deep shuddering breaths.

'Do you know the way out of this sector?' he asked at last, reaching down for the bottle. He filled the tumbler again.

'No,' Tom replied. 'There's no way through.'

'Of course there's a way through! How do you suppose the authorities pass about the city? You need the proper documents, that's all. You haven't got any, I take it.'

'No.'

'You shall. That's no problem. I have a spare pass for a trusty lieutenant. That's you. What do you say?'

Tom could say nothing. The excitement he felt was tempered by the fear that he might betray himself. To cover his confusion he reached out for the glass which Marcus seemed to be holding towards him, took it in both hands and drank. The liquor splashed into his mouth. It was like fire! His throat burned and ached, his eyes watered and a pain ran down his insides.

'We drink to it!' enthused his companion, taking a much larger gulp himself. He clapped Tom on the shoulder.

From outside in the street there came the sound of passers-by. Marcus went to the window, which had no curtain, and peered through the grime on the pane.

'It's time,' he said. He raised his voice: 'Ready, Fang!'

'Time for what?' asked Tom, his throat still stinging.

'He's got to earn his food. And mine. It's what I keep him for.'

Tom followed him into the next room, where the dog was on

104

its haunches, trembling. It was impossible to tell whether the animal shivered from the excitement of going out or because it was in a state of terror. Marcus reached high on the wall for a stout leather muzzle which he thrust onto the vicious snout. He slipped the chain over its head, and then all three were outside in the narrow alley, which was rapidly filling with people.

The sun had risen and glimmered dimly through thin cloud. All along the street there was a bustle of people, mostly men, and all walked in the one direction. From time to time smaller paths joined the main thoroughfare and groups of people emerged to mingle with the throng.

'Where are we going?' Tom asked, wondering at the sudden flux where but minutes before there had been emptiness.

'Don't know,' said Marcus. 'Those at the front know the way and we follow. There's no fixed place for it.'

Tom decided to ask no further questions, but gazed instead at the people around him. Most were dressed very poorly, their heavy coats threadbare, the boots creased and down at heel. At first few words were spoken – Tom remembered the silence of the deserted streets by the east gate – but as they grew in number they seemed to lose their reserve and soon there was a babble of voices and a whirl of gesticulating arms.

All the time Fang pulled on in front, opening a wide path for them: nobody, having cast eyes on the wild-eyed brute, wished to be within range, despite the muzzle. It tried incessantly to open its teeth and a thin spittle dripped from its jaws. Tom saw people nudge their companions and point to the shaggy-haired beast, and there was a muttering and nervous laughter.

'That devil has *my* money,' he heard one of them whisper.

Marcus said nothing and looked neither to right or left. His lined face carried an expression of great concentration. Only when they reached a large waste area, where the crowd spilled out and began to form a large jostling circle, did he show any interest in his surroundings. The ground was bare and hard, with patches of brittle snow in the hollows. It dipped towards the centre and the ragged flock stood back from this lower ground, making a rough arena of it.

'Marcus, ho!'

A tall bearded athletic man pushed through the crowd towards them carrying a contraption of leather and steel in his hand. When he came closer, Tom saw that it was a harness. Now he understood the wasted hairs on Fang's chest: the harness had a thick leather breastplate, from which protruded a wicked metal spike. Tom recoiled in horror.

'Who do we fight?' asked Marcus, following the man towards the centre.

'An unknown beast,' he was answered. 'The people from the fourth precinct have put it up.'

'It has no chance,' said Marcus in a tone which forebad reply. 'What breed is it?'

'They're keeping silent about it.'

Marcus reached into a pocket and pulled out a wad of paper. He held it out to Tom.

'Money,' he said. 'A lot of it, so don't lose it. You see the men up by the big tree there? Put the money on Fang.'

It was difficult to fight his way through to the bookmakers. There was a busy throng around them and a great deal of cash was changing hands. When Tom at last squeezed his way to the front a fat little man bounced forward and took him by the shoulder.

'Here's a young punter of promise!' he cackled, capturing everyone's attention immediately. 'Learn the skills of betting early, my son, and you'll not want for anything in your old age.'

Behind him his colleagues were chalking prices on a blackboard. At a rickety table a young man scribbled on small pieces of paper.

'So let's see the colour of your money, young man. We're not proud here, we're not. The smallest coins accepted!'

Tom held out the thick pile of notes, conscious that all eyes were upon him. The bookie faltered for a second, seeing the sum he was offered, but quickly regained his composure.

'That's it!' he shouted, waving the notes in the air for all to see. 'Start as you mean to go on, my son. There's gambling blood in you, praise be!'

There was a murmur from the crowd, which edged forward excitedly.

'And where should the money go?'

He came closer and saw that Tom did not understand.

'Which cur takes your fancy?'

'Fang.'

106

Now there was a greater commotion and the bookie turned to his companions with a broad smile that suggested relief.

'So the world isn't of one mind, after all,' he said, still holding the money aloft. 'Here's a supporter of the old champion, my friends.'

Some of the onlookers shook their heads at Tom, while others waved their hands at him to catch his attention.

'Don't do it, lad! Change your bet! It hasn't a chance today!'

But Tom stood his ground.

'Here's a man who knows his mind,' rejoiced the bookie, turning to the young man at the desk. 'A thousand on Fang.'

'No, no! Wait a while! Give him a chance!'

'He's made his choice.'

'Take it back, boy! Change your bet!'

The fat man, enjoying the commotion, handed the notes to one of his colleagues and passed Tom a slip of paper. There seemed to be nothing but squiggles on it.

'Might as well tear it up and throw it away,' he heard someone say as he made his way back to Marcus. 'Not a chance today.'

There was now a flow of people from the betting area towards the arena. Around the inside of this, at intervals of about twenty paces, stood a ring of men carrying stout spears. They wore metal protectors around their legs. Tom found Marcus and the man with the beard bent over the dog to fix the harness. The metal spike thrust out evilly. The last strap was being adjusted when there was a stupendous roar from the crowd. It was a terrible roar, suggesting fear and passion and rage. Tom, who was not tall enough to see what had caused this spontaneous explosion, started back in alarm.

'What is it?' asked Marcus, testing the leather.

His companion, who had raised himself on his toes to look into the arena, said nothing for a moment. He seemed shaken.

'It's the other hound,' he said at last. 'It's a monster.'

'Huh!'

Marcus' expression was dismissive as he straightened up and led Fang towards the one opening through the crowd. Tom and the bearded man followed him through the ranks of spectators to the arena. Was it a pitiful glance each man seemed to give the shaggy brute?

107

Once in the arena, Tom understood the violent clamour. The other dog, held back by no fewer than three men, was truly of a monstrous size. It stood more than a head taller than Fang, and its body – contrastingly sleek and a light tan in colour – seemed to dance with muscle. It pawed the ground. Its eyes were a rich red. Its upper lip bared to reveal sharp and gleaming teeth.

Marcus, kneeling to release Fang's muzzle, showed no sign of concern, but Tom could not believe that he was not trembling inside. Fang, now that the business was about to begin, strained wildly to be at its adversary, snarling loudly, the ferocious eyes turning up in their sockets until they were almost lost to view.

There was a brief ceremony in the centre of the arena, which Tom, sick with fear, hoped would last for ever, and then the two animals were released and careered towards their first bloody collision.

The commotion was almost unbearable. Tom found himself covering his ears and turning his eyes away, but the noise hammered through his hands. The crowd exulted, bayed, but even this heavy sound failed to extinguish the savage yelping of the two beasts, the barks of pain, the vicious growling.

He opened his eyes. The spectators surged forward, yelling wildly, as the animals flung themselves at one another, the terrible spikes always racing ahead of them. They rolled over and over, the ground crimson beneath them. As they lurched towards the front rank of spectators two of the men with the spears darted forward and struck them blows to force them back into the arena. Fang, one eye closed and swollen, found itself trapped beneath the heavy body of the other dog and writhed and snapped. The spike had missed its body but now the huge animal heaved and thrust down again and the sharp metal grazed Fang's flank and blood spurted in the air.

Tom turned away again, loathing it, and saw that Marcus' face glowed with a terrible enthusiasm. His mouth was open, but speechless, his hands beat the air, he swayed to and fro with excitement. It was as if he wished to be out there, in the arena, battling with the threshing, murderous dogs. Tom watched him, appalled. This was the man who could help him, whom he must seem to make an ally of. His eyes had a crazed expression, the thin lips were drawn back in a gape of depraved exultation.

'Kill, Ripper, kill!'

The supporters of the larger creature urged it on and, indeed, its superior size seemed to be carrying the contest. The beasts were adept at dodging the advancing blade and there were repeated collisions of the shoulders, one of which sent Fang spinning to the ground where it was temporarily at the mercy of its rival. Twice the blade struck home and Fang staggered away, howling but still defiant.

But now it revealed its experience. It tore at the huge Ripper, made as if to strike and then, at the last moment, veered away. Surprised, the larger animal hesitated for a crucial second and found itself attacked from the side. Fang leapt upon the exposed flank, the sharp spike burying deep. Its teeth hit into the flesh of its adversary again and again. They tumbled over, panting and snapping, and when at last they separated and struggled to their feet it was the other dog which limped away, badly torn, not relishing the fight. Its skin was laced with running streams of blood.

'Again, Fang! Take him now!'

'Turn Ripper, turn!'

How could they enjoy so cruel a battle? Tom held his hand over his mouth for fear he would disgrace himself. He must not let his horror show. All around him the excited faces were turned upon the wrestling dogs, the grating voices raised to urge them to greater violence. Would he, too, react like this once he had lived among these people for a while longer?

But one other person did not share the general emotion. With a shock, Tom recognised a face from the House of the Star – that of the grizzled-haired man with gold-framed spectacles. He seemed to take no interest in the sport but bestowed his impassive gaze upon his fellow spectators. As at the inn, it was impossible to gauge what he felt. Tom only thought how strange it was that he should be here, and he turned away so that their eyes should not meet.

By now both dogs were close to exhaustion. They attacked, it seemed, merely from habit. Fang's matted fur, saturated with blood, stood up in spikes like black spearheads. Ripper's handsome brown coat was criss-crossed by broadening crimson rivers. Occasionally one would stumble and fall even when its opponent was some way off, but always the fear of the oncoming spiked harness put a new impulse into the weary legs and the feinting, leaping and biting continued all over again.

The spectators, sensing that the end was near, grew more hysterical in their cries. There was money to be won and lost. The men with the spears pushed the crowd back with arms outstretched, though never taking their eyes from the thrashing animals.

Ripper, as the heavier of the two, began to gain the advantage of its weight, pinning Fang to the ground, where the two lay gasping, and taking sudden violent snaps with its vicious teeth. Tom saw no way in which the shaggy black creature could escape, but he had taken no account of its cunning. Its submissive posture must have been exaggerated to deceive its enemy, for it suddenly heaved and convulsed and was free. Even as Ripper struggled to its feet Fang lunged forward, keeping the spike low down and slightly raised. The larger beast collapsed onto its back, feet pawing the air desperately. Fang, in a frenzy, struck again and again, suddenly sure of its triumph. Its wild eyes blazed as it thrust and thrust and thrust.

Tom could not watch, but heard from the noise of the crowd that the battle was over. There were groans, a few exclamations and then, for a few seconds, a strange silence, a terrible silence. From the dogs there was no sound at all. And then there was movement, a shuffling of feet and the rapid dispersal of the spectators, funnelling into the narrow alley from whence they had come, leaving slips of torn paper on the ground behind them.

Marcus, having won a great deal, was in good spirits as they returned. They made slow progress because of the crippled condition of the poor lacerated animal that followed behind, but Marcus never gave a glance to the rear.

'They thought they'd surprise us,' he said scornfully. 'Who was surprised, young Tom?'

'He's badly hurt.'

'Of course he's badly hurt. He usually is. We won't fight him again for a while yet.'

The crowds had completely evaporated, so that the alleys

through which they passed were once again empty and austere. Although the sun had broken through the thin clouds, the air was chill, painfully so.

'Six times he's been challenged,' gloated Marcus. 'Six times he's seen them off.'

'Is it always to the death?'

'Unless they run. And it's not possible to run.'

When they reached the house the dog struggled to its room and collapsed in a corner, too exhausted even to lick its wounds. Marcus paid it no attention at all, but poured two glasses of the colourless liquid Tom had tasted before. He sat back in his chair, a serene expression of self-satisfaction on his face.

'We taught them a lesson,' he said.

Tom wetted his lips with the drink but took none of it into his mouth. He sniffed at it, but could smell nothing.

'Here's to those,' said Marcus, raising his glass, 'who meddle.'

Tom raised his own glass, put it to his lips and dipped his tongue in the drink. It burned.

Outside there were faint sounds to indicate that the city went about its secretive business. A distant hammer clanged on iron. A saw bit into wood, rhythmically. There was a trundling noise, as if of machinery turning. After a while Marcus rose to recharge his glass and, instead of returning to his chair, he sat on the arm of Tom's.

'So you're ready to help the cause,' he said. 'To search and destroy.'

'Whenever you like,' Tom replied. 'I'm ready.'

'I can promise you excitement,' Marcus told him, 'and enjoyment. Especially enjoyment. There's nothing so pleasurable as destroying enemies of the cause.'

Tom played the lip of his glass around his mouth, pleased by the calmness he was able to display.

'And this time,' went on Marcus, smiling with his pleasure, 'we've an especially fine bird to bring down.'

'Bird?'

'In fact, two of them. Two of the fair sex, young Tom. That's who we're after. We'll pluck their feathers one by one. Are you game?'

Tom nodded vigorously.

'Do we know who they are?'

'Do we know? Why of course we do! One, to be sure, is getting on in years and doesn't merit another thought. But the other, young Tom, is a speciality it'll be a delight to ensnare. It's quite lip-licking!'

His eyes were loose with excitement.

'Mother and daughter, they are, and the young one a most delightful creature. The loveliest flaxen hair, young Tom, and eyes of the most heavenly blue!'

19 Meditation

The picture, propped against a pile of books, stared stead-fastly back at him through the gloomy light of the late afternoon. Tom, alone once again in his room at the House of the Star, watched it carefully as if at any moment it might twitch into life. Next to it lay the papers, charred at the edges, which the mad old man had pushed into his pocket.

Would his father be surprised if he knew how keenly Tom sought him? No, no: surely he would understand. Would he be horrified to know of the experiences he had so far endured? Again, he would understand.

The face in the picture was of a strong, warm-hearted man. Tom knew this by looking into the eyes. Of his flesh-and-blood father he had no memory at all: or if he had, it was submerged beneath the character created by his mother's stories of the early years. The image was filtered through his mother's loss and yearning, so that it seemed to represent an ideal, godlike human being.

And yet, surely he could see that in the picture too? There was a reassuring honesty in that weather-beaten face and a keen intelligence in the expression. Tom knew that this was a man worth following, wherever the journey took him: he would not be disappointed.

In the large room below, the evening's entertainment had begun. He could hear the rhythm of Old Weasel's instrument and the occasional shout rose, muffled, through the floor. For the inhabitants of the inn the days merged into one another almost unheeded, each a copy of the one preceding it, while for him there was incident and change and there might not be days enough.

The violence which seethed below the surface of city life had been apparent to him ever since he had arrived, but yesterday's meeting with the vicious Marcus and his involvement with the terrible fight between the two dogs had served to emphasise the danger he was in. Now he remembered not only the bloody tussle in the makeshift arena but his later journey home to the House of the Star. How tremblingly he had held out the pass Marcus had given him, with what relief had he hurried through the passages that led from one sector to the other, emerging at last from a door indistinguishable from all the others in the mean grey street.

He was ashamed of his trembling. He knew that he could not remain a prey to events, to other people's plans and schemings, and survive. He must act for himself. He must exercise cunning: perhaps, in his own way, he must be ruthless too. But what would his father think of him then?

The eyes seemed to offer him reassurance. 'Do what you do for the best reasons,' they seemed to say, 'and all will be well.'

Yet he knew that this was too simple. The alliance with Marcus offered him a way to rediscover the girl with blue eyes and so, perhaps, would lead him to the fabled underground city. At the same time it was a dreadful threat: Marcus would not hesitate to act brutally towards him if his suspicions were aroused. How should he protect himself?

There were things that he had always considered evil. To kill was horrific. Suppose – just suppose – that to kill Marcus was the only way to reach the underground city. In his childhood days at home (how far off they seemed!) he had often played with his village friends at games of warrior gangs involving dire death and destruction. But they were only games. Was it ever right to kill a man, really?

'Do what you do for the best reasons'. Yet even Marcus believed his own cause was just. He blindly destroyed people in order that the Red Blade should rule the city. Tom saw the error of this quite clearly – Marcus wanted to create his ideal city, ignoring the price that would be paid. He schemed and killed for a controlled, well-ordered city but overlooked the fact that it would be a city in which murder and cruelty had become commonplace. It wasn't possible to ignore the actions that people took to achieve the results they wanted. These actions left their indelible imprints behind them.

Even so, could a death sometimes be justified? If – he reasoned desperately – if he *knew* that for Marcus to die would mean the triumph of good over evil? But that was no use. Of course he could never know it. We could never know for certain the ends of our actions.

Did that mean, then – he shuddered to imagine it – that if Marcus found the girl and intended to kill her he, Tom, should do nothing to stop him, even if it meant killing Marcus instead? No, no, clearly this couldn't be right. Here there was a clear end to the action proposed. If he did nothing to prevent it, he would be guilty of allowing it to happen. It would be no use to say it was nothing to do with him. He would have the choice either to do nothing or to resist: it wasn't possible to escape the choice, to say the responsibility wasn't his. So if he had to kill Marcus to save the girl, surely then this was what he should do.

Tom gazed at the picture for strength, but he knew that the strength must come from inside himself. He had never before in his life had to tussle in this way with his conscience and his courage. How could he learn to be secretive, single-minded, even perhaps ruthless, without becoming warped and dishonest in the process? Must be *be* like Marcus in order to confront Marcus? The consoling thought came to him that his father had surely been afflicted with the very same doubts. He did not question that his father was a good man. Yet if he had survived, if he was really in the underground city alive, surely he, too, had had to use his strength and his wits. It must be possible to be both tough and honest!

So long had he been engaged in these difficult speculations that, on raising his head, he was surprised to see through the window that the daylight had now completely gone. He drew the curtain across, suddenly feeling extremely weary, and smiled sardonically at his own presumption. To think that he should have been so blithely considering Marcus' death when his own was so very much more likely. He was, in truth, in a precarious situation.

Further morbid thought on these lines, however, was prevented by a heavy knocking on the door. Tom quickly took the picture and the papers and slipped them under his pillow. The knocking grew even more vigorous and seemed to be accompanied by hefty kicks until, before he had reached it, the door gave and swung open.

20　The Hunted

The man who stepped inside and threw the door shut behind
him did not, it was immediately apparent, have any violent
intention. He stood heaving for breath, a finger pressed to his
lips. It was the shabby old fellow who seemed to spend his entire
life in the room downstairs. His battered hat was missing,
revealing a thin matting of fine white hair which fell in a shock
about his ears.

They faced each other in complete silence for what seemed a
very long time. Tom noticed again the stained and crumpled
trousers, and saw that the worn slippers gave loose covering for
what were otherwise bare feet. Finally the old man tottered
forward and subsided heavily onto the bed. He fumbled at a
pocket and produced, clumsily, his familiar pipe. The smoke,
thick and pungent, drifted slowly towards the ceiling.

'Safe,' he sighed tremulously, but still looking anxiously
towards the door as if at any moment it might open. 'She's
gone.'

'She?'

'The Sphynx. Terrible woman.'

Tom, whose imagination had prepared him for a more
sinister explanation, almost laughed out loud.

'You're frightened of her?'

The smoker nodded, his eyes moist and grateful.

'Fearful woman. Fearful woman.'

Tom sat in his chair, fascinated. He had never passed more
than a few words with his uninvited guest and yet, for a reason
he did not understand, he found him strangely familiar and
easy to talk to.

'But why should you fear her?' he asked. 'Has she threatened
you?'

'She will. She will.'

The old man spoke slowly and fell into silence once more. He

116

pulled on the pipe lovingly, the smoke rising thickly from the side of his mouth. He seemed to disappear for a while, his thoughts far away, until he suddenly sat upright and held out his hand.

'Clutt,' he said. 'That's my name, or one of them. That's what they call me downstairs. You're a good lad.'

Tom, who could not reach without standing, leaned forward to grasp his fingers.

'I'm Tom,' he said.

'Oh yes indeed,' said Clutt, as if clearing up a doubt that Tom had about his own identity. 'Quite right. We all know you, young Tom. You didn't hear anything outside just then, did you?'

'No. Nothing at all.'

'There aren't any locks, that's the trouble. It's difficult to hide.'

Ash from his pipe drifted onto his lap, but he appeared not to notice.

'It's the rent,' he said after a while. 'I owe a month's money.'

'And she's threatened you?'

'Ha! You've seen her eyes Tom, have you? They're a constant threat. True isn't it? They're always coming at you. She doesn't need to speak, that one.'

Tom again had the feeling of familiarity with the old man, though he had certainly never met him before his stay at the House of the Star.

'Can't you find the money?' he asked.

'Oh, I'll find it,' answered Clutt. 'It's due to me. The delivery's held up again, that's all. Communications aren't what they were in this city, young Tom.'

'And can't you explain to her?'

'Explain! To that one!'

Clutt shook his head wonderingly and occupied himself again with his pipe, packing the tobacco with a horny finger and taking vigorous sucks at the stem.

'But, then, I suppose I may have to eventually. It's just that she panics me. Women always do, but she's the worst I ever met. Did you ever know one like her?'

'She's very fierce,' Tom admitted, smiling to himself.

'They have a way of unsettling you, women have,' went on

117

Clutt, speaking in a slow, dreamlike manner. 'They've always got a plan, and they've always got a place for you in it. There's no leaving alone with them.

'I'm a man that likes to be let alone to think my thoughts and go about my business, with a bit of social chatter just every so often to pass the time of day. You follow me? I don't want all that here-ing and there-ing and how about this-ing. That's a woman's way.

'She's the worst of the whole lot.'

Tom sat back in his chair to watch his guest puffing at his pipe and declaring his simple philosophy. Clutt obviously felt no pressing need to talk, and between his random comments whole minutes passed during which he cradled his pipe and gazed into smoky space.

'It was a bossy woman that drove me away from home,' said Clutt eventually, with a meaningful glance in Tom's direction. 'I couldn't see any escape from her if I stayed.'

Tom, who could think of no appropriate answer, only nodded solemnly.

'I shouldn't be surprised if she's still the terror of the place. A tall, boney red-haired woman. I shouldn't be surprised if you'd met her yourself, Tom.'

'Me met her?'

'It wouldn't surprise me, I say. But if you had you wouldn't forget. She'd have her fingers on your soul.'

Tom smiled politely, rather unsettled by the strangeness of Clutt's conversation.

'I don't think I can have known her,' he said.

'Well, perhaps not. Perhaps she's passed on by now. I'm not a young man, after all. But she had the fierce dominating personality of those women who come from our part of the world. Untameable.'

'*Our* part?'

'Well!' Clutt laughed. 'It can't be said that we own it in a legal sense. But don't we feel that it's all ours – those proud mountains and the deep pure streams?'

Now Tom realised with a start why the old man had seemed so familiar, why he had sat talking so easily with him. He had not been aware of the accent of his homeland, but it had spoken to him unconsciously.

118

'You, too –' he began, but quickly checking himself for fear of betraying his secrets.

'To be sure, yes! Have I lost so many of the ways that you couldn't tell all along? Ah, when you stood up on the table and sang that song it was as though you'd taken hold of my coat and spun me round in a circle. I'd forgotten it all, you see – it was so long ago.'

He toyed with his pipe again, fussing with the tobacco in the bowl. He sucked and sucked until a thin wisp of smoke crawled upwards once more and then, his cheeks collapsed inwards, attacked the business with a will until the miniature furnace was soundly kindled.

'I wasn't much more than twenty, you see. A farmer's son. Not much of a future, but I was contented enough with the way of the world. Then the lady in question began to lay snares for me and I upped and sought my fortune in the city.'

'And did you find it?'

'No lad. No fortune. But the life has been good enough, good enough.'

They sat in silence, old man and young boy joined together by a wreath of grey smoke. Clutt closed his eyes and wriggled his feet out of his threadbare slippers. He seemed completely at rest.

'The strange thing is,' he said after some while, 'that the last time I heard that song was in this very house. "You reckless moon, mare with no rider . . . " A strange thing, that.'

'You heard it here?'

'I did. Sung in a proud and boisterous fashion by a fellow who stayed here for a night or two.'

'Who was he?'

'Don't know. I never enquired. He was from our parts, sure enough. Not a bad voice.'

Tom was out of his chair and perched on the bed close to the old man.

'What kind of man was he?' he demanded urgently, forgetting his caution. 'Could you describe him?'

'Oh, it was a long time ago, laddie. A great deal gets forgotten.'

He must not give his secret away. He must certainly not show his picture. But he could not contain the excitement in his voice.

'Nothing at all? Can't you remember how he looked?'

'Let me think, then. Give me a moment.'

The moment stretched into a period and the period into a passage, until Tom thought the shabby old fellow had nodded asleep. His chest rose and fell, and the pipe cooled and lost all signs of life.

'A poet, I think they said he was. Well known in his way, though that meant nothing to me. I don't read much. We never had time for reading in our family. A life on the land. They called him, I seem to remember, the Poet of the Wilderness. That was it. He left very soon.

'He was fairly tall. I have the picture of him standing there, singing that song. A robust man, the sort of man other people notice. I didn't speak to him, though. My life in those parts was long ago.'

Tom grasped him by the shoulder, helplessly.

'His eyes. How were they? Did they seem honest eyes?'

'What a question!' Clutt laughed wheezily. 'To be sure, I've no idea. Why do you ask me that?'

'I don't know.'

'Homesick, I dare say. That's only natural.'

His memories exhausted, Clutt slid off into his own mental world once more. The subject was closed. His body reclined on Tom's bed but his thoughts were far away. A contented smile moved his lips. Tom returned to his chair, his own thoughts in tumult. Who was the stranger at the House of the Star? Was it conceivable that it had been his father? And, if so, what was the meaning of the coincidence?

Down below, the usual rowdiness was in full swing. The floor seemed to throb with the sound. But now, as he imagined the scene downstairs, he found that the soldiers, the regular guests, Old Weasel, dwindled to mere shadowy presences hovering in the corners, while at the centre of the room stood a tall, imposing handsome man who dominated the company; a man from his own distant part of the country, mysterious, quickly disappearing. What had brought him to the House of the Star? Where had he gone?

'You're a good lad, Tom. A good lad. But it's time I was gone.'

Clutt, who had come out of his reverie, struggled to his feet but immediately hesitated.

120

'One more favour though, eh? Take a peek out of the door for me. Quietly, now.'

The corridor was empty. Tom beckoned to Clutt, who shuffled outside and stopped.

'The third door along, Tom,' he whispered nervously. 'Would you mind? A small favour.'

Tom led the way, once again smiling to himself. How strange for a grown man to be so afraid of a woman! They crept forward silently, and he pushed the door open.

He could not believe what he saw. All the furniture seemed to have been picked up and thrown around; drawers had been emptied; even the curtains had been tugged from their rail and hung in shreds. He felt Clutt push his way into the room beside him

'My things,' he said brokenly, passing his pipe rapidly from one hand to the other and back again, left to right, right to left. 'My things.'

They stood side by side, shaken, until there was a sound in the corridor and, turning, Tom found Clem and his large wife coming up behind them

'Clutt!' exclaimed the Sphynx loudly, raising her shoulders as if to take a swing at him 'Been skulking have you? Foolish man! There was no way you could have escaped *me*!'

21 Ransacked

Tom swung round angrily.

'Why did you do it?' he demanded. 'He's done you no harm.'

The Sphynx totally ignored the accusation and clamped a firm hand on Clutt's shoulder. Strangely, he seemed too overcome by the shock of what he had discovered to be terrified of the woman he had abjectly hidden from only minutes before. The tears formed in his eyes.

'We've no room here,' the forceful woman lectured him, 'for people who avoid paying their way. That's not very wise of you at all, Clutt.'

'The money's coming.'

'But the future tense is no use to me, Clutt. We have to live in the present.'

'By tomorrow. I promise it.'

Clem, who seemed rather uneasy about his wife's fierceness, eased his way past her into the room. When he came upon the disarray within he turned on Clutt with puzzlement in his eyes.

'What's this here, then? What's happened here?'

Clutt was unable to reply. He merely waved a hand towards his scattered belongings. But Tom felt the fury rage inside him.

'As if you don't know!' he shouted. 'You thought you would punish Clutt by breaking up everything he had. It's cruel, its inhumane!'

'Foolish boy.'

It was the Sphynx who spoke. She, too, now stood inside the room, surveying the chaos. She folded her arms together and her large bosom swelled with a powerful emotion.

'Disgraceful!' she said simply.

There was a silence, during which Clutt shuffled forward into what had been his ordered little home. He bent to retrieve an object from beneath the bed. What it was the onlookers were unable to see. He knelt to the floor where a drawer lay tipped over, its contents spilled out in a heap. He lifted it up, fitted it back in the chest to which it belonged and placed the object inside. Then he closed the drawer. He had, all this while, the trance-like air of a sleepwalker.

Tom spoke quietly.

'You didn't know?' he asked.

'A stupid idea. Do you think we would wreck our own building?'

Now Tom felt not only perplexed but humiliated too.

'Why should anyone do this?' he asked.

But the Sphynx ignored the question.

'Courage, Clutt!' she ordered. 'They've not touched *you*, man. I'll have someone here immediately to put the place to rights.'

With that she strode away and the atmosphere in the room lightened considerably. Clem put his hand on Clutt's arm and led him to the bed.

'Sit you down,' he said. 'We'll sort it out, old chap.'

There was not a thing in the room which had been left untouched. The few books Clutt possessed stood straddled on their open leaves as if each had been thoroughly shaken before being discarded. Two pictures had been taken from the wall and tossed into a corner where they lay among slivers of broken glass. The bedclothes had been stripped.

'Why?' Tom asked again.

Clem, who had begun to pick objects from the floor, seemed about to reply until, with a sharp cry, he stood rigid, staring at the wall. The colour in his face drained away. Just below the ceiling, the paint spattered in dabs and drips, was the emblem of the Red Blade.

'Even here,' he whispered hoarsely. 'Even here!'

The paint was still wet, for at that moment a large blob, which had obviously been gathering all the while, broke open and a scarlet stream ran down the wall like blood from a wound.

Clutt sat moaning on the bed, too far gone even to light his eternal comforter, which protruded awkwardly from a pocket, occasionally breathing specks of old burnt tobacco. Clem sat by him and shook his shoulder.

'There was nothing to find, was there?' he stated, demanding a negative answer. 'You were hiding nothing.'

'No.'

'You speak honestly now, Clutt. There was nothing?'

'Nothing.'

Tom began to push the furniture into position, glad of something to do. He could not bear to watch either the old man's brokenness or Clem's sudden terror. They made him feel menaced himself. Of course he was menaced. He thrust the chest of drawers against the wall, the edge of it digging into his shoulder.

'It's because you're a stranger, Clutt, that's why,' Clem said, reasoning to himself. 'In the bad times it's always the strangers they suspect.'

Clutt only whimpered by way of reply.

'Even though you have been here half a lifetime,' Clem added.

Tom lifted a small chair from the floor and swung it upright. He must escape. Now. Tonight. They would surely come for him next. Was it wise to run? He ignored the question: he understood too little of anything to judge the wisdom of running. He only knew that he felt his life hung on a thread.

'And worse times are coming,' Clem said ominously, carefully avoiding the young man's eyes. 'I wouldn't be a stranger for all the world.'

22 Friends

The light inside the cafe was so dim that Tom stood for some moments in the doorway before he made out the figure of the waiter, cloth on arm, standing by the bar. There were but three customers at various tables, eating in silence.

'You offered me work.'

The waiter came forward, smiling.

'Good lad. I had a feeling we'd see you again. When can you start?'

'This evening. Now.'

He was led through the door behind the bar, along a short corridor and into what was unmistakably the kitchen. Great clouds of steam swirled about their heads. There was the sound of bubbling liquid and a clatter of plates.

'Lucy – here's someone to help out. The lad I spoke to you of.'

The words seemed to be swept up into the encircling billows, never to be heard, but they in fact conjured up a gradually materialising human form, which took shape among the vapours. The drama of her ghostly emergence was enhanced by her appearance – a huge red woman, pouring with perspiration, stripped to the waist, her flesh hanging in folds, culminating in a face of greater width than length and split in two by a broad grin. The lower part of her body was clad in pyjama-like trousers made of white cotton, and her feet were bare.

'Is this 'ims gonna help? Bless you, boy.'

And with these words she threw her arms around him and hugged him, wrapping him in hot, wet flesh until he felt he would suffocate. But no sooner had she released him than she was sucked up by the belching steam once more, only her disembodied voice left behind.

'We needed someone. Bill's been working 'is legs off, haven't you, love?'

Bill nodded, pointlessly for she could not see him.

'Are you giving him Lugg's room?'

Bill nodded again and Lucy swam back into view.

'Nice little room is Lugg's. He liked it before he took off. Small, but nice. You show 'im, Bill.'

Tom was taken from the kitchen through a door that led to a narrow and steep staircase. Lugg's room was indeed small, a tiny box of a room containing little furniture and one round window high on the wall opposite the door. It was nevertheless as 'nice' as Lucy had promised. It was clean and had a pleasant smell and what little there was struck Tom as attractive and well matched.

He put what few possessions he had, including his precious picture, in a small cupboard by the bed. At this moment he suddenly became aware of the eery singing he had first sensed while in the white room. It seemed to well up from far below, and yet it appeared that his companion did not hear it.

'You make yourself at home, lad. Now I can't keep calling you lad, can I? Do you have a name?'

'Tom.'

They thrust out their hands and shook them solemnly and warmly.

'You make yourself at home, Tom, and when you're ready come down and join us. You're among friends here.'

And friends they very soon seemed, the more so because they were for a while marooned with only themselves for company. The next day, after a clear warm morning that held the promise of spring, it began to snow with an earnestness that made the winter's earlier offerings seem meagre indeed. Beginning with a few small crystals that spun lazily down, it turned by degrees into a swirling, blinding mass of large flakes that seemed to choke the very air. Windows filled with it, turning the rooms behind them into shadowy caverns. Doorways were sealed with its fragile cement. The rare city bird, returning to ledges that had disappeared, flew around confused, afraid of becoming part of the falling whiteness. The harsh outlines of the city grew softer and rounded as the streets gradually climbed the walls of the buildings and became impassable.

Tom stood in his apron by the window of the night cafe and

126

watched. His immediate problems were solved. Until this snow cleared – and still it fell and fell – he could do nothing but stay here and serve any customers local enough and hungry enough to force their way through the drifts, and so far there had been none.

As afternoon turned imperceptibly to evening Tom settled down with Bill and Lucy at one of the tables and played a board game. Tom was unfamiliar with it. There appeared to be an extraordinary number of complex rules which formed the focus of a whole sequence of bantering arguments between Bill and Lucy, during which Tom simply gazed at the board, enchanted. It seemed possessed of a rare beauty, with its detailed drawings and diagrams interspersed with numbers and instructions, all crudely printed and hand-coloured. The various items represented included a migrating flock of birds, whose formation across the clouded sky created the likeness of a human face; a man from whose mouth flowed a galaxy of stars; and a rainbow which became fire at one extremity and ice at the other.

Bill and Lucy, who had told him to watch them play for a while – 'you'll soon pick it up' – had offered no clue as to the purpose of the game. Neither did the written instructions, which contained such items as 'Swords fall upon the dream of the insane king' and 'Take nine in consolation for the loss of a silver moonscape'.

Despite his ultimate failure to grasp the logic of the game Tom could not but take pleasure in the first moments of good-natured and innocent entertainment he had known since his arrival in the city. And the sight of Lucy and Bill dissolving into laughter at their inability to agree over the rules was enough to infect Tom with similar convulsions which became so uncontrolled that they left him lying on the floor gasping for breath before they had run their course.

For a week nobody called. The three of them found small jobs to do in the daytime, talked and played in the evenings. It was warm inside, and intimate. In the cafe area their voices echoed and the light from outside was an even more muted green than before. When at last the snow stopped falling and the drifts slowly collapsed and began to recede one or two people kicked a path through to the cafe again.

To Tom's surprise one of the first to appear was a man he had seen both at the House of the Star and at the grim fight between the two dogs. It was the man with grizzled hair, gold-rimmed spectacles and impeccable dress. Today he wore, beneath his heavy top coat, a lilac shirt with a silk cravat of deep maroon and a jacket which seemed to reflect the colour of both.

What was even more surprising, however, was the deference Bill paid to this guest. He hurried to clear his plate away when he had finished eating, seemed anxious that the food, the drink, even the humble seating should be to his liking, and on one occasion actually addressed him as 'sir'.

Tom challenged Bill about this later in the day, when there was a pause in their work and they drank large mugs of hot soup in the kitchen.

'His name is Porlock,' Bill said. 'He's a real gentleman, Tom, that he is. A refined sort of man.'

'But you seemed to treat him differently,' Tom persisted. 'As if he were special.'

'Ah well, Tom, so he is. Special in a manner of speaking.' (He seemed unusually guarded, embarrassed too at not being his normal frank self). 'He's a business contact, you might say. Yes, that's what he is undoubtedly. And a real gentleman, too.'

This seemed to close the conversation, but Bill's strange manner disinclined Tom to let the matter drop.

'I've seen him before,' he said. 'Several times. Mostly at the House of the Star.'

'You know that place?'

There seemed some alarm in Bill's expression, and Tom was angry with himself for having let fall the unguarded remark.

'Yes. I've been staying there. That man, Porlock, is also often there.'

'Well, that's as maybe Tom, and to be sure I don't know a thing about it. No I don't. Let me tell you, Tom, that this city is a dangerous place, and I'd be very surprised if you knew the twentieth of it. The point is that we don't talk about much else but our own concerns and the weather we're having and the food we put into our stomachs. You like this soup, eh?'

'Delicious.'

'And you'll have noticed I'm sure, as you're an intelligent soul, that Lucy and me haven't asked you a thing about yourself. Nor will we, rest assured. You can tell us what you like and we'll listen – we'll listen with great interest, Tom. But that's for you to decide. We won't ever pry into your affairs, old fellow. You're among friends here, and friends don't ask questions.'

Later, while he was resting in his room, Tom had a visitor of his own. The dwarf appeared, wearing boots so high they almost throttled him but still only just high enough for the tops to be above the snow. He took off his wet outer clothing and sat in Tom's best chair, quite without his usual swagger. His face was pale, his hands shook.

'So you found your way to the east sector,' he said. 'May I ask how you managed it?'

Perhaps he meant to assume his usual inquisitorial manner, but the edge had gone from his voice.

'At first,' Tom replied, 'I came over the rooftops.'

'No. I don't believe that. You couldn't.'

'I did. There were spikes down the side of one of the buildings, with the sign that you gave me – the eye – on the wall. There were crossings between the buildings and then a door and a long steep flight of steps down into the street.'

The dwarf, convinced by the description, only shuddered.

'That sign,' Tom asked. 'What does it mean?'

'We don't know.'

'Don't know?'

'Of course we use it as an emblem to distinguish friends from enemies, but the meaning has been lost. We believe it was used by the masters of the underground city. There is much that we don't understand.'

They sat in silence for a while. Tom thought how much had happened since last he met the dwarf, and how that had changed their relationship. He felt now that he need keep nothing back, that they were indeed united against the evil that he had seen all around him.

'Afterwards,' he volunteered, 'I met a man called Marcus whom I first saw as a prisoner of the commander. He's an agent of the Red Blade and he thinks that I sympathise with him. He's given me a pass.'

Here the dwarf passed a hand over his face in a despairing gesture.

129

'I'm glad you have told me this, Tom,' he said. 'It proves your honesty. I know the man Marcus and I've seen you with him. We are in terrible trouble. The commander and many of our colleagues have been arrested by the Blade. They are being tortured; they cannot all hold out. You must tell me all you know.'

Tom began with his arrival in the city and his experiences in the house with the green and white rooms. He told the dwarf everything and found that the telling left him exhausted but strangely happy: sharing his problem had halved it. He mentioned his brief encounter with the mad archivist and the papers he had found in his pocket.

'Papers? Let me see!'

Tom brought them out from their hiding-place and the dwarf unrolled them and began to scrutinise them, every so often reading a word or a phrase out loud.

'I must take these,' he said finally. 'I don't know what to make of them.'

'He was strange,' Tom said. 'The soldiers took him away.'

When he came to leave, the dwarf grasped Tom by the arm almost tenderly.

'Time is running out,' he said. 'Don't let us down, Tom.'

'I shan't,' he replied, with more confidence than he felt.

His main task was taking orders and scurrying back and forth with the trays. Although he felt happy with Bill and Lucy in the night cafe, he could not help comparing the gloom and hush of the place, the surliness of the customers, with the boisterous gatherings at the House of the Star. Here eyes were averted and little was said.

An hour before dawn on the morning after the dwarf's visit the man called Porlock came again. He ordered a large fish breakfast which he ate fastidiously, carefully dissecting the salted flesh and placing the slender bones in a neat row on his plate. Tom noticed that Lucy had selected the best she could find and had added an extra portion of marinated potatoes and dressing.

Melted snow from the man's boots must have trickled across the floor, for Tom had just delivered a steaming pot of coffee to the table and was turning away when his foot slipped on the polished surface and, in a bewildering instant, he was on his back, striking his head against a chair. The man, with little expression, leaned over to help him to his feet, and as Tom lay there, looking up at the face in the greenish gloom of the night cafe, he realised that he had been through this very experience before; that he had known this face before the House of the Star; that he had once before looked up at it washed in green light only, on that occasion, for it to fade into darkness and to be replaced, upon his waking, by the brightness of the white room.

He realised, too, that Porlock instantly divined his recognition. The hand that held his arm and helped him to stand retained its grip once he was standing. It forced him down to a chair.

'So.'

His voice was low and hoarse.

'What games are you playing, boy?'

Tom sat silently, not knowing how to answer, the grip biting into his arm. Porlock signalled with his free hand and Bill locked the door and lowered the blind. He looked perplexed, but obeyed another wag of the fingers and disappeared into the kitchen.

'Well?'

'No games,' Tom said breathlessly. 'I'm trying to find someone – in the underground city.'

At this Porlock released his arm and brought his bespectacled eyes close to Tom's.

'You *know*?'

Tom nodded.

'As I was leaving the house I heard sounds from below. At the time I didn't understand. Since then – '

'Well?'

'I have heard the stories and I believe the city exists. I want to go there.'

'You are in hideous danger.'

'I know that.'

'This man Marcus I have seen you with. What do you know of him?'

'That he is hired to kill by the Red Blade and that he is searching for the girl with blue eyes I met in the white room.'

131

'Sonia.'

'Ah.'

It was strange to hear a name attached to a girl he had thought of only in terms of her eyes and her hair and, above all, her kindness.

'He is looking for Sonia and her mother,' Tom continued, 'and I am hoping to find them too.'

Porlock regarded him carefully.

'Hideous danger,' he said again. 'If you realised, child.'

'I'm not a child,' Tom protested boldly. 'I think I understand the danger. It's the only way to find the underground city. Unless – '

The meaning of his unspoken sentence was surely obvious, but Porlock gave him no help at all.

'Unless you can take me there,' Tom concluded.

'No. That's not possible. Or shall we say, it's highly improbable.'

'Why?'

'Because very few are shown the way. Many would wish to go, but the risks of betrayal are too great.'

Porlock pulled a colourful handkerchief from a pocket and wiped his glasses, methodically.

'I too am looking for Sonia and her mother,' he said at length. 'I wish to take them to safety. You know that their usual route has been sealed off?'

'Yes. There's no way in.'

'Fortunately the soldiers found nothing. The entrance was well disguised. There are, of course, other routes but they're not known to the two ladies in question.'

There was another silence during which Porlock gazed into space with the expression Tom knew so well. It was impossible to tell what he thought. Tom had found the man rather sinister in the past, but at the moment he felt only a burning excitement.

'I well know,' Porlock continued eventually, 'that there are many people, good people, who would like to find the underground city. It cannot be. Not until certain prophecies are fulfilled. You must not breathe a word of what you know.'

Tom thought of the dwarf and said nothing. It was too late to unsay what he had revealed.

'You can help me if you will.'

'And then – '

'I can promise you nothing; it would be dishonest of me to do so. I shall do what I can and you must leave the matter there. Will you help me find Sonia and her mother?'

Tom nodded.

'Marcus has many more people working for him than I have. You have told me that you understand the risks.'

'I must take them.'

'You realise that I have in turn risked my life in talking to you. I shall go further. I shall come regularly to this place during the next few days. If you intend to betray me I shall be waiting for whoever they send. Mine is but one life and you can threaten no others.

'Until that happens I shall continue to believe in you.'

The going was difficult, in parts even more difficult than he had anticipated. Combined with the problems of actually walking were the problems of finding the right house, for the snow had made the streets even more anonymous than before. But although fearing himself lost on several occasions, he eventually found the evil alley and the decaying house. The snow had not improved its appearance: indeed, against the shining whiteness of the ground the walls looked even shabbier and the door more rotten.

Tom felt his heart beating against the wall of his chest, yet knew that he must calm himself if Marcus was to suspect nothing. He tried to think himself into the role of assassin until, standing there in the snowy street, he felt his face assuming the contours that he associated with hardness. Having thus steeled himself, he banged with his fist upon the door.

Fang's distant growl was accompanied after some seconds by a peculiar creaking and rumbling sound from within. The door opened slowly. The face that peered out into the dim dawn light was an unexpected one. Straddled on a strange wheeled contraption, his legs hanging uselessly on either side, was the bellows-pumper.

23 Enemies

A hand grasped him by the wrist and tugged him viciously inside, so that for the second time that morning he found himself flat on his back. This time, however, there was no offer of help. The bellows-pumper flung the door shut and, working a long lever backwards and forwards, manouevred his weird vehicle closer to Tom's spreadeagled body.

'Head over heels!' he crowed, leaning down with a lopsided leer on his face. 'So *you're* the young man who's wormed his way into Marcus' confidence. Now fancy that! What tricks life plays on us! What cruel luck for you, eh my mannikin?'

Tom said nothing, feeling a numbing sense of hopelessness steal over him.

'Such a pity,' continued his captor with familiar sarcasm, 'that we didn't have time to make a blacksmith of you. But you simply disappeared!'

The dog continued to growl thickly through the inner door until the bellows-pumper shouted a command. The noise ceased abruptly.

'As for your blacksmith friend, I'm afraid he isn't with us any more. He decided to take up flying but found himself a little too heavy. Such a waste!

'But then, you knew that didn't you, my cherub? Nearly took flight yourself. What a pity for you that you didn't – much less gruesome than what lies in store.'

Tom picked himself up, brushing dust and doghairs from his coat.

'So sorry,' crooned the bellows-pumper tauntingly. 'What excruciating manners – I didn't offer you a chair. Please be seated. Put your feet up and enjoy yourself. Just there. That's right.'

To Tom it seemed colder inside the house than out. The wretched state of the room, with its cracked plaster, moss-

grown walls, rotted window-frames, the unclean damp smell –
this squalor echoed his own miserable situation.

'Where's Marcus?' he asked.

'Oh indeed, where's Marcus? Where's Marcus? Because
when Marcus arrives he'll have a little sport, won't he! To think
of being fooled by a young sprat with big innocent eyes. Marcus
won't like that, not a bit. Marcus carries a long sharp knife, you
know. Did you know that?'

'Where is he?'

The bellows-pumper only chuckled to himself and began to
pilot his vehicle in a circle around Tom's chair. He thrust the
lever back and forth with manic energy until he was travelling
at such speed that it made Tom dizzy to watch him.

'Not much good in the legs, I grant, but strong enough of
arm! Like to test it, would you?'

Tom, ignoring the remark, received a sudden blow on the
head which knocked him half out of his chair.

'Feel it, did you? That was a lazy one. I can do better!'

This time Tom was prepared and ducked beneath the
clenched fist.

'Good, good! I like a challenge. Steady now!'

Round he came again, and Tom threw himself away from a
blow that was never delivered. The bellows-pumper seemed
beside himself with mirth, cackling deliriously, so that Tom
was off guard when the fist was swung again. It caught him full
on the nose and he felt the blood run down over his lip.

'Two-one!'

Tom, dazed, instinctively raised his own fists, but his tormentor seemed already to have tired of the entertainment,
wheeling away out of reach and bringing his conveyance to a
halt.

'Like some more games to wile away the time, eh?'

There were two doors, Tom reflected, assessing how he
might possibly escape. The dog was behind one of them; the
bellows pumper blocked his route to the outside world. Could
he outpace the vehicle in a sudden dash? There was also the
window. The individual panes were too small to allow him
through, but if he threw himself against it the woodwork would
surely splinter and collapse.

Perhaps it was a glance that gave him away, for the bellows-pumper rapidly wheeled himself to the inner door and pushed it open. Fang brushed past him and bounded into the centre of the room, barking loudly. Its fur, torn and still matted where the blood had run, gave evidence of the recent fight, but the beast's spirit seemed to have recovered completely.

'Hold, Fang!'

At the order the dog immediately stopped in its tracks, its yellow eyes aimed at poor Tom, who pressed himself back into his chair.

'A surprise visitor, Fang, but very welcome. Like the smell of him, do you? Think he might taste good?'

The bellows-pumper not only showed no fear of the animal himself but seemed to have an uncanny hold over it. Tom watched in wonder as a mere motion of the index finger brought Fang across to the chair, head cocked to one side.

'A kiss, my pretty one?'

And as the bellows-pumper bent his head Fang raised itself on its haunches and licked his face, lavishly. He laughed all the while, contentedly.

'I need my sticks, Fang.'

The dog now disappeared for a moment into the other room and returned holding both of a pair of crutches in its huge jaws. The bellows-pumper took them and dropped them into slots obviously made for the purpose on his vehicle.

'Now I'm ready to leave,' he said.

'Leave?' exclaimed Tom with mingled amazement and undisguisable hope.

'There I go, treating my guest abominably again! My sincere apologies, lambkin. Excuse my uncouth manners. But I know you'd love to meet your friend Marcus again as soon as possible. I'll get him for you, that's a promise. Delivered in person.'

The bellows-pumper ferried himself to the street door, but at the last moment swung round.

'However,' he said, 'it would be thoughtless to leave you with no company at all. Shall I leave you the dog, perhaps?'

Tom said nothing but held tightly to his chair.

'On guard, Fang!'

The brute leapt forward, snarling, and lay on the ground not a yard from Tom's feet. From its throat came a prolonged and ominous growl.

'A dear pet, you'll find. Affectionate and faithful. Rather playful sometimes, it's true, but a real treasure.'

He paused in the doorway.

'You really should wipe that blood off your nose,' he said.

Tom, unthinking, reached for his handkerchief and, with an ugly roar, Fang leapt to its feet, the fur on its back erect, its teeth bared. This quite delighted the bellows-pumper, whose stuttering laughter could be heard for some time after he had slammed the door behind him and wheeled himself off down the street.

A silence fell upon the room. Tom desperately scoured his memory for the merest hint of how to deal with a savage dog. Fang rested with its snout on its extended front paws, to all appearances asleep yet patently not so. Experimentally, Tom made the slightest movement with his foot: the creature's ears instantly pricked and the eyes unfolded.

'Oh Great Invisible One,' he prayed silently. 'Help me now.'

Surely the supreme spirit was not a frequenter only of rooftops under the moon. Surely it was possible to sense the power even in a miserable hovel such as this. Yet once again Tom found himself unable to open himself to the experience: his fear still mastered him.

Back in his own part of the country, he suddenly recalled, there was a strange old man who spent all his life out on the mountains. They said he 'communed with nature'. There were many stories about the life he led – how he foraged for his food and how he lived alongside the creatures of the wild. Once, it was said, two young children had strayed from their home and, while wandering lost on the mountain slopes, had come face to face with a wolf. The old man appeared just as it was about to attack, and he called to the wolf with peculiar sounds. It turned away from the children, meekly slunk to the old man's feet and, after further admonishing noises, loped away never to be seen again.

'Good dog,' Tom whispered hopefully. 'You're a good dog, Fang.'

At this the beast became alert and a growling sound seemed to run up and down between its throat and its stomach. Tom tried a soothing sing-song effect.

'*Good* dog, *good* dog, *good* dog. . . . '

137

But the growling only increased and Fang thumped its tail menacingly on the floor. Perhaps if he hummed a monotonous tune.... Now the animal sprang to its feet and barked savagely.

There was clearly no way in which he could escape. The danger which he had confronted so bravely when it was an idea in his brain was almost impossible to bear when it grew close in the person of Marcus. Even now the bellows-pumper must be telling his story: within moments they would be upon him, Marcus thirsty for revenge. He carried a long knife.

Like a prisoner in the condemned cell, Tom found himself insanely fascinated by every detail in the room around him, the last objects he would ever see in this life. The very growth on the walls which he had found so repulsive now seemed precious to him as being part of the world he knew. These short feathery fronds would be here when he had gone. Why was human life so brief? The cracks in the plaster seemed to be speaking to him in words he could not understand. The smears on the window-glass: why had he not noticed their intricate patterns before? There was so much he had not noticed, had not appreciated, and now it was too late.

The hairs along Fang's back quivered and its head turned to one side. An ear lifted. A low growling started up again and then the dog was on its feet, though never moving an inch away from its prisoner. The door was kicked open, and in strode Marcus.

'Hello young Tom,' he said, approaching the chair.

Tom's senses reeled.

'What – no voice? Lost it in the snows, have you?'

He went to a cupboard, stooped to bring out a bottle and a tumbler. He filled this to the brim and gulped a mouthful down.

'Got a bloody nose, have you? Gave as good as you got, I hope. Here, Fang, out of the way!'

But the dog would not move. It stood hunched in front of Tom, its head lowered, one eye following Marcus around the room.

'Has there been anybody else here?' Marcus asked, dropping into one of the battered armchairs.

'Anybody else?'

'A man, Tom. Another man. I was expecting someone.'

Tom's body seemed to understand the situation before his brain had grasped it. He shook and all but fainted away.

'Are you unwell?'

'No, no. I banged my nose, that's all.'

'Ha!'

Marcus tipped the tumbler to his lips, all the time keeping his eyes on Fang.

'What's the matter with the dog?' he asked.

'Nothing.'

'Nothing, is it? Fang – to your bed!'

There was no movement save the lowering of the animal's tail.

'He doesn't go. You see that?'

He stood up and came closer.

'There's something wrong here. Why doesn't he obey me?'

Tom improvised wildly.

'It's my fault, I think. I gave him some scraps to eat. I had some food with me. He wouldn't go away.'

Marcus squatted, looking into Fang's eyes, considering. Master and dog stared unblinkingly at one another for a long time.

'So that's it,' Marcus said at last, rising to his feet. 'Greedy are you, Fang? What I give you isn't enough, eh? I thought I'd beaten the bad habits out of you, but you've a few more lessons to learn, that's clear.

It seemed that the dog knew what was about to happen even before it heard the chain being taken from the wall in the next room. It whined and fretted, its paws trembling, but still it did not move. Tom put his hands over his eyes, horrified and remorseful. How could he have brought about this cruelty? Yet he could not stop it.

The blows fell, three or four of them, before the dog retreated, whining and snapping uselessly at the flailing chain. It was driven back into the other room, Marcus cursing it even as he continued to whip the harsh metal down upon its body. It was some while before he had finished and had shut the door and come back into the room, taking up his drink again.

'They need bringing to heel,' he said simply.

Tom gratefully escaped from his chair and stalked up and down the room, free to move his arms and legs again.

'I would have come sooner,' he said, 'but I was snowed up.'

'So were we all. But your sense of timing is excellent. The time is ripe, Tom lad!'

He drained his glass, picked up the bottle and hesitated.

'Question is,' he said, 'do we wait for the fellow I told you of or do we strike while the iron is hot?'

'It's usually wise,' Tom suggested, 'not to delay.'

'Or, to put it another way, shall we have one more drink before we go to give us strength for the work in hand?'

'What work?'

'Ah, now this will excite you, my little confederate. It's those two birdies I told you of – the mother and her succulent daughter. I think we've found them. A joyous moment this is going to be!'

He put the bottle on the floor and upended the tumbler upon it.

'Feeling a bit bloodthirsty are you, my young slasher? Like to see how the deed is done?'

Tom could only nod, weakly.

'Then as drinks can wait, and as people don't always keep appointments, I think it's best we set to our mouthwatering duties. Don't you agree?'

24   Across the Water

Marcus paused only to scribble a note, which he pushed underneath the bottle. Tom trailed after him through the door and into the alley, all the while glancing warily this way and that for any sign of the returning bellows-pumper. Did he hear the creaking of those wheels?

They set off along streets he had not entered before, all of them as mean and narrow as any he had yet seen in this inhospitable city, the snow piled up to either side. Marcus volunteered no information as to where they were going to meet their prey, nor under what circumstances, but his eagerness drove him at such a pace that Tom found himself breaking into a trot to keep level.

After some while his nostrils picked up a scent which was immediately familiar although he could not put a name to it. The smell was not of itself pleasant – in fact it seemed somehow unclean – and yet it stirred a strange excitement in him. He said nothing, however, only straining to keep up until, turning a corner, they found themselves confronted by water.

A wide river flowed sullenly past carrying lumps of ice and assorted flotsam. Tom, amazed, watched spars of wood swirl by, a leaky barrel, lengths of discoloured cloth knotting and unwinding as they passed. Above his head an iron winch projected from a large building that seemed to be a warehouse. There was a landing stage and a desolate stretch of quayside.

On the further shore, in the grey distance, the city continued as if without interruption – more grim buildings, narrow passageways. Some way upstream a monstrous bridge spanned the water. Marcus paced along the empty quay, his face clouded, and the evil exhilaration seemed to leave him for a moment.

'Where's the ferryman?' he snarled. 'This is his place. How does he expect us to reach the island?'

He waved his hand downstream and Tom saw a small hump of land rising out of the dingy water, scrubby vegetation behind a narrow grey beach. The wind ran chill across the river, painfully stabbing at their faces.

'Ah – he's left us a present!'

Marcus' unpleasant smile returned when he saw tied close-by the ferryman's shallow boat.

'If the fool's not here he won't miss it, will he? How's your rowing arm, Tom?'

Tom smiled.

'It used to be good.'

They descended steps cut into the quayside, moving carefully at the bottom, where there was a carpeting of green weed. As they stepped into the boat Tom noticed that Marcus seemed less than confident, bending low and almost crawling along as the boat rocked to and fro. He nodded to Tom to sit in the centre and take the oars. Slowly, clumsily, he reached back to untie the rope and Tom began to row with a confidence that betrayed a past familiarity with boats.

What memories he had of family excursions to their nearest river! How he had loved to take the oars and bear his shrieking sisters into the deepest waters, his mother trailing her fingers in the passing bubbles and laughing merrily at the fun. The oars seemed familiar in his grip. For a moment his relationship with Marcus seemed to have changed entirely – he confident, masterful, the other quiet, hunched, even frightened.

Marcus, facing him, made no effort to help. In fact he made no movement at all. He sat rigid at the back, clearly impressed by Tom's ability.

'You've a way with boats, lad,' he said. 'You've handled them before.'

Tom nodded.

'Well, it's not for me. I like dry land under my feet. I'm useless in the water; couldn't swim to save my life.'

He gave a little laugh, as if to excuse himself the rare weakness.

'You need both feet anchored firmly to the ground when you thrust a knife between the shoulders, eh boy?'

They drew closer to the island. The water lapped around it, leaving a creamy scum behind each time it retreated. There was

142

no sign of life, so that Tom was surprised to hear a faint shout on the air.

'What's that?' Marcus demanded urgently.

Tom, looking over his shoulder, could see nothing. When the cry was heard again, however, he realised that it came not from the island but from the land they had recently left. A figure waved frantically from the quayside, small in the distance but unmistakable because of the wheeled vehicle in which it sat.

'What is it?' Marcus asked again.

Tom shook his head.

'Don't know,' he said desperately.

The cry came again, and a word separated itself: 'Beware!'

Now Marcus, clutching the side with a grasp that whitened his knuckles, turned to look back. The bellows-pumper continued to wave his arms and shout. The word 'trust' carried across the water.

'Wait!' Marcus ordered.

Tom pulled on one oar, trembling. His companion strained to hear the words being shouted from the quayside.

'Turn back,' he said after a few moments. 'Head back to the shore.'

Tom stopped rowing and shipped his oars.

'Back, I say. Do you hear? Turn her!'

As he uttered the command Marcus made the mistake of instinctively rising to his feet, swaying forward as he did so. Tom instantly shifted to one side, dipping one oar into the water and hauling on it as strongly as he knew how. As the boat rocked violently he grasped at Marcus as if to steady himself – yet knowing that it was not to steady himself – and, locked together, they tumbled into the icy water.

They sank beneath the surface for a moment, the breath dragged from their bodies by the coldness of the water. By the time they had resurfaced the current had swept the boat beyond their reach. Marcus clutched desperately, his open mouth sucking in air, but Tom shook off the grasp, kicked himself away. His coat was so heavy that at first he seemed not to move at all. He frantically struggled at the buttons, then the arms, fighting to be free of it. Three times he sank under and felt he had no strength to keep going, and yet each time he emerged,

143

his chest heaving for air. At last the coat came away. He struck
out for the shore.

An arm rose from the racing water, and then the head, for the
last time. Marcus screamed, but although the wretchedness in
that cry tortured Tom he continued to swim away, battling
against the current. He swam painfully, heavily, until at the last
an eddy carried him swiftly in and he stumbled onto his knees
on the dirty sand. His body shook and ached with fatigue. The
water slapped at his legs as if trying to reclaim him.

'Come on, mister. You're safe now. Come on, then.'

A man came running towards him. He was fat, and the
running left him as breathless as Tom. He crouched down and
peered at the wet boy through two large protruding eyes which,
combined with a receding chin, gave his face such a carp-like
appearance that Tom began to wonder whether he had indeed
reached land or whether he had slid to the depths and was being
greeted by a creature of the river.

This fancy was dispersed when the man had regained his
breath enough to speak. His voice was high and reedy and came
in gasps.

'Not much ... hope for Marcus ... went under ... no
chance. ...'

'You know Marcus?'

'I've brought ... the ladies ... in the gardens. ...'

At this moment he, too, caught sight of the bellows-pumper
at the far-off quayside. He answered the wild gesticulations
with a broad two-armed wave of his own.

'Look,' he said. 'I must fetch him.'

Tom, feeling weak and ill, sat heavily on the ground,
shivering.

'Stay,' he pleaded.

'Must go,' the man said. 'Back soon ... must get him ... you
go to the gardens, see ... dry off ... or you'll die of the chill.'

Without waiting for any further stuttering conversation he
lumbered along the strand and pulled a boat from out of the
bushes. He shouldered it into the water, leapt into it and began
to pull strongly for the shore.

Tom, his spirits low, struggled slowly to his feet. He had no
idea what 'the gardens' could be, but his misery was too
complete for him to care. Coldness left him numb, save for the

144

aching in his arms and legs and the violent pumping of his heart and lungs. He walked leadenly to the fringe of low bushes and pushed his way through. He was surprised to come upon a high wall, with a small black door set into it.

The wall and the door seemed to sway before his eyes as he approached and for a moment he felt as though he would fall. The door was of heavy iron, and although he turned the handle he could not at first push it open. He braced himself against it and, at last, inch by inch, it gave and he tottered inside, immediately collapsing from the effort. He lay for a while, eyes closed, head throbbing.

He opened his eyes upon a green world! Never had he seen such a place, nor could he have imagined one. Wide lawns led to dense shrubberies of luxuriant tropical growth. The air seemed scented and heavy and, even more astounding, it was warm: many degrees warmer than the air that scoured the city streets and blew across the river. And yet above was the same lowering grey sky, blocking out the winter sun.

Already the heat had penetrated his clothes so that his body, so recently frozen and wretched, became comfortable and relaxed. Steam began to rise from his clothes, until he was transformed for a while into a column of mist. Standing, he moved on towards verdant shrubberies, feeling that it grew warmer still, until the heat became oppressive and sweat poured from his feverish brow. Between the tangled growth of shiny leaves and vines he could see a trellised path, and he was drawn to it, at the same time wondering and alarmed.

The air around him now buzzed and droned with the sound of insects, and perhaps it was the high-pitched sound combined with the torpid heat, but he suddenly seemed no longer alone. Were there voices, whispers? He began to move faster, glancing about him as he did so, and then broke into a trot. The greater activity combined with a mounting panic quickly enervated him and he fell to his knees, sweat pouring and head pounding. His eyes closed and salt stung his breath, coming in short gasps. He remained in this state for several minutes until slowly, stage by stage, his panic subsided and he climbed to his feet once more.

Listening carefully he was sure he discerned movement in the thick undergrowth, and he plunged in, scattering leaves

145

and blossoms as he fought his way through. But the growth was too thick so that he made little progress, and this combined with a cavernous darkness drove him back to the pathway. He determined to make his way back towards the grassed area where he was safe from ambush, and he set off once more along the path until it opened upon lawns.

The brightness of the open space contrasted strongly with the overhung path, and it was several seconds before he noticed the two women seated on the grass and looking intently at him, one rather old, the other about his own age. He was transfixed. Sonia smiled at him and he, to his constant shame henceforth, instead of rushing forward and greeting her, simply stood where he was and burst into tears. And there he remained standing until Sonia went to him and guided him back to where her mother sat.

He fell forward on the grass, and for a long time he was semi-conscious, knowing where he was and knowing them to be there, but unable to think clearly and certainly unable to move. He felt them turn him over, and there was a cool feeling across his forehead. He lay with eyes closed, hearing the murmur of their voices without understanding what they said.

Slowly his spirits revived. He felt himself rested and breathing more easily. His mind began to stir. Yet, when he opened his eyes, he saw that the green world was still about him and he felt the air warm against his temples.

'Where are we?' he asked.

'Shhhh.'

'I must know.'

'On an island. But say nothing. Rest.'

'What is this place? Why is it so warm?'

Sonia smiled down on him, but nervously.

'It's the vents.'

'No Sonia. You must not speak so.'

'I'm sorry, mother.'

They fell into silence once again, but Tom fought against the desire to sleep. He thought of the man with the face like a fish rowing to pick up the bellows-pumper at the quayside.

'Were you watching me just now? When I was on the path?'

'Yes. We were hiding. We're waiting to meet a man called Marcus. He's coming to help us.'

146

'He's dead.'

'No – don't say it!'

'I was with him. He drowned. It's best for you that he did.'

Mother and daughter exchanged glances of combined bewilderment and horror.

'Listen,' Tom said. 'We haven't much time. You recognise me, don't you? You remember that you helped me?'

The mother shook her head but Sonia said simply: 'I didn't think ever to see you again.'

'That Marcus was an agent of the Red Blade. You will have to believe me. He intended to kill you both. There is another man who even now will be in a boat on his way to the island with the same purpose. Are there any other boats here?'

'I don't know.'

They made their way from the gardens, Sonia with a determined expression on her face but her mother seemingly overcome with despair. She had to be led along, through the overhanging greenery to the iron door.

'Such a paradise,' Tom said wonderingly. 'Why is there nobody here?'

'They are afraid,' Sonia explained. 'There are stories about the place, superstitions.'

Outside, the air was again so chill that their hands and cheeks ached with it. Tom, without a coat now, felt the cold penetrate to his bones. The three of them pushed through the scrub to the shore and saw the bellows-pumper already halfway towards the island. They stumbled along, frantically searching for a means of escape. A humped shape on the mud sent a shudder of anticipation through Tom, but closer inspection revealed the rotting carcass of an upturned boat draped with wet sacking.

By now the oncoming boat was close enough for the bellows-pumper to yell taunts at them, and he rejoiced ecstatically in their impending doom. Tom tried unavailingly to shut out the shouted threats and abuse. They came to the end of the island, soon traversed the width of it and began to hunt along the further shore. They had no more than ten minutes.

'Porlock is seeking you,' Tom said, as he and Sonia searched, for a moment, in the same clump of vegetation.

'You know Porlock too?'

'Do you trust me?'

147

Sonia paused as if to consider her reply and at that moment there was a cry of despair from her mother. She had sat herself down upon a large stone and covered her face with her hands. Sonia ran to her side, stroking her and imploring her to stand up and go with them.

And then Tom found the boat. It was old and green with slime, but there was no obvious sign of damage. He yelled to the others and heaved it onto the sand. At first there seemed to be no oars, but he kicked and scrabbled furiously among the bushes until he found them, side by side and serviceable. They pushed the boat to the water's edge and clambered in.

How far away were the bellows-pumper and his pilot? Even now they might be landing on the other side of the small island. Tom pulled strenuously on the oars, glancing briefly over his shoulder at the landing he must aim for. There were quays on this bank of the river, too, and he fancied that he saw people moving on them, perhaps going about their business.

Sonia sat with her arm around her mother's shoulders, which heaved with her continual sobbing, as Tom pulled nearer and nearer to land. He was well across the river when he saw the man with the fishy face come running along the shore of the island, look over to the boat with its three occupants and run back again to alert the bellows-pumper.

'We haven't long,' he said. 'Where do we go when we land?'

Sonia shook her head helplessly.

'I don't know the city,' she said.

'Don't know it?'

'Hardly at all.'

'And your mother?'

Sonia spoke quietly into her mother's ear and received a vigorous shake of the head in reply.

'It's a long time since she travelled about,' Sonia explained. 'We've been ... elsewhere.'

Tom, understanding, said nothing. The boat with their two pursuers now came round the head of the island and he pulled even harder on the oars.

'We had to leave the house you met us in,' Sonia said.

'I know,' he replied. 'I know all that, Sonia.'

She spoke almost brusquely.

148

'How is it that you know so much?' she demanded.

But now they were at the landing-stage and no reply was necessary. As he manoeuvred the small boat into position he saw, further along the quay, that men were working, carrying and loading. Nobody troubled them, however, as they tied the boat and clambered onto the slippery quayside.

'Hey! Hold those three!'

The voice of the bellows-pumper carried across the water and one or two of the men looked up from their work. Tom seized hold of Sonia and her mother and began to run towards the nearest alley.

'Hold them, I say. In the name of the Blade!'

25 Rats

They ran between large cavernous buildings, workshops and warehouses. There was the clattering sound of following footsteps which, however, soon died away. Tom, knowing that pursuit was inevitable, made abrupt changes of direction, never once pausing to look behind.

He would have pushed on even faster, but Sonia's mother was already gasping for breath and straining to be free of his grip.

'Stop, Tom,' the girl pleaded at last, shaking his arm. 'She can't. You'll kill her.'

So now, after a brief rest which seemed to him an age, they proceeded at walking pace, through dingy deserted thoroughfares. From within the buildings they occasionally heard sounds indicating that people were working but there was a strange, an eery hush about an area so obviously designed to be thronging with labour.

Tom, catching Sonia's eye, found an expression on her face he could only describe as one of horror. Yet she had seemed so composed in the boat in the face of their great danger.

'We'll get away,' he said as cheerfully as he might. But she ignored his false optimism with an expressive frown, as if disturbed for quite other reasons.

'This place,' she said at last. 'To think that men made this.'

'I don't understand.'

'The city,' she asked, 'is it all like this?'

'More or less.'

'So severe. So without – joy.'

They came to another meeting of ways and Tom, intent on choosing the best route, merely shrugged.

'It's a city,' he said. 'Men must have buildings to live and work in, after all. Beauty is quite another matter.'

He felt, as he said it, that it was a wise remark, but she only looked at him witheringly, as if in fact he were a child.

'You don't believe that, surely? That this is the best man can create?'

'I don't know,' Tom faltered, feeling at a disadvantage. 'It's the only city I've known. I come from the country.'

'Ah,' she said simply. 'If you but knew!'

After a while Tom encountered a familiar problem. Their repeated turns and backtrackings only brought them back to places they had visited before. They were in another self-contained sector of the city and had reached its limits.

'We must find somewhere to hide until nightfall,' he said.

The old lady, tears permanently in her eyes, nodded gratefully at the thought of resting her tottering legs.

'There's no escape,' she mumbled pathetically, and once having said it she repeated it over and over – 'no escape, there's no escape.'

'There, there, mother,' Sonia cajoled her as they led her inside a large hangar-like building. 'We'll do what we can.'

Tom again found himself admiring Sonia's calmness and her realism: she made no attempt to pretend to her mother that their situation was anything but desperate, yet she refused to despair.

There was a ladder leading to a high open loft on which were standing dozens of heavy crates. They helped the poor woman up – Sonia, who climbed first to show that it was possible, by repeated words of encouragement, Tom, standing a rung below her, by the reassuring pressure of his hands on her elbows. At the top it was dark and evil-smelling, and there was a heavy scuttling sound as they groped their way towards the inner wall. They all instinctively held back for a moment.

'It's nothing,' Tom said. 'I think I kicked a stone.'

But Sonia was as ruthlessly honest as before.

'Rats,' she said. 'They live here. But they won't hurt us.'

They found dry sacking and made as comfortable an area as they could in the corner. The mother lay down, an arm crooked over her face, shaking. Tom and Sonia sat in silence for a while.

'We can't remain here for long,' Sonia said eventually. 'They'll make a search.'

'Tonight we'll find a way out.'

151

She made no answer. No doubt she thought he was uttering meaningless phrases again, mere words. He felt that she judged him unkindly.

'I've survived worse trouble,' he heard himself saying too loudly, his face flushing. 'At least I haven't been hiding myself away while other people were in danger!'

There was no reply. It was impossible to unsay what he had spoken. They sat in a silence much heavier than before.

'Why did you say that?' she asked eventually.

'I don't know. I'm sorry.'

She glanced at him, keenly.

'You think I've led a sheltered life.'

'You admitted yourself that you don't know the city. It frightens you.'

'It appals me. I had thought it was like that only by the east gate – the area I know.'

'You lived in that house where I met you – and in the underground city. There are many people who would like to find that city, good people. They are not permitted. Meanwhile, their lives are threatened.'

He had not realised that Sonia's mother was listening, but now she whimpered and clutched at the girl's sleeve.

'Say nothing. You mustn't!'

'It's all right, mother. I know what I should not say.'

She leant towards Tom in the darkness.

'You must understand that I can't talk of those matters. But how do you think it is that my mother and I are in this wretched situation – if we lived a sheltered life, as you think?'

'I don't know. The entrance was sealed up. You were betrayed, perhaps.'

'Perhaps. We did not live cloistered in that house, you know, like members of a religious order. We were along those who took the risks. It was while we were in the eastern sector that the way was closed to us.'

'Who sealed the entrance?'

Sonia paused before replying and then continued in the same quiet tones.

'It had to be done quickly, according to a pre-arranged plan, as the first sign of danger. There was no time for mother and me to be told.'

152

'And you know no other way of finding the underground city. Porlock told me so.'

The mother's sniffling now turned into heavy sobs, and Sonia lifted the trembling head onto her lap and gently stroked the dishevelled hairs at her temple.

'Tell me of your adventures, Tom.'

So he began, and spoke for a long time, explaining that he sought his father and describing the events that had occurred since he left the house with the white room. Sonia listened gravely, interrupting him only to clarify some point he had left obscure, occasionally lifting a hand silently over her mouth in a gesture of amazement or horror. When he came to the death of Marcus she shook her head wonderingly.

'We shouldn't be alive now,' she said, 'if you hadn't....'

She left the sentence incomplete.

'No,' said Tom quickly. 'I didn't kill him. He fell in. I turned the boat and we lost our balance. He couldn't swim.'

Yet he knew that this was not an honest remark. In fact he could not bear to think of those moments in the boat when he had acted on an impulse, not hesitating, tipping them both into the icy current. As if in consolation Sonia reached out to squeeze his hand – and at that moment they heard voices in the street outside. She did not release her grip.

'We'll try this one,' they heard. 'You search the workshop on the other side.'

The light was fading outside, so that even the large area downstairs was shadowy, its features indistinct. They heard the steps of three or four men, and then the sound of heavy objects being moved.

'I say they've flown.'

'There's nowhere they could go.'

'Slipped back to the river, maybe.'

'A lot of good that would do them. The guards are shoulder to shoulder along the quay.'

Sonia's mother, unable to hold back a terrified whimper, thrust her face into her daughter's lap. Her body shook convulsively. Tom held his breath, knowing that the searchers were growing closer, until the ladder suddenly rattled against the floor of the loft.

'Here's a likely place.'

153

'You going up?'

'I don't like heights. I'll hold it steady for you.'

'There's my hero! Hang on, then.'

Steel-tipped boots clanged against the iron rungs. The floor trembled. A head came over the edge, a dark shape in the gloom. Tom, crouching low in the corner, felt Sonia's hair fall across his forehead. He could see only that the man started in the other direction.

'Anything useful up there?'

'Lot of crates, that's all.'

'Valuables? We ought to get something for our trouble, don't you think?'

'Some hopes. I'll have a feel inside.'

There followed a furious scrabbling and a fearful scream. Something brushed past Tom's shoulder, gone in an instant.

'What's the matter, man?'

'My hand – the devil!'

'What is it?'

'I'm bitten. Help me down. A blasted rat.'

They heard the boots on the ladder again, moving more quickly this time.

'I'm bleeding. Look! Vicious brute.'

'You found the nest, I'll be bound.'

'Vicious. Give me a cloth.'

The voices died away, leaving a silence which even the four-legged occupants of the loft forebore to break. The old lady, trembling still, sat up and looked about her.

'They've gone?' she asked. 'We're safe?'

'Safe, mother. Try to sleep.'

Sonia smoothed out the sacking and plumped up a makeshift pillow for her mother to rest on. Now that the immediate crisis was past she seemed to relax a little, and within a few moments she had fallen into a deep slumber. Sonia and Tom watched her with relief. For a long time they said nothing, only listening to the rhythmic breathing and feeling the bitter cold of the evening slowly infiltrate the recesses of the warehouse.

Tom considered what he could do. A return across the river was clearly impossible. The chances of sneaking down to the quayside unseen and finding a boat must be very small and he did not doubt that the bridge he had seen was heavily guarded.

He thought of Bill and Lucy in the all-night cafe and experienced a pang of what felt almost like homesickness.

The only hope was escape to the next sector of the city, yet they had been unable to find a way through. He had the pass. Had the bellows-pumper alerted every part of his organisation to watch for the three fugitives? Tom began to formulate the beginnings of a plan.

'Don't laugh at me,' Sonia said suddenly, still speaking in hushed tones, 'but when you first arrived at the house – when we looked after you – I thought of you as a little brother. I never had a brother, you see.'

'I shouldn't have thought,' Tom replied quickly, 'that I'm an inch shorter than you.'

'No, no. It was because you were unwell, I think. Exhausted. You needed protection. I don't think of you at all in that way now.'

And how *did* she think of him now? Tom was surprised to find that it mattered to him that he should know. He could not ask the question, however, and, stifled with embarrassment, he pushed himself to his knees.

'We must go,' he said. 'It's dark now.'

'I'll wake mother.'

It seemed cruel to rouse the old lady, but Sonia did it kindly, shaking her hand and speaking softly close to her ear. Gradually the eyes opened and she sat up. In fact the sleep seemed to have calmed her, and she listened to their suggestions and prepared herself to leave. Tom first descended the ladder and spent some minutes in the alleys outside, ensuring that the way was clear. Then he returned, called up to them, and helped them down to the ground.

'When we find someone in authority,' he explained carefully, 'I shall produce the pass. You must remain in hiding. I shall then try and get us all through.'

This sounded straightforward, and none of them chose to question the simplicity of the operation. They advanced silently through the streets, Tom leading the way around each corner. The air, he noticed, though still raw (and especially to him since he had lost his coat) seemed nevertheless a little less chill than for several weeks. The snow, still packed high at the sides of the thoroughfares, was dimpled

155

along the surface where, during the day, patches had begun to thaw.

After some minutes there was a sound that he had heard more than once in the streets of the city, a sound which, because of its past associations, filled him with alarm. Yet it was what he wished to hear.

'The guards,' he said. 'If you wait in this alley I'll go forward to meet them.'

He asked the question Sonia had not answered before.

'Do you trust me?'

'We trust you.'

Sonia pressed her mother's hand and the old lady nodded, trying to smile but only bringing the tears to her eyes. The marching footsteps grew louder and Tom, not wishing to arouse suspicions, walked boldly in the middle of the street. As the guards – a platoon of eight – drew closer, he raised an arm in confident greeting.

'At last!' he called. 'You don't know what a search I've had for you.'

The platoon halted and the captain stepped forward. He looked Tom up and down carefully.

'Looking for us?'

'Well, I've got a problem. I've a need to get through to the next sector, and although I've got a pass I'm blowed if I can remember the way through.'

'Been through before, have you?'

'Yes, of course. I'm always here and there about the city. But I don't know this sector as well as some.'

The captain continued to look thoughtfully at Tom. He turned to his men, as if to judge their reaction.

'Let's see your pass.'

Tom pulled it from his pocket. He and the captain turned to allow the light of the moon to shine upon it, and he discovered, with a lurching feeling at his heart, that his swim in the river had made the ink run so that the words were scarcely decipherable.

'What's this?'

'I had a tumble in the snow,' Tom said quickly. 'I was helping a colleague to make an arrest when the fellow grabbed me by the throat and rolled me over. I lost everything from my pockets.'

156

He swallowed hard and looked over at the guards, attempting a cynical smile.

'I'm pleased to say he lost a lot more than that!'

One or two of them chuckled and the captain, though still hesitant, handed the document back to him.

'I don't know whether they'll accept it,' he said. 'Come this way.'

They were in fact only a couple of minutes from the corridor to the next sector. The captain rapped on a door which opened to reveal two heavily armed sentinels, one an elderly fellow with a lined, weather-beaten face, the other considerably younger and livelier. Tom told his story over again, and again waited in suspense as they examined the paper.

'Whose signature is this?'

'I don't know,' Tom replied. 'I work with a man called Marcus. He obtained the pass.'

'Marcus?' asked the younger one, interested. 'That the one with the dog?'

'Fang. Yes.'

'Look here,' said the other. 'That's his mark there.'

'So it is. A wild dog, that.'

'A champion,' Tom said. 'He's unbeaten.'

'More's the pity. I lost money on that creature. I was in the east sector when it fought last time out.'

'And what a fight!' enthused Tom, taking advantage of the change in the conversation. 'That Ripper was a demon, wasn't it?'

'Size of a lion, I'd say.'

'And what teeth!'

'I didn't see how it could lose.'

'But Fang's got cunning, don't you agree?'

'Oh, he's smart all right.'

The captain, feeling rather out of the conversation, made a brief speech of farewell and marched his men away.

'He's smart,' the sentinel continued, 'but one day he'll meet his match. He'll get too old for it.'

His companion, apparently having no interest in dog-fights, handed Tom the pass.

'I should renew this,' he said. 'There's some as wouldn't allow it.'

157

'I'll do it in the morning,' Tom said. 'In the meantime I need your help.'

'In what way?'

'Well,' Tom continued, playing the actor's role with more confidence as the minutes passed, 'I've a couple of prisoners who don't know they're prisoners.'

They laughed.

'How's that, then?'

'They're two ladies who're wanted for interrogation. They don't suspect me at the moment, and I'm anxious that they come quietly as far as possible. If I bring them through, will you give them a smile and a nod?'

The younger one nudged his colleague.

'At the very least,' he said. 'What have they done?'

Tom put a finger to his lips.

'Can't say,' he told them. 'But they could swing for it.'

'Fetch 'em, man. Let's be seeing these treacherous beauties!'

So Tom hurried along the street and led Sonia and her mother to the doorway and the passage through to the other sector. The two sentinels, surprised at Sonia's youth and beauty, smiled even more broadly than Tom could have hoped for, bowed as well as nodded and waved extravagantly as the three made their way along the windowless passageway. Tom, urging the others to say nothing, passed easily through the guards at the other end and then they were for the moment free, alone under a moon which rode fast among its heaving clouds.

'Where now?' asked Sonia, her face showing relief and delight.

But Tom did not answer for a moment. To his astonishment he recognised some of the buildings they passed. He had been in this sector before. At first he could not say where he was, but soon they came across the delapidated monument he had discovered on an earlier journey through the city streets, the strange inscription on its base.

'I know this!' he called out, brushing away the snow. 'Look, Sonia – these words. They were also written on the wall of the white room. "Wear me as your spiked heel: I will bite into ice for you". What do they mean? Whose words are they?'

'They are part of a poem.'

'But why here? And why in that room?'

158

'It is a poem which is important for many people.' Sonia was reluctant to say more. 'I think those people must have erected the monument.'

'And who destroyed it?'

Sonia only shook her head, and her mother, who had now recovered much of her composure, said: 'There are things you must not ask. We cannot answer.'

Now they passed along streets he knew well. They came to the market square, and he remembered the long chase and how he had hidden under the cloth that covered the stall. Tall buildings rose on either side of the narrow thoroughfares, with scarcely a window to be seen.

'In a moment,' Tom said, 'we shall be at the place I told you of – the House of the Star. It's a place which holds great danger for us. I believe I was first sent there because it houses agents of the Blade. But I believe there may be friends there, too.'

'I can't expect you to accept the dangers if you don't want to, but I know that for myself I must go in. It's the only chance I have.'

Now they turned a corner and saw the sign of the star swinging in the evening breeze. Sonia answered immediately.

'We'll take the chance with you,' she said.

26   On Trial

Tom was totally unprepared for the scene within. First he
found the door guarded by a sinister fellow in dark clothes and
black beret who half-dragged them inside and motioned them
to seats by a small table. Although the large room was crowded,
he was immediately aware of a strange, brittle silence, so unlike
the usual clamour of the place – a silence which was broken by
an angry, declaiming voice, raised for all to hear.

'And who, I ask you, had a greater opportunity to betray our
Movement than this treacherous creature you see before you?'

The voice – it was scarcely credible – was that of the normally
subdued Clem. But there was a greater shock in store: for the
object of his accusation was none other than his own wife, the
redoubtable Sphynx.

A long table was drawn up before the huge, glowing fire. At
one end sat the Sphynx, bolt upright, her face expressing
extreme distaste. Clem stood with his back to the flames,
addressing his remarks to a cluster of hunched, predominantly
elderly men Tom had never seen before and who were grouped
at the other end of the table. Like the man at the door they were
sombrely dressed and wore black berets. They seemed to Tom
like flies on a carcass.

Now he looked around the room and saw, among the throng,
many people he recognised. But this evening there was no
thought of talking and joking with their neighbours. Most of
them gazed at the floor, as if not wishing to be involved with the
drama being played out before them.

'Look at her now – carefully. Is guilt not written across her
features?'

Slumped in a comfortable chair near the centre of the room
was his fellow-countryman Clutt. His head lolled on his chest,
which rose and fell gently as in sleep, yet one hand still firmly
clutched the inevitable pipe. Tom saw the stammerer and, on a

160

low chair close to the fire, Old Weasel, his instrument between his knees and silent. Old Weasel wore his customary black beret; he was gaunt and old like the strangers, yet he seemed to Tom a different kind of creature. Was that only because he had befriended him?

'Oh, I studied her behaviour for a long time before I could believe in her infamy and was ready to report my findings to the local committee of the Red Blade.'

Tom caught the eye of the city guard with pearly teeth who on so many occasions had been the life and soul of the company. Now – although he must surely support the rough and ready court proceedings they were witnessing – his expression was curiously cold and distant. His fellow guards sat close by, heavy and mute.

'Three days ago she was absent for one whole morning and, being suspicious. . . . '

The words evaporated in Tom's brain as he saw, sitting alone with a glass and a decanter, the elegantly attired figure of Porlock. He maintained, as ever, his air of the disinterested spectator, fixing the proceedings with a steady gaze through his gold-rimmed spectacles. He was turned away from Tom, but must surely soon see him if he had not done so already. Tom glanced at his two companions, who sat close to one another, clasping hands. They must give no sign that they recognised the one man who might yet save them.

Tom looked again at the group of strangers, menacing in their brooding attention. He trembled. This was no charade, no evening's entertainment. Beyond them, on the wall, was the dagger emblem with its dripping blood.

'. . . until I discovered evidence which links this woman with associates of the enemy.'

Tom thought of his own helpless position – a stranger to the city who had run away from the House of the Star. The evidence surely pointed a crimson finger in his direction. But he found the plight of Sonia and her mother prevented him from concentrating on his own danger. The old lady once again seemed on the point of collapse, her lowered head shaking, but he noticed how Sonia not only caressed her mother's hand reassuringly but forced herself to show a calmness she could not feel. She might have been a local girl dropped in for a warming

161

nightcap rather than a fugitive hunted at this moment by agents of the Blade.

How he longed for happier times when he might wander the world with Sonia! He heard little of Clem's chilling betrayal for dreaming of ways in which they might escape, even imagining the first moments when they were free to talk, to share their thoughts. These sensations were so new to him as to seem suddenly absurd, with the consequence that he returned rudely to the present just as Clem wound up his denunciation.

'... and I ask you, therefore, to take her to the Citadel for the final judgement and sentencing.'

There was a leaden hush while the old men inclined their heads towards one another and muttered inaudibly. Clem avoided his wife's eye, turning towards the fire, which seemed to snap and snarl in his face. A few of his guests, who this evening seemed more like prisoners in the House of the Star, shifted in their seats and stole furtive glances at their neighbours who studiously avoided them. Tom stretched his fingers to touch Sonia lightly on the arm, but he dared not say a word.

One of the old men signalled to Clem, who now bent his head among the black berets. Perhaps this conspiratorial action was more than the Sphynx could bear, for she now rose to her feet and in her full and disdainful voice began to berate her husband.

'Oh you poor jack-rabbit, you! To tell such lies and incriminate your own wife! Who ever heard of such abject behaviour? The degradation that cowardice will drive a man to!'

But the hostelry was no longer hers. The voice that had been accustomed to striking terror in her customers had no effect on the present masters of the place. She was waved back into her chair while the whispered consultation continued. She was defeated.

'So concludes the case for the prosecution,' announced Clem after a while. 'Who will speak in defence of this noble lady?'

For the first time the old men took an interest in the other inhabitants of the room. They turned lined, unforgiving faces upon the assembly, as if to challenge a champion of the Sphynx to stand forward. The silence was now so absolute that the spitting of the logs upon the fire could be heard at the furthest point, like snakes in a pit.

162

Could the Sphynx indeed be an opponent of the Blade? Tom had felt all along that there must be friends as well as enemies at the inn. He thought back to the incident which had caused him to flee the building: the ransacking of Clutt's room. He remembered the Sphynx's anger, Clem's dread on seeing the dagger symbol on the wall.

'I-I-I'd like to say s-something.'

Incredibly the stammerer stood and made his way forward, approaching the large table.

'A counsel for the defence, eh?'

The stammerer, having made what must have been a supreme effort, now seemed unable to continue.

'Well? What evidence have you to put before this tribunal?'

'E-e-evidence?'

'You're speaking for the lady. Let's hear what facts you have to defend her with.'

Watching the stammerer forlornly struggling for words, his face white and taut, Tom felt ashamed. He knew he could not will *his* legs to propel him forward, however just the cause. Yet this poor man had been humiliated once before. Tom remembered the pathetic procession around the room, the guards having their boisterous fun, and he remembered how then, too, he had done nothing, only felt anger and pity.

'I have n-n-no evidence. I m-merely want to say h-how g-g-good she's been to m-me since I've st-st-stayed at this pl-place.'

Here the old men looked at one another with raised eyebrows and Tom almost expected them to laugh out loud. That the brave man should have put himself in this position simply to speak for the Sphynx's kindness to him only increased Tom's admiration.

'Generous, was she?'

'Y-y-yes.'

'Generous to whom? That's the question. To the wrong kind of person, my friend. What's your station in life?'

'I'm a c-c-clerk. G-g-grade three.'

'A clerk, eh? That covers a multitude of sins! For why was the lady so generous to you? That's what we'd like to know. Work in a sensitive area, do you?'

'N-no. S-s-sanitation.'

'Ah! Sewers and the like, eh? Escape routes for criminals. That what you've been up to?'

'No.'

It was obvious that Clem taunted the stammerer for the sport of it rather than out of any belief in his guilt. It was equally obvious that, brave as the intervention had been, it had helped the Sphynx not at all: perhaps the reverse.

'There are severe penalties for people who waste the time of tribunals,' barked Clem, changing tack. 'Have you nothing more to say?'

'N-n-no.'

'Then sit down my friend before you're marked down for a trip to the Citadel. Sit down!'

Tom watched the stammerer return to his chair and slowly lower himself onto it, stiff, in a state of shock. No one said a word to him. There was another conference at the table, and it was some time before Clem straightened up and addressed his remarks to the whole congregation.

'The tribunal will have more people to question. Nobody may leave until its business is finished. There will, however, be a short break in the proceedings and you are requested to enjoy yourselves.'

Seeing that there was no response whatsoever, he banged a fist on the table.

'Talk – you understand? Drink! Do what you would normally do!'

He swung round on Old Weasel, who sat immobile, nursing his instrument.

'Music! Come on – play! Enjoy yourselves, all of you!'

The first notes were plucked and people began to mumble incoherently to their neighbours. After the initial murmuring there was a sudden welter of sound, as if everyone raised his voice at the same moment in a great release of tension. There was a great deal of shoulder-slapping and punching among the city guards, and even a forced laugh or two.

'I don't think,' Sonia said wryly, 'that this was a good time to arrive.'

Tom again marvelled at her composure.

'Have you seen Porlock?'

'Yes.'

'Don't show that you know him.'

At this moment the gold-framed spectacles turned in their direction, but they did not pause. Porlock might never have seen them before in his life.

'Are you frightened?' Tom asked.

'Only as I was yesterday and the day before.'

The music, plangent behind the babble of voices, became suddenly, poignantly familiar. Old Weasel's fingers plucked the tune he had sung in this room all that time ago, and the notes seemed to speak to him through the confusion and terror he felt, offering him reassurance. How thankful he was then to the old minstrel, the great survivor. He almost believed that his own survival was possible.

Not for long, however. Clem and the men in black berets began to turn their attention towards the imprisoned customers at the tables. The old men nodded and passed brief comments as Clem, standing behind them and leaning forward, singled out individuals with a pointed finger. That finger swung towards Tom and stopped. The questioning seemed to intensify and one of the group took a glass from his pocket and held it to one eye, peering intently.

'Sonia,' Tom said quietly. 'Do you know these men? Will they know you?'

'No. I don't think so.'

'I wish I hadn't brought you here. You would have been safer by yourselves, the two of you. I've put your heads in a noose.'

'Don't speak like that.'

Old Weasel's tune changed again. Not for a second had he looked towards Tom as he played. He concentrated on the strings of his curious instrument, his spindly fingers rocking from one to the other without a pause. Nor did Porlock turn in his direction again: he examined the people at the long table with his usual careful scrutiny, apparently quite without concern, let alone fear. The Sphynx, for so long the dominating character of the inn, sat humbled in her chair, her eyes downcast. Despite Sonia's presence by his side, Tom felt horribly alone.

'Silence! Enough!'

Clem raised a hand and immediately, with the speed and finality of a guillotine, the low murmur snapped into a silence as deep and ominous as that which had seemed to hollow out the room before.

'The tribunal is reconvened. If your name is called, stand forward and answer respectfully.'

Now there was another awful moment while he once again consulted his superiors. Faces in the throng were drawn and white with fear, hands clutched for comfort at glasses, chairs, the edges of tables. Finally Clem took up his position once more.

'The lad Tom,' he said flatly.

His head swam. He rose, but could not feel his legs. He brushed past the seated customers heavily, clumsily – a glass toppled to the floor and shattered – but was unaware of making contact with them. The men with black berets were like malevolent monkeys. They seemed to jabber angrily.

'Where's your respect?' Clem demanded.

'Respect?'

Here one of the old men spoke for the first time, inclining a ravaged face towards Tom.

'You did not stoop before the sign,' he accused, his voice thin and cruel. 'It is not your practice, perhaps?'

'Stoop?'

'Bow the head!' broke in Clem in an exasperated manner, but the old man silenced him with a wave.

'Were you brought up to honour the Blade?'

'I come from far away,' Tom replied instantly. 'I had not known of the sign before I arrived in the city.'

'How long ago?'

'Just before the first winter.'

Now another of the tribunal intervened.

'What brought you here, boy?'

'My parents died. I came to stay with a relative.'

'Name?'

Tom faltered, ludicrously unprepared, but a loud voice saved him.

'Brach. Edward Brach. Fourth district. His uncle. No room in his own house.'

The words were uttered by the Sphynx so quickly and forcefully that nobody was able to stop her before she had provided Tom with his alibi.

166

'Silence!'

Clem glowered at his wife, then beckoned Tom round the table to stand before the glowing fire.

'So dear uncle Edward sent you here, did he?'

'Yes.'

'Oh I'm sure that's what the records say, my young friend. *She* had charge of the records. But if she speaks up on your behalf there's not much hope for you, and that's a fact.'

'He paid for me to stay here. He had no room.'

'Poor fellow. Came visiting, did he?'

'Once or twice.'

'Big fellow? Bewhiskered? Wore riding boots?'

'No.'

'Not that one. Let's think. Did he limp rather badly? Had a watch on a chain?'

'Neither.'

'Hm. A visitor for young Tom. . . . Yes, I have it! A little chap, so high. A dwarf, no less. Oh yes, I've known a dwarf come seeking you out.'

'That wasn't my uncle.'

'Ah – not! Who was he?'

'A friend.'

'And what a friend!'

Clem whispered in the ears of the tribunal, who shook their heads solemnly.

'He's known to us, your friend. He's a marked man. How did you come to meet him?'

'He tumbled in the snow,' Tom replied quickly. 'I helped him up and brought him in to warm him.'

How had he learned to lie so effectively? Yet once would not be enough. It was as if he were on one of the toboggan runs of his childhood, clinging desperately to the careering sledge, skirting one hazard after another, no time for self-congratulation before the next protruding rock thrust up from under the snow.

'And the ladies you've brought with you. Your aunt and your cousin, no doubt?'

'No. Just acquaintances.'

He had meant to prevent Sonia and her mother suffering from the association with him, but as he spoke the words they sounded like a betrayal and he wished he could unsay them.

167

'Just acquaintances! On the contrary, I'm sure we shall find them most interesting. But that pleasure we'll delay for a little. Tell us first what you've found to do in this great city of ours since your arrival.'

He began to tell of the places he had visited, the sights he had seen, the people he had met – some of them genuine, others fictitious. He had been a tourist in the city, enjoying the cut and thrust of the market, admiring the architecture. As he spoke he looked about him and found that the eyes of the people he knew were averted from him, that there were sorrowful expressions on their faces. Did they know that his case was hopeless? Nevertheless, he pressed on, forcing a manic cheerfulness into his voice.

'A lover of our city, it's evident! All credit to you! By which gate did you enter?'

'The east gate.'

'And how did you pass through to this sector?'

'I forget the route.'

'There is no open way.'

'My uncle had a pass.'

'Oh blessed uncle! Too bad he shouldn't be with us tonight. You know his address, of course?'

'He never told me. I've not been there.'

As he responded to this interrogation the outer door opened. In the silence between question and answer there came a familiar creaking sound, and the man guarding the door stepped back to admit a wheeled vehicle and its sinister occupant.

'We come now to your unexplained disappearance. A most suspicious circumstance.'

Tom, the panic immobilising him, offered no reply. The bellows-pumper, however, made no immediate intervention in the proceedings, resting his chin upon folded arms and seeming content to survey the spectacle. More accurate, perhaps, to say that he savoured it. There was a thin smile on his lips and Tom saw that he bowed with mock graciousness towards Sonia and her mother.

'Why did you leave us so suddenly?'

'I followed your advice,' Tom said. 'When one of the lodgers' rooms was ransacked you told me that strangers to the city were threatened. I was frightened.'

168

For the first time Clem seemed discomforted, as if Tom had touched on an incident he would rather forget.

'You had no advice from me!'

'I thought you meant me to run.'

'Then you're a fool!'

This outburst seemed to unsettle Clem, and he gave a nervous sideways glance towards the old men of the tribunal. One of them called him over, and there was more whispered conversation. Tom became aware that Old Weasel was attending to the great fire, throwing wood upon it, and when he took up the log basket to replenish it from the pile that was kept in a small room off the kitchen it seemed to Tom's overworked brain that a wisp of smoke followed him. Although most eyes were still turned towards the floor, he found that Porlock studied him dispassionately as ever, while the bellows-pumper smiled jauntily, provokingly. The only other person to answer his gaze was Sonia, whose dear face appeared the more beautiful because he felt that after this night he would never see it again.

'Like to visit the Citadel, would you?' Clem resumed eventually. 'Like to enjoy a taste of true justice.'

'I've no wish to.'

'I'm sure you haven't. But that's what's in store for you, my lad. That's the course of action I propose to the tribunal.'

He turned to his captive audience.

'Who'll speak for him? Who'll defend the indefensible?'

Again the old men swung round. This time, however, there was no brave champion to speak for the accused. The silence seemed to press in on Tom, as if it would crush him.

Slowly, the wheeled contraption rolled forward. The bellows-pumper began to snigger, a horrible sound that reverberated around the room. Working his lever back and forth, he grinned merrily at the people he passed until he brought himself close to the great table.

'Don't know who'll speak for him, but I'll damn him!'

A susurrus swept through the onlookers like the wind under a barn door.

'You know the agent Marcus – a bold man, loyal to the Blade in bad times as well as good? This creature' – he flung a contemptuous arm in Tom's direction – 'killed him.'

'No, no. I – '

'Drowned him. I saw it myself, but hours ago.'

The tribunal, unprepared for an indictment so specific, sat silent, hanging on the bellows-pumper's words.

'He's known to me from the eastern sector, where he escaped us over the rooftops. We fired the flares and brought down his companion – a treacherous blacksmith – but this one gave us the slip. When I met up with him again he was worming his way into Marcus' confidence.

'I followed them to the river. They were rowing to the Isle of Flowers, and when I called across the water this cockroach tipped the boat, wrestled Marcus overboard and swam to the shore.'

He worked the lever on his machine, manoeuvring it until he had his back to the men in their black berets, giving himself a view of the crowded room.

'But this one, your honours, murderer though he be, is nothing to our other captives. Take a good look at the two ladies at the table there. Innocent-looking, wouldn't you say?'

Heads turned to Sonia and her mother. Sonia's statuesque calm contrasted vividly with the old lady's pitiful demeanour. Tears coursed down her face, which crumpled with fear and anguish. A moaning sound escaped her lips.

'These are the two most wanted people in our city. Enemies of the Blade, indeed, but more than that – much more than that, your honours.'

The bellows-pumper swung himself round again, making the most of his revelation.

'They know the way to the city underground!'

Now there was, for the first time this evening, a spontaneous outburst from the whole assembly. The sudden commotion was a mingling of shock, of disbelief, of excitement, of wonder.

'It exists!'

'They know the way!'

'Didn't I say it was true?'

'Another city! There's another city. . . .'

One of the tribunal pushed himself to his feet.

'It is forbidden to speak of that place. It's the Blade law. These rumours of some mythical city.'

170

But the bellows-pumper would not be silenced. As the babble increased all around him he raised his voice.

'We need no longer pretend, comrade. We have nothing to fear. The city exists, and we have the way to find it!'

The first wave of sound, even as it ebbed, regathered like the foaming oceans and seemed to tumble about their heads. But, dimly at first, Tom became aware that the nature of the sound was changing, that a new sensation began to flow through the room and that it was a sensation of panic. Then his nose picked up a smell which was at first indistinguishable from the smoke stench from the blazing logs nearby but which soon became more acrid.

'Fire! In the room beyond!'

'For mercy's sake – let us out!'

'Water! Where's water?'

Great folds of billowing smoke wafted in from the kitchen area. Tables were overturned, glasses smashed, as the nearest customers leapt to their feet, backing away towards the centre of the room. The old men of the tribunal, who had scarcely moved a muscle during the proceedings so far, scurried about like ants caught in a forest fire. It was Clem who took the decisive action.

'Guards to the door! Let no one leave the building!'

The doorway to the kitchen was now totally obscured by the pall of smoke, which rose to the ceiling and began to drift across it to the furthest side of the room. Clem, without hesitation, plunged into the swirling fog, which swallowed him in an instant.

One man who had made no move at all despite the general hubbub was Old Weasel. He sat with his instrument, his face expressionless – and, at once, Tom realised how the fire had started. He had not imagined the thin trail of smoke which had followed Old Weasel with the log basket. Why had he done it? The answer was at once obvious and unbelievable: to save Tom if it were at all possible. Yet surely the great survivor had broken his own lifelong rule; had risked his own life.

He saw Tom's enquiring look and, raising a finger to the frail and bony skull which was the seat of all his cunning, was close enough to say simply: 'Old age has made a fool of me.'

The sooty figure of Clem, arms across his face for protection, staggered through the smoke.

171

'Five strong men!' he gasped. 'We can do it. The fire's not yet taken hold.'

Two men shuffled forward, but others shrank away so that Clem had to step in among the throng and seize them by the shirt fronts.

'Come on!' he yelled, abusing them for their reluctance. 'There's water through here!'

Finally he mustered a small party of pressed men who stripped off their jackets, held them over their mouths and charged headfirst through the smoke. Tom, unrestrained, hurried among the panic-striken crowd to where Sonia and her mother still sat at their small table.

'Quickly! Follow me!'

There was no escape through the street door, which was now defended by members of the city guard. These were busy pushing away frantic individuals who had completely lost their wits and were clamouring to be out in the night air. Nor, of course, was there a way to the rooftop, since that route was cut off by Old Weasel's conflagration. Tom led the way up the inner staircase to the bedroom area, elated to be free of his persecutors although he knew that it offered no way out of the building.

'Where are we going?' Sonia asked breathlessly.

He made no reply. How could he tell them that there was no escape? He led them forward, along the corridor towards his own room. Even as he reached for the handle, however, there was the sound of hurrying footsteps behind them and a brusque command.

'Stop! You won't get away through there!'

27 Steps

It was Porlock. The old lady threw herself onto his chest and clutched at him, sobbing with relief. With Sonia on the other side, he helped the weeping, almost senseless, figure along the corridor.

'This is my room,' he said, pushing a door open. 'We'll be safe in here for a few moments.'

Tom, trailing behind, found his brain almost choked with questions.

'The Sphynx,' he said, 'is she really an enemy of the Blade? Is she with you?'

'An enemy, yes. But she is one of those people who still seek the underground city. She knows nothing of my position.'

'And Clem?'

'It is as you see. He is a dangerous man.'

They helped the poor shaking creature onto the bed, where she lay trembling, her eyes closed. Sonia sat at her head, stroking her cheek.

'It is not the time,' Porlock rebuked him gently, 'for *you* to be putting questions to *me*. There is much that I could discuss with you, Tom, but I will simplify matters by asking one thing.'

He reached into a pocket and withdrew an object that was instantly recognisable. It was the picture Tom had carried with him from his home village.

'Of course,' Porlock said, 'I searched your room at the all-night cafe. This is yours?'

'Yes.'

'Why do you carry it?'

'That is the reason I am in the city,' Tom replied. 'It's the man I am seeking – my father.'

Porlock appeared deeply shocked by this information. He studied Tom's face, then the picture, then Tom's face again.

173

'You are saying' – he spoke slowly, deliberately – 'that this is your father? You tell me this in all seriousness?'

'It's true.'

Porlock turned away from them for a moment, still examining the picture. Sonia's mother was now whimpering quietly, while from below the firefighting could be heard as a muffled commotion. Tom expected the door to burst open at any second.

'Come.'

Porlock crossed to a corner of the room, knelt down and lifted a small section of floorboard. He put his arm inside the gap. Tom heard a click and a large panel swung open in the wall.

'This is the way down.'

Tom felt his lips quiver, sudden tears burn his eyes.

'To the underground city? You're taking me?'

'I am taking you, Tom. But I am also taking these two ladies, and I think you might give some assistance.'

They helped Sonia's mother to her feet, consoling her as best they could. Through the wall there were steep steps and then, almost immediately, a passage with windows which looked down upon the darkened street. Porlock closed the panel behind them and they followed the passage along the length of the House of the Star. At the end was a door.

'Few have passed this way,' Porlock said, opening it.

Stone steps led down. As Tom waited his turn to begin the descent he looked from the window. A thaw had begun. The whiteness of the roofs was laced with thin black runnels of melted snow.

A movement at street level attracted his eye. Outside the inn, and gazing up it seemed to the very window at which he stood, was the boy with the green scarf. He appeared so small and pathetic from Tom's vantage point, so vulnerable. He raised an arm, a beckoning gesture. What innocent childish world did he inhabit? What carefree hours did he spend playing about the city streets? He beckoned, and Tom felt the allure of those untroubled times of childhood, free of striving, free of responsibility.

He turned away and followed the others down the steps.

PART THREE

Revelations

28 Another World

O, but the descent was darkness – and anticipation of arrival was lost in the slow and dangerous progress through the tunnel. Each step was tested by a groping foot, and each steadied by a hand that was guided by the rough wall. And there was, alongside the darkness, silence, saving the soft padding sound of footfall on stone, for no one spoke for fear of confounding the senses. The smell was dampness, wet earth – the walls running in patches, the hand dragging through slime – and there seemed no end. Was the staircase slowly turning? It was impossible to be sure. Tom felt a numbness grip his mind. He could hear Sonia's mother breathing, a low rasping sound; Porlock had begun to mutter to himself. . . . And then there was a suggestion of light – not even so much as a glimmer at first, yet Tom found himself distinguishing the figures of his companions which seemed gradually to detach themselves from the clinging blackness.

Light after darkness is usually welcomed, but in this instance the sight of the staircase falling away steeply before him, with no obvious end, unnerved him. The gradual curve appeared now to have been illusory for he was staring down a long straight shaft that cut diagonally through the rock of the earth's crust. Further down, the rock walls appeared to become glass and it was through this glass that the light was flooding in. Tom knew that he must sit down before giddiness overcame him and sent him tumbling the remaining length of the staircase. The others seemed to understand and halted.

'Don't worry,' Porlock counselled him. 'It is always so the first time.'

They re-started, Tom now concentrating on the wall beside

him. His eyes kept track of a rock-face growing smoother as they descended until the smoothness of rock became the smoothness of glass, and instead of staring at a wall he found himself looking into seemingly endless space: a vast domed ceiling supported by columns, between which were revealed further domes and columns, and then beyond, yet more – a huge honeycombed space – and below, the city!

Words . . . of what use are words? Words can only diminish what Tom experienced. Here was space after the confines of the tunnel, brightness after shadow; here was a tumble of buildings and pathways, styles heaped upon styles, long tiled roofs pierced by brick chimneys growing into white stone columns that sprouted balconies and walkways which, winding upwards, led to houses of glass that hung like lanterns from the cavern's ceiling. Brick walls became stone walls, became wooden walls, became glass walls; elegant façades grew into pleasing grotesqueries of contorted detail; picturesque cottages resolved themselves into sheer curtains of glass that plunged several storeys to become transparent pavilions; and, threading between these structures, were' streets, magical streets, lined with spherical lamps – the space on either side seeming to recede endlessly between columns – while below and below (was there a ground level?) these passageways skirted chasms that seemed to contain more windows, more walkways, sudden splashes of green vegetation, more roads, more chimneys, more bridges, more roofs. . . .

Tom felt as an ant must feel having crawled into the stonework of a Gothic cathedral, to emerge at the highest point of the transept arch: and, indeed, as the cathedral's ceiling would be bright with painted pattern, so this ceiling was bright with painted pattern – gold stars faint against blue sky, clouds rolling past sunny skies, birds wheeling in formation, the skies of the upper world frozen in a luminous sheen of paint upon the roof of this subterranean world.

And then the streets themselves – warmth, the scents of summer flowers. So much he could sense already, but how? The people moving with purpose, calm, lacking the furtive shadow-creeping of the surface; a man cleaning a window, a slow regular comforting movement; another two talking on a corner, unaware of the world, happily engaged in their own

178

private thoughts; the smiles, the greetings, the fresh complexions – why not paler in this underground world? – the delightful detail of the buildings that held the eye, preventing their enormous size from overwhelming and becoming oppressive; window boxes (could those really be plants? But they must be, for wasn't that an old lady, kind-faced, white-haired, poised with a watering can above the box, apparently lost in thought and smiling benignly at the street below?); walls with inlaid ceramic plaques and niches for sculpture, not the horrifying images of the surface city but images of grace and delicacy; everywhere variety, pleasure, ornate vents, bow windows, lamps glowing soft colours from shadowy corners – for one of the glories of this elfin place was the artificial light which created pools of colour and though never gloomy was nowhere either harsh or glaring, so that one seemed to float from soft green to pink light, or from cool blueness to apricot, while in the distance the lights twinkled deliciously as if one were moving through a gigantic jewel box.

Tom trembled with a pleasure he had never before known. If his life were to end at this moment, in these streets, it would have been fulfilled by the mere sight of such a place – though death would seem the crueller for snatching a life which lingered on the very threshold of delight.

Porlock halted before a door, plain save for a glass porthole at face height; and indeed within a minute a face had appeared at the glass – a face which broke into a broad smile at the sight of Porlock. The door was flung open and Porlock was engulfed in the arms of a huge man. Tom stared, disbelieving. The blacksmith had surely been killed: he had fallen so far ... but, who then was this? The smile broadened even more when the blacksmith saw Tom.

'So you made it, little man! We both made it!'

He tousled Tom's hair and then clasped Porlock's shoulder once again.

'Thanks to this gentleman. Thanks to his compassion.'

Porlock shook him off, goodnaturedly but with a trace of embarrassment.

'Enough of this,' he protested, leading the way inside.

As Tom followed behind he observed to his horror the misshapen bulk of the blacksmith's body, his painfully slow

179

limping motion. The blacksmith, suddenly turning, read his mind and simply smiled.

'The main thing, little man,' he said, still rejoicing, 'is that we both made it!'

29 Evening Chorus

They sat in a delightfully cosy room, well fed and holding mugs of steaming punch. Since the conversation rarely touched upon things that concerned him, Tom found himself drifting into his own thoughts. There were so many things that he wanted to know, so many questions to ask, but he knew they would have to wait. For now the time belonged to old friends with news to exchange, and the lion's share of the conversation fell to the blacksmith and Porlock.

Beyond leaded windows Tom could hear the sounds of children playing and, with a shock, he realised how much of his own childhood had fallen away. He thought back to the boy who had first entered the surface city, and he seemed to be a different person. So much had happened in the outer circumstances of his life that the changes that had taken place within him had passed unnoticed.

As the evening wore on the light began to dim at the window. It will soon be dark, he thought – and the implication of the thought startled him back to attentiveness.

'But why is the light fading?' he asked. 'Why, down here?'

Sonia smiled across the room at him.

'Man needs sleep and the darkness is for sleeping. It's almost time for the evening chorus.'

She went to the window and flung it wide. A few moments later, from the distance, a bell was heard and this became the signal for the people within the room to burst into song. At the window Sonia sang with a particularly strong and beautiful voice, and her voice and their voices became mingled with other voices as the whole city swelled with the singing of every citizen – one enormous crescendo of sweet sound that Tom found delightfully and unexpectedly familiar. It was – incredibly, it seemed to him – a song that his mother had sung (softly, bent over his bed) when as a young child he had been unable to

181

sleep. He found his eyes filling with tears at the memory, and he began to sing the words that he knew so well. And as the singing progressed, so evening became night and the lights in the roof of the cavern diminished to stars and Tom joined Sonia at the window.

As the song ended and the voices faded away, a vast silence fell upon the city, which seemed more enchanted than ever.

'You know the song,' Sonia said, standing beside him in the darkness.

'Oh, so very well! It's a song of my home country.'

Now there was movement in the room. The blacksmith stooped in the doorway, wishing everyone a blessed good night, and Porlock rose too, pausing for a moment to smooth the creases from his finely tailored trousers. Having experienced the beauty of the city, Tom now understood Porlock's fastidiousness of dress, the carefully matched colouring in everything he wore.

'Sonia, don't keep the young man up too long. Show him to his room shortly, eh? Tomorrow is a busy day.'

Nodding, she closed the door behind him.

'That song,' she said. 'It's from your home country, you say.'

'Yes.'

'How strange.'

'Why so?'

But she shook her head, as if unwilling to explain.

'We have sung it every evening for years past.'

And now Tom realised the nature of that ethereal singing which had tantalised him at various times while in the city above. It had been no figment of his overworked brain. He had been listening to the music of this enchanting place without ever knowing it.

30   The Doll

'At last you've arrived . . . the time is ripe for action . . . we've been waiting. . . .'

Who was talking? Where did the voice come from? Tom rolled listlessly on the bed in the heat of the room.

'We've been waiting.'

'Why have you been waiting? What's expected of me? I came to find my father – who are you?'

Tom sat up, open-eyed but only partially awake. He was alone in the darkened room but still he could hear the voice: 'we've been waiting' – the walls whispered it; the air was full of it; it came from no person but still whispered loudly and insistently. 'We've been waiting.'

'What must I do?' cried Tom, this time aloud. But there was no answer and the voice seemed to die as he became more alert. Silence. He tried once more to sleep; lay back on the bed; but sleep had deserted him. It was a dream, perhaps.

He walked to the window and, opening it, stepped out onto a small balcony. The stars glimmered high above him. He made out Orion, with its studded belt; the Twins, Castor and Pollux; the scattered lights of the Great Bear; the lovely pale orange of Arcturus . . . and sensed, almost immediately, that they were adrift, inaccurately placed both in relation to one another and to the time of the year. Tom knew his night sky and how it looked as winter departed. Yet he was in no way disappointed by this dome of velvet with its glittering constellations. The city was at peace around him, bathing him in its tranquility. Nothing stirred. How he longed to be a part of it! But he felt – he could not say why – that this peace could not yet be his, that this was merely an interlude until. . . .

What was it that was expected of him?

The balcony was a little way above the pavement. Tom climbed over and dropped softly to the path beneath. It led upwards between houses until the street ended with one of the dizzying chasms that were so much a characteristic of this strange place, and the path continued as a bridge whose low balustrades Tom kept well clear of. Beyond the chasm the pathway forked, one way leading narrowly down between glass-fronted buildings, and the other climbing by means of a stairway to a wide square. Tom chose the stairway. Everywhere seemed deserted, although some windows were lit and he seemed to sense rather than see movements beyond the glass. The streets, lit at intervals with coloured lanterns, returned to Tom that feeling of total bliss he had experienced when he had first arrived, and his restless sleep with its unanswered questions seemed never to have occurred.

It was a rhythmic chanting, only just heard, that led him to enter an archway which opened onto the square. Beyond was a courtyard where an old man knelt before a large yellow sphere that rested upon a low plinth. As he knelt he rocked slowly to and fro and chanted. His eyes remained fixed upon the sphere and he ignored Tom, or was unaware of his presence. Tom however, felt no sense of intrusion and stood and watched, first the white hair at the top of the man's head and then, as it reappeared from each deep bow, his face – a wise face, heavily lined and seemingly weather-beaten by decades of exposure to sun and wind.

The curious nature of this last fact escaped Tom at first and he continued to stare, almost hypnotised by the regular rhythm of the movement and chanting. The words he could not understand, but they seemed to him an ancient dialect of his own language. And then something curious did strike him: the old voice continued to chant its set phrases and at a certain point, and always the same point, the voice clicked unnaturally.

'Excuse me.'

Tom decided to confirm a suspicion that was slowly forming in his mind. There was no answer. He knelt by the figure and rested his hand on the frail arm, immediately starting back – startled even by a discovery he had expected to make. His hand had rested not upon warm flesh but upon a cold, hard surface that was clearly not human. The nodding, chanting figure was merely a doll, an automaton, whose mechanical vigil had been designed by earlier hands in earlier days.

It was uncanny. Tom was shaken. There was something eery about this lifelike puppet performing its mechanical rites beneath an artificial daylight and moonlight. How much more of the city was not as it seemed? How many of the figures that he had seen performing their comforting, routine jobs as he had walked through the streets, were but dolls? The old lady watering the window box: had she paused in thought like that throughout centuries? The man cleaning the window? The people talking privately and unconcerned about the passers-by?

Tom left the courtyard, his feeling of euphoria replaced by an eery, a sickening uncertainty. He felt suddenly alone. He retraced his steps, crossing the bridge with scarcely a thought of the abyss beneath. Coloured orbs dappled the street in rich minglings of emerald, lemon, magenta, but he had no eye for them.

He was close to the house when he almost walked into an elderly lady carrying a lantern and emerging from a narrow opening between two buildings. She opened her eyes wide in surprise and then, lifting the light in order to see Tom's face clearly, she smiled a friendly greeting.

'You're about late, young man. Youth needs its sleep. You leave the night streets for old insomniacs like me. Blessings be with you! Goodnight!'

She was indeed real, and as Tom watched her shuffle away a new surge of confidence filled him. He climbed the balcony, entered his room, lay once more upon the bed, and this time fell into a deep, undisturbed sleep.

31   Prophecies

'Mirrors and machines,' Sonia laughed. 'Mirrors and machines.'

She led Tom through the city under the perfect copy of a glaring mid-morning sun. They passed between copses of trees whose delicate foliage cast a cool shadow on lush grass, while birds called among the branches.

'But what is reality? If, as you say, so much that we see is illusion – if distances and perspectives are deceptive – how do you know what is real?'

Sonia took him by the arm.

'It's *all* real, Tom. Why does it matter that it has been especially created? Isn't the beauty enough?'

Beyond the next buildings a river rippled through a distant meadow and tumbled in a series of cascades over large rocks.

'It's very beautiful.'

They entered a square which was dominated by a large white circular building. Earlier, while they had been breakfasting, Porlock had appeared and asked with a peculiar insistence that Sonia bring Tom to the debating chamber. Now they entered the impressive carved stone entrance and mounted a flight of wide marbled stairs which curved to a first-floor balcony. Sonia pushed open a door and Tom found himself in a vast gallery which looked down upon the chamber itself.

The light was muted compared with the glare outside and he realised, as his eyes became accustomed to it, that it was tinged with green. On one wall, so large as to be seen from all parts of the interior, was the painting of an eye, with bright blue iris. He and Sonia were alone in the viewing gallery, but as he looked over the balustrade to the circular chamber below he saw that an assembly of several dozen people was already engaged in earnest discussion. Although there were men and women of all ages, there was a preponderance of elderly men, many of whom clutched large black books to their chests. One of these was speaking in a low voice – so low that Tom struggled to understand the words he spoke – while a few yards away the figure of Porlock stood impatiently, as if waiting the chance to intervene.

'The eye,' Tom whispered. 'What does it mean?'

'There is no single meaning. It stands for knowledge, for justice and truth.'

'It is also used by the people in the surface city who wish to overthrow the Red Blade. I was helped after I first met you because of the design on the buttons of the coat you gave me.'

Tom felt in his pocket for the metal disc the dwarf had given him.

'Look.'

'Yes, it's identical. The symbol of the all-seeing eye is very ancient. It existed before this place was brought into being.'

'Members of the Blade bow to their scarlet dagger.'

'It is different with the eye,' Sonia said. 'The eye sees within. There is no need to bow before it.'

Down below Porlock had begun to speak. Tom peered over the balustrade to watch him. He had removed his gold-framed spectacles and held them in one hand as he answered the old man with the book.

'Why does he want me here?' Tom asked.

'I don't know. He wouldn't say.'

To Tom's surprise, Porlock spoke of the very people he himself had mentioned only moments before.

'There are people in the city above us,' he declaimed in a rather grand fashion, 'who need, who crave, our sustenance and support.'

'And why do they need it, pray?'

'You know as well as I. The Red Blade grows more powerful by the day. Leaders of these brave people are at this moment being tortured and killed in the infamous Citadel.'

'But is it a concern of ours?'

Several of the old men fussed at their books. It was obvious that Porlock faced a united opposition. A man with a long grey beard pushed himself to his feet, an outraged look in his eye.

'The ancient writings tell us that there are two worlds. The two worlds shall remain asunder.'

187

There were loud noises of agreement and a clamour of voices quoting lines from the large black books. Sonia shook her head sadly.

'The debate has been continuing in one form or another for weeks. Porlock has support, but there are many of the ancients who rely on the old texts and will not move.'

'Is Porlock powerful?'

'He has influence. Only in recent years have watchers been allowed in the surface city, and that was his doing.'

'Watchers?'

'Those of us – mother and I, Porlock himself, a few others – who have been trusted to live in the city and observe what passes there. But we may only watch. It is forbidden to intervene.'

'The rule here sounds rather strict.'

She smiled.

'How should a place like this exist without rules for the good of us all? The people here are no less human than those in the city above – as you may hear!' (The voices rose once more in a furious babble). 'But we live by an inherited wisdom.'

'Bound up in those black books?'

Now Sonia laughed.

'They are not the law. The law can be made and unmade. But many of the old ones treat them as the exact truth.'

New voices had joined the debate, urging various conflicting courses of action. It was some time before Porlock spoke again, and then he changed the direction of his argument.

'If my learned colleagues are satisfied that we have no duty to those who suffer in the city, let them consider our own survival. For that, my friends, is now at stake.'

This brought about a frightened commotion.

'Nonsense!'

'On what evidence?'

'Explain yourself!'

Porlock calmly wiped the glass of his spectacles before continuing.

'I have reported to this assembly more than once that the Red Blade grows more cunning as well as more powerful. It has a dozen agents in every sector. We have, within the past few days, had to close the way to the house by the east gate.'

188

Now a heavy silence fell upon the company. Porlock turned his gaze slowly around the hall.

'The way had been discovered. We closed it with minutes to spare. Minutes, my friends. Two of our number were almost lost because of it. The way can never be re-opened.'

'Who betrayed us?'

Porlock turned to his questioner.

'If we had a betrayer, my friend, we should be thankful. There would be a solution, would there not? But the matter is not so straightforward. The Blade has investigators everywhere. As they gain in strength so will they by chance – by pure chance, I say – so will they discover our secrets. This is why we cannot, we must not, ignore the horrors of the city above us.'

This time Porlock's words had more obvious effect. There was no eagerness from the old men to shout him down: they sat, mute, shaking their heads enigmatically. A woman of about thirty stood up and began to question him briskly.

'What exactly are you proposing?'

'That we make contact with the forces for good in the city and offer our support.'

'When we number but a few hundred and have no weapons?'

'Yes.'

'And what good, what possible good, will that do either them or us?'

Porlock folded his arms.

'My friends, there is no point in suggesting that we have physical strength. What we possess is moral strength. The very knowledge of our existence and our support will invigorate those who stand against the Red Blade.'

Now the debate became more complicated. There were those who opposed the use of force in principle: the black books were consulted again. Others were of the opinion that moral strength would be of little avail in the violent city above. Speaker after speaker rose to make a contribution.

'A few hundred,' Tom repeated. 'Is that all there are of you?'

'And no weapons. We live in peace.'

He sat rigid, astounded. He had expected something very different. Only half-listening to the debate, he found despair overcoming him. If the community was so small, why had he not yet been reunited with his father? If his father was not here, what chance had he now of finding him?

Porlock, having restoked the fires of the debate, sat back stroking a hand over his grizzled hair. He cast a quick glance up at the gallery and nodded towards Tom before turning away.

'Does he bring many people to the underground city?' Tom asked.

'Of course not. It's a rare honour. There are so many who would wish to come – who would give everything they have.'

'The blacksmith was brought here.'

'He was terribly injured. Porlock knew him to be a good and trustworthy man.'

They sat in silence for a while, their eyes turned to the gathering below. It was clear that Porlock's second intervention had swayed many people to his side, but there was still a seemingly immovable opposition by the old men. They had a text for every argument, always a story from times gone by to parallel anything that was happening today. Eventually Porlock rose to his feet once more.

'We have listened,' he said gravely, 'to detailed recitations from the ancient texts. Although they do not have the force of law, they demand great respect from us all, and it is only because others among us are more learned in this respect that I have not hitherto referred to them myself. . . .'

He paused, and there was a silence during which, it seemed, his audience attempted to gauge whether he perhaps spoke with irony. Sonia, for her part, looked on with an expression of bewilderment.

'My distinguished friends will know well those writings which foretell the rise of the Red Blade. We are all aware, are we not, that this repulsive sect was initiated many years ago by a stranger to the city – "Like a tick entering the wool of the sheep" does it not read? "And like a tick he will drink the blood of the city". Aren't we all aware of those prophetic lines?'

There were nods of the head all round the chamber. Sonia, Tom noticed, seemed no less bewildered than before. Porlock's voice grew ever more ponderous as if to match the sanctity of the books from which he quoted.

'And do I need to remind you, my friends, of the passage

which follows – another passage of prophecy? This one is, until now, unfulfilled. Until now. . . . '

He again paused. One or two of the old men began to move their lips, soundlessly rehearsing the lines.

'"But another will follow seeking a father. . . . "'

At this point several members of the assembly began to utter the words, softly, so that Porlock led a chorus. Tom clutched the balustrade so that his fingers ached.

> Secretly he will enter the city –
> like a steel comb he will enter the sheep's wool,
> rake out the clinging vermin. . . .

Porlock spoke challengingly.

'Do we not believe in prophecy? That each prophecy will in time be fulfilled?'

The man with the long grey beard stood slowly to face him.

'We do believe so, friend Porlock. But you must explain yourself.'

Porlock swung round and raised his arm to the gallery.

'The time is nigh. One has followed seeking a father.'

Amid the commotion which followed Tom realised that he was being beckoned to descend to the chamber. Overwhelmed by what he had heard, he was scarcely aware of his progress down the wide marble stairs and into the auditorium. Faces swam at him in the greenish light and he would surely have fainted away had not Porlock placed an arm around his shoulders and led him gently to the centre of the throng.

'One has followed,' Porlock repeated. 'I want you, Tom, to answer all the questions that I and these people ask you. Speak openly, for they are friends.'

Tom nodded, unsure whether words would come.

'You have come seeking your father. Tell these good people how you came here, and from where.'

He began, falteringly, with a description of his journey. He told of the cold, lonely nights, the days of wandering without food, his clothes torn and soiled. He explained why he had come, how life had been in his home village, what he had expected of the city – and what he had found.

They listened, curious, even moved. When he had finished,

though, he was aware of an air of puzzlement in the chamber. There were whisperings and shakings of heads.

'A fascinating story, friend Porlock,' one of the assembly commented at length. 'But why the fulfilment of prophecy?'

'Are you deaf that you cannot hear?' Porlock demanded. 'Or blind that you cannot see? You have heard the story. You have heard this young man tell you where he comes from.'

The bafflement of his audience had in no way diminished, but it seemed that Porlock relied on this perplexity for the effectiveness of his next move. For now he reached into a pocket and withdrew an object which Tom at once recognised.

'Is this, Tom, the picture of your father which you carried with you to the city?'

'Yes.'

'And is it not, my friends, a remarkable picture?'

He held it up and turned it slowly so that everyone should see it. There were sharp cries of surprise, howls even, an incredible cacophony of exclamations, a furious babble of excited voices. Tom felt Porlock's reassuring arm around his shoulders once more as the noise seemed to go on and on for ever. The picture was passed from hand to hand, each recipient grasping it eagerly and poring over it with attention to every detail.

Then they began to ask him questions. What kind of man was his father? What could he remember of his early years? Why had he decided to follow his father to the city? He answered as best he could, repeating some of his story, often having to shake his head and admit that he did not know. Eventually – the interrogation having abated somewhat but the interest of the assembly remaining as keen as ever – Porlock had a whispered conversation with a group of the old men and led him towards the door.

'Our thanks to you, Tom, for your clear and honest answers. The remainder of our debate must be in private.'

Sonia had come down to escort him to an antechamber. They dare not look one another in the eye for the awesomeness of what they had heard. He followed her into an iridescent cavern, where a fountain played into a shimmering pool lit from below and the further recesses seemed hung with gleaming ice, fold on fold of stalagtites, despite the bright shafts of sunlight which illuminated the place from some hidden grille. Sonia sat on a low bench by the fountain, her fingers trailing in the water.

He could not talk about what had happened. Indeed, he could scarcely think clearly about it. Was he therefore the fulfilment of a prophecy? He glanced towards Sonia and her eyes, which had been turned on him, quickly looked away. They were suddenly shy of one another, awkward.

'The light in the chamber,' he said at last, his voice echoing. 'It was green – as in that room I stumbled into. Why is that?'

'All our meetings are held under green light. It's the sacred colour.'

They fell into silence once more. He, too, sat by the fountain. The water was clear and very cold. He shook his fingers and beads of water sprang sparkling through the air.

'Victory!'

It was Porlock, who came striding towards them and unashamedly embraced them each in turn.

'Fine work, Tom. We've won the day. Now we've work to do.'

He turned to Sonia.

'Fresh clothes and the necessary papers for our young gentleman, if you please. We leave within the hour!'

32   Disillusion

But Tom's heady sense of destiny was not to last.

After swift preparation he had taken his leave of Sonia (whose tearfulness reminded him of their first farewell at the house with the white room) and followed Porlock through streets he had not travelled before. The stairway was a different one – wider, and with two cables of thick rope stretching up into the obliterating darkness. At intervals were strung large wicker baskets which must move up and down on a pulley system, but the lids were on and he could not see what they contained.

As they began to climb, Porlock looked over his shoulder and gave a short laugh.

'I'm sorry about all that prophesying nonsense this morning,' he said. 'The fact is, those old fogeys won't listen to reason. You have to pander to their fanciful notions. Nothing like a few of the ancient texts to fire their imaginations!'

Tom, taken aback, merely kept on climbing.

'You heard me appeal to their humanity: no concern whatsoever for the people in the city above! So I explained the dangers we ourselves face. They chose not to believe in them. Nothing for it but to make up fairy tales.'

'You mean,' Tom asked wildly, 'that you don't believe me?'

'Believe you? Of course I do! You're an honest fellow, Tom. I knew you'd not let me down.'

'But the picture. . . .'

'Your father, that I don't doubt. The question is – who is he?'

'I don't understand.'

'The moment I discovered that picture I saw the resemblance to a certain man. I need say no more, I think – a mere resemblance. And your story fits neatly. Coincidences. But I know these old men with their thick black books. They can't resist the suggestion of a mystery, the hint of prophecy. They swallowed the bait!'

Tom halted abruptly, his surprise turning to anger.

'You used me,' he accused. 'You've been dishonest with me!'

'I promised you nothing.'

'You led me to believe that I would find my father. You've deceived me. He isn't here.'

'I don't know where he is.'

Tom sat down heavily, his legs weak, a sick feeling in his stomach. He covered his head in his arms and wished he could cry, but felt only a burning ache where the tears should be.

'For shame!' Porlock chided. 'All's not lost.'

But Tom would not hear, and the words floated away down the steep steps. Porlock made as if to proceed upwards, perhaps calculating that this would spur Tom into action, then came down again. Eventually he shook Tom's shoulder and spoke loudly and sternly.

'My duty is to the many good people in this city and the city above. Am I to prefer their deaths to the disappointment of a boy who has undertaken an impossible mission? Find a lost father in a place so vast! Should I not seize the chance to save so many?'

Tom listened, without answering. He remembered his own soul-searching at the House of the Star, when he had asked himself what actions were permissible to reach a desired end. Again there came the dreadful vision of the boat and Marcus drowning, and he knew that it was for the best and yet that he could not accept it, that he had killed a man.

'Stay here,' Porlock continued, 'and you're no better than the old men, with their antiquated texts and their fine words and their blindness to the perils of others. Stay here and you'll be forever stuck fast in your own selfishness.'

'The people here won't betray me as you have done.'

'Betray!'

'Sonia would not lie to me.'

Porlock sat on the step and his voice grew softer.

'Yes, I could have told you that your quest was hopeless. What good would that have done you? Didn't you want to reach the underground city? You talk of betrayal and lies. These are mere words. Life isn't so simple that a man can never tell a lie in the cause of justice.'

Tom, although he felt too bitter to reply, yet recognised the truth in these words. He opened his eyes and looked back down the tunnel. It would not take long to retrace his steps. Porlock rose to his feet.

'Without you,' he said, 'I am likely to fail. Why should the people in the surface city trust me? But you know them. You can vouch for me, for the underground city.'

His voice grew severe again.

'Submit to your feelings of anger and frustration if you will. By all means take your revenge on me. But recognise, Tom, that the decision is yours.'

He began to climb the steps, but slowly, as if he expected Tom to join him. And, indeed, without making any conscious decision to do so, Tom found himself on his feet and following. Their progress was steady, necessitating frequent rests during which they stood lightly panting, leaning against the damp wall. They had gone far beyond the light before Porlock spoke again.

'Don't think too badly of me,' he said. 'If this business goes well I shall help you all I can.'

How dense the blackness was! He dare not look behind, yet it was unnerving to stare ahead into the void. Occasionally he strayed too close to the wall and his shoulder brushed one of the baskets. Then the slight creak of the wickerwork seemed to flood his senses, which were starved of other stimulation.

'There are only three ways to the city,' Porlock revealed during one of their rests. 'The one by the east gate is closed, as you know – probably for ever. The route by which I took you underground has also been sealed off. I heard as we set out that the House of the Star was badly damaged by the fire we witnessed.

'This way is therefore the only one that remains open for us.'

It seemed that they would climb for ever. Tom could not believe that the journey down had been so long. His legs ached and he was stung by sweat.

'The lights!'

It was a few seconds before he realised that he was not imagining the flickers of illumination some way ahead. As they drew closer he found that they were set into the wall, waving a shaky light over the damp rock. He could make out the strands of rope, too, which here seemed to plunge downwards, away out of sight again. Or perhaps it was that they themselves were climbing more steeply and in another direction.

'The door,' Porlock panted. 'Somewhere here.'

They stood together, fumbling desperately as if the door might no longer be there, leaving them marooned in darkness.

'Yes, here!'

Porlock led him through. They emerged in a narrow staircase, lit by a high window. It was immediately familiar. Although at first he could not think where he was, he knew that he had been here before.

33   Handshake

A few steps and they were engulfed by swirling steam. They coughed and fought for breath. The kitchen of the all-night cafe! They stepped inside and there was Lucy, beaming broadly at Porlock and gathering Tom within one vast and motherly arm.

'Look at this! Bill, you come here! Visitors!'

Bill appeared, holding out his hand to Porlock, whom he treated with his customary respect, and nodding happily at Tom.

'Don't tell me, young Tom – you've come from down there!'

'That he has,' Porlock said severely, 'but it's better that the whole world doesn't know it.'

'Ah! I'm sorry. I got carried away. No one else here just now.'

They went into a back room, Tom marvelling that his old friends should know about the underground city.

'You've been down there?' he asked Bill in a whisper, afraid of Porlock's sharp tongue.

'Once or twice, yes. But we live up here. We're needed.'

'Needed?'

'For the food, you see. You noticed those baskets on your way up? Nobody suspects a cafe for buying large quantities of food. We send most of it down.'

Porlock fluttered his hand in irritation.

'We've urgent business to attend to. We need to make contact with one of those who use the rooftops.'

'Do I know him?'

'He's been here before,' Tom said. 'A dwarf.'

Bill clapped him on the shoulder.

'You're in luck,' he said. 'He's often here asking for you. He sits in the corner, shrinking into the shadows.'

'Hunted,' Porlock said.

'You think so? Poor soul!'

'What does he say?' asked Tom.

'Nothing, save to ask if you've been seen. I just shake the head. Few words as possible, that's my motto. He sometimes takes a small meal but never finishes it.'

Porlock seemed satisfied.

'As soon as he arrives,' he said, 'bring him in here.'

The hours would have dragged had Tom not busied himself in the kitchen with Bill and Lucy. He left Porlock contentedly reading in the back room and spent his time carrying saucepans, adding salt and pepper to concoctions bubbling on the huge ranges, and helping to wash and dry a prodigious collection of utensils which seemed to be in constant use. It was strange to think that the food they were preparing would be sent down the long tunnel to be consumed by Sonia and the blacksmith and the other people he knew.

It was mid-evening when Bill waved Tom into the back-room, following moments later with the dwarf in tow. Tom was shocked by his wretched condition. Not only did his clothes seem ragged and dirty, but he had the look of a fugitive, ill-fed and desperate. He eyed Porlock in a manner which suggested at once familiarity and wariness, and addressed Tom in a broken voice.

'I want words,' he said. 'Alone.'

'You can talk in front of Porlock,' Tom replied. 'He's a friend.'

'Alone, I say!'

Porlock complied immediately.

'Your caution is commendable,' he said, standing.

The dwarf followed towards the door, as if to ensure that Porlock would leave, swinging round urgently once it had closed.

'I'm in terrible trouble,' he blurted out. 'I can't evade them much longer. They're closing in.'

'I know,' said Tom. 'There's a man I call the bellows-pumper because of the circumstances in which I first met him. He is a man without the use of his legs.'

'That's the man! That's the man, Tom!'

'You know him?'

'Ha! You ask me that? That's a good question!'

199

Tom was accustomed to a strangeness in the dwarf's manner, but he had never before seen him in this wild, manic mood.

'Would you believe that he was a friend once? Can you see him as a friend to any man? But yes, he was. A friend!'

He paced up and down, with abrupt changes of direction.

'Even an enemy of the Red Blade, he was. Oh, yes! Not that he ever hated the Blade as I did. Took against it more from a spirit of adventure, I'd say. He had his legs then, you see. A bold young man he was!'

'And what happened?'

The dwarf seemed reluctant to give a direct answer to this question. He continued his energetic parading around the room until, coming close to Tom, he stopped suddenly and thrust his face forward.

'He fell. Down and down. Smack!'

'An accident?'

'Of course, an accident. It was far from here – another part of the city. We were on the rooftops, devising a new route. And . . . we got into difficulties. No way back. We were on a ledge, a narrow ledge. There was a sheer drop. . . .'

His eyes still stared towards Tom but they looked right through him. The dwarf was on the ledge again, high above the city. Tom saw beads of sweat break out on his forehead and his hands clenching and unclenching.

'He fell?'

'I couldn't turn. He began to slip – called out to me. "I'm going," he said. "I'm going." I couldn't reach out. I had to hold on. He went over the edge and was gone. I heard it.'

There was a silence, during which the dwarf seemed to return by stages to the present.

'You've seen what happened. He lived, but his legs were gone. He blamed me for it – all of us. He joined the Blade and has pursued us ever since. Now he's in these parts and our people are being persecuted. Many are dead. Many are tortured.'

'What have you learned that can help us?'

The question was put more as an accusation than as a plea. The eyes interrogated him.

'I've been to the underground city,' Tom said simply.

The dwarf laughed bitterly.

'So you choose to mock! Good may it do you! I hope you enjoy our suffering!'

'I've been there, I tell you. With Porlock. He is from the underground city. It exists. I've found it.'

Slowly it became apparent to the dwarf that Tom was in earnest. The effect was dramatic. His legs buckled beneath him and he collapsed full length on the floor. His eyes were not closed, but he seemed unable to move a muscle as Tom stooped over him and began to lift him up. Perhaps Porlock had been listening beyond the door, for at this moment he entered the room and helped Tom carry his burden to a chair.

'It's a wonderful place,' said Tom, seeing from the dwarf's expression that he could understand, although the shock had left him temporarily paralysed. 'There is colour, and distance, and beauty.'

The words tumbled from his lips, unordered but rich with praise for the new world he had found. He spoke of the sights he had seen, the people he had met. The dwarf listened for some minutes, a smile gradually playing along his lips.

'And there is water,' Tom said, 'cascading from nowhere into limpid pools, and there are birds in the trees with songs and trills you would never believe....'

The dwarf sat up in the chair, his eyes brimming with tears.

'Oh, wonders!' he whispered hoarsely.

Porlock, as brisk as ever, drew up his own chair and, ignoring the dwarf's display of emotion, began to explain his mission.

'We have often met without knowing one another. Now we are united in a common aim: the overthrow of the Red Blade. I know you to be one of those who use the rooftops. Tom will vouch for me as a representative of those underground. Time, we both know, is short.'

The dwarf nodded.

'The people underground,' Porlock added, 'are ready to support you. I have been charged with offering that support.'

The dwarf continued to nod rhythmically, although for a while he said nothing. He stood up and began to pace the room again, at first uncertainly, then with the same quick movements as before.

'We can be ready within days,' he said in a low voice, half to himself. 'In some sectors the units are fully prepared. Else-

201

where there's work to be done. A few have no spirit for it – though that may change.

'The messengers could be despatched immediately. That means the whole city could be alerted within hours. Speed is vital.'

Porlock interrupted.

'Your organisation,' he asked. 'Has it been infiltrated by agents of the Blade?'

'No. How can we tell? Certainly we have lost many valuable leaders – the eastern commander. . . . Too many of our number are fainthearted, but we are strong enough to strike them, with your help.'

He took to muttering to himself, planning the exercise that would be undertaken. He counted on his fingers, waved his arms, nodded his head vigorously, so that Tom was unable to prevent himself smiling at the performance. Finally he turned towards Porlock.

'How many men do you have under arms?' he asked.

'Under arms, none.'

'None! You mean . . . none?'

'We are not a warlike people.'

'Not warlike, is it!'

The dwarf began to shake with a sudden fury.

'You presume to offer your help when you have no fighting men?' he cried savagely. 'You lead me to believe you are ready to stand with us shoulder to shoulder – and then tell me that you are "not a warlike people"! What kind of fool's paradise do you inhabit?'

Porlock, stern of expression, made no reply.

'When men have been dying, persecuted by the Blade! They cry out, stretch out their hands for help – and are offered a bland smile. From a people who are "not warlike". That, my friend, is the kind of support we can do without!'

He looked up at Porlock, a bitter sneer on his lips.

'Or do you think we should preach truth and beauty to the Blade so that they throw down their weapons and submit? We are perhaps misguided in opposing force with force. We've misjudged the enemy. We've imagined the cruelties, the murders!'

Porlock allowed the thunder to pass, though the dark

202

clouds on the dwarf's face certainly showed no signs of dispersing.

'I'm sorry,' he said. 'That kind of help we cannot give. What we do offer is genuine, however.'

'Genuine – but useless.'

'You must decide that for yourself.'

They were treated once more to a display of gesturing and mumbling as the dwarf argued the possibilities to himself. He had, for the moment, forgotten them. He paused, arm raised, lips silently moving; then swung round and marched along the length of the room, an urgent humming sound rising in his throat. He leant against the wall, shaking his head from side to side; ground a fist into the palm of the other hand; played his tongue reflectively over his lips.

'There is one way.'

'What's that?' Porlock asked.

'It's a plan we have considered. It requires only a few men at the outset – highly trained men, but only a few. To assault the Citadel.'

'That's impossible!'

'To enter the Citadel. You know that the supreme ruler lives on the top floor and is never seen? The top floor is shuttered. Nobody knows how well it is guarded, exactly where the ruler is to be found. We have discussed the possibility of crossing to the roof of the Citadel and attempting to seize the ruler. With the Blade demoralised, we would attack in force.

'I believe we would succeed, but it's obviously a perilous task and our leaders have been reluctant to attempt it.'

'What would make them change their minds?'

The dwarf screwed up his eyes and tilted his head to one side.

'The belief, perhaps, that the underground city exists and will give support. Especially if the nature of that support is not explained to them. Let's say they imagine a vast army stands by in readiness.... You understand me? A little deception is excusable, don't you think?'

'In view of the urgency of the matter.'

'Indeed. The main thing is to act – and act soon.'

To Tom's amazement Porlock and the dwarf extended their hands and shook them, like comrades. He thought of Porlock's speech in the debating chamber, persuading the gathering by means that were less than honest, and he compared this with the dwarf's present intention of deceiving his own leaders. Both would argue that they were justified by the turn of events. Neither, it was clear, felt anything but satisfaction in their agreed course of action. This was apparent in the conspiratorial smiles with which they made their farewells.

34   Into the Citadel

The wind gusted across the flat expanse of roof so that the
three of them – Tom, Porlock, the dwarf – found themselves
huddling together for protection. Close by, a team of
experienced climbers prepared for the assault. They wore
black clothing for camouflage in the darkness, and had the
paraphernalia of their trade slung about them: ropes, grap-
pling hooks, knives. Across a wide and dizzy gulf, its roof
slightly lower than the one on which they stood, lay the
forbidding grey pile of the Citadel. The snow had melted,
save in small pockets which never saw the sun by day, but
there had been a light rain which made the surface glisten and
this, combined with the swirling wind, promised to make a
footing treacherous.

'See the top floor of the Citadel,' called the dwarf, cupping
his hands around his mouth. 'It's always in darkness, with the
shutters closed. It's lower down that the guards patrol.'

As if in response to this remark (though he had in fact been
engaged in conversation with his colleagues) the leader of the
group suddenly motioned everyone well back from the edge of
the roof. He dropped to the ground and inched forward on his
stomach to peer across the divide. The dwarf put his mouth to
Tom's ear.

'There are guards on each floor,' he explained. 'They come
and go at regular intervals. The crossing must be done within
the space of a few minutes or we shall be seen.'

The leader stood and beckoned his team forward again.
They worked speedily, apparently without fear of their precarious position. One sat with his feet out over the edge while
he knotted rope, for all the world as though he were a mere
foot or two from the ground. Tom had noticed that one of the
men carried a crossbow: this was now taken to the edge and an
arrow tied to a length of rope. It shot across the chasm and

stuck fast. Two men now grasped the rope and hauled on it, testing it for strength.

'Down!'

A sentry had evidently appeared on another floor. Each man flattened himself on the roof, motionless, until a signal brought him back to his post. There followed a heated discussion, raised voices occasionally carried on the wind, but undecipherable. The leader detached himself from the group and approached the watching trio.

'It's the devil to get a decent hold. We've done the best we can, but it's uncertain. We need a light weight to go first.'

'Me!' exclaimed the dwarf in terror. 'You mean me? I can't! Not near the edge!'

'You only have to hold on,' the leader said carelessly. 'If the rope comes away at the far side you hang on and we'll haul you up. It's time we're up against. If one of us goes and it comes away we'll have to start over again.'

But the dwarf backed away, shaking.

'Can't! Not possible!'

Tom remembered that the dwarf had spoken before of a terrifying experience on the rooftops. He remembered, too, his own escape when the rope had snapped on the icy bridge between the House of the Star and the eastern sector. Yet he found himself stepping forward.

'I'll go. Tell me what I have to do.'

The leader nodded approvingly.

'Well, you're not so very small, my lad, but lighter than any of us, to be sure. Quickly, now.'

They stood around him, anxious to be at their task. He was shown how to grasp the rope; how to pass hand over hand; told what he must do when he reached the other side; how to react should the rope come away. There was no sentiment among these men – merely a sharp tap on the shoulder to tell him it was time to go.

He launched himself into space, feeling for a moment gloriously free as he swung forward and began to carry himself across. The awfulness of it struck him seconds later. A dash of wind rocked him sideways and the rope shook violently, vibrating under his fingers. He clung on, his shoulders already aching from the effort. He kept his head up, his eyes on the few

206

stars that glinted among the clouds. Hand over hand he advanced, close to panic but knowing he was watched from the roof behind. Knowing, too, that if he failed the mission itself might come to nothing. The citadel grew closer, but very slowly. His arms burned with the effort; he could not feel his hands. What if his numbed fingers lost their grip? What if the wind tore them from the rope?

He was near enough to the building to make out the small scarlet dagger on each of the shutters masking the windows on the topmost floor. No light escaped from between the slats. He wondered whether hidden eyes were watching his jerky progress across the gulf, hidden sentries waiting to seize him. Further down lights burned behind large windows, and anyone looking up could not fail to see him. He came close to the arrow which, buried in woodwork, was his only support. Was it possible that this alone kept him aloft, prevented him from plunging down and down to the distant street? It seemed so fragile: it shook in the wind. The leader of the assault party had been so matter-of-fact about the crossing, but if the arrow should shake free he would be swung down into the side of the building behind him, battered against the brickwork before plummeting to the ground.

The wind shook him and spun him round as he reached out a hand for the roof. He needed to pull himself up, away from the rope, but he froze between the two – propped awkwardly against the building but not daring to let go of the lifeline. The wind slapped him again, tugging his arm out into the void. His shoulder began to slip from the wall. He heard himself moan with the effort as he threw both hands towards a small projection and began to haul himself upwards.

Once safe on the roof he could not believe that he had come so far. The rope stretched away like a slender thread and on the far roof the men who watched him seemed small, remote. He quickly took the end of the rope as he had been instructed, untied it and fastened it to a strong support. It was heavy in his fingers and wet from the drizzle which had started up again. Knotting it was difficult. When he looked up they had all gone: he could see no one. He stood alone on the roof, underneath him the very headquarters of the infamous organisation he had grown to fear and loathe. Suppose he were left here, stranded. . . .

But they must have been avoiding another sentry, for he saw that now the first man had started forward, a coil of rope unwinding over one shoulder. He picked his way across the gap at incredible speed, body and limbs in perfect harmony. As he put a foot on the roof he gave the slightest of nods to Tom by way of acknowledgement, checked the knot he had made and fastened his own rope. The next man, too, brought a rope with him, so that the rest of the party – after another brief disappearance – swayed across on a makeshift bridge. The last to come was Porlock.

'Good man!' he said, taking Tom by the hand.

'But where's the dwarf?'

'He couldn't. His nerve has gone. He'll wait for us.'

A rope-ladder was slung over the edge. The team went to work, each man carrying out his duties at great speed and in complete silence. One after the other they disappeared from view. Finally a head and shoulders re-emerged and the waiting pair were gestured to follow.

The way in was through a pair of shutters which had been forced. The wood was soft and rotten, and as Tom brushed it with his shoulder one section broke off and fell away into the darkness. He saw it turning and turning, hitting the wall and spinning down and down until it was lost from view. A window had been broken – the rainy squalls must have disguised the sound – and he climbed through it.

A long corridor lay in heavy darkness. The assault party had clearly encountered not a soul during their entry. Along one side were the shuttered windows. On the other there seemed to be doors at regular intervals and two of the group approached the first of these, while another pair took up positions close by. There was only a faint light from the broken window but it was enough to run along the blade of a long knife. Porlock motioned to Tom to keep well back and, needlessly, put a finger to his lips.

The door, surprisingly, was not locked. The men, on a signal, hurled themselves inside. It seemed but a second for the whole group to be in the room – and little more before they all came out. One of them, who Tom now saw carried a small light, shook his head wonderingly and they moved on down the corridor. Tom and Porlock, bringing up the rear, paused in the doorway. As their eyes adjusted to the gloom they were able to make out, dimly, rows of glass cases with specimens of some kind mounted in them – insects, perhaps, or spiders. There was an unpleasant smell of neglect and decay. Porlock drew Tom away.

The men in black regrouped around the second door. Their technique was identical, and again they hurried out and continued down the corridor. This room was completely empty. The third appeared to be some kind of shrine with a huge scarlet dagger emblem on the wall, glowing faintly in the darkness: but a shrine that had long since fallen into disuse. It was eery, unsettling, almost preposterous. They had expected guards, lights burning long into the night, perhaps, in some intelligence centre: instead they found silence, darkness, emptiness.

Every door opened easily, to reveal no sign of human habitation, yet still the group advanced stealthily, prepared at any moment to be surprised. They came at last to a door which clearly led to the floor below, but which had been efficiently sealed. There was no way of passing through it without arousing every sentry in the building. Then how. . . ? Tom saw the question on every man's face. How did the ruler of the Blade communicate with his underlings? Or was their information, perhaps, at fault? Did the ruler not inhabit the top floor as everyone believed, but operate from elsewhere in the building?

There was one last door, at the very end of the corridor. The knives were once more held in readiness, two men put their shoulders to the woodwork. Tom watched as they turned the handle and stepped swiftly inside. This time they did not immediately come out again. Tom and Porlock heard low exclamations.

They crept forward and peered inside. Darkness. A glass chandelier hung heavy from the ceiling. The floor was thickly carpeted. There were bookcases around the walls and, before a large shutterless window, a massive desk littered with objects it was impossible to distinguish. Tom started back. The moon, passing from behind a cloud, shed a fleeting illumination over the interior to reveal that the room had an occupant presiding over chandelier, bookcases and the cluttered desk. He sat in a leather chair under the window, grinning and gaping – a brittle human skeleton.

35 Life in Death

The hardened men who minutes before had risked their lives
with scarcely a thought now shrank back, stricken expressions
on their faces. Only Porlock retained his composure, taking the
flickering light from the man who carried it and playing it on
the bones, which gleamed a sickly white. Tom, notwithstand-
ing the horror in the chair – which seemed to stare at him from
its ghastly hollow sockets – edged close to his companion. The
objects on the desk were now seen to consist largely of papers,
and they stooped to read them.

Dust covered everything; time had starched the paper;
sunlight had faded the writing. A spidery scrawl was now
visible as a kind of faint echo of the original, so that they had to
dwell on each cluster of signs to decipher the meaning. The
script was in the fashion of an earlier time and the language,
too, had an antiquated ring.

'He who discovers this,' the first words ran, 'has discovered
the secret of the Red Blade. But he has discovered it too late.'

Porlock lifted the sheet and the corner crumbled in his
fingers.

'For here is a paradox. I am the Blade and I am no more. Yet
the Blade lives for ever. Gaze on me and you look upon life in
death.'

Tom declined to obey the instruction and turn. He drew
closer to Porlock and was not ashamed of his fear. Porlock
himself seemed unsettled. The members of the assault party
were shuffling out of the door, regrouping in the corridor
outside.

'Power is with a ghost, because the living wish it so.'

These strange words completed the first page. Porlock, with
great care, slid it gently to one side, but it instantly cracked in
several places and the edges began to flake. The second sheet,
not bleached by the sun, was rather more easy to scan.

'I, a stranger, found a people needing strength. I offered them strength. They seized it. They worshipped the sign of the Red Blade.

'Men are weak. They crave control. The Blade controls. The Blade will always control. I have ensured that it shall be so.

'Gaze on me and you look upon life in death.'

Porlock, moving aside this second sheet and blowing away the particles that broke from it, gave Tom a questioning glance as if to ask whether he wished to leave. He shook his head and bent it once more over the desk. The writing on the third sheet was more closely packed.

'The chain of command is hidden from every eye. No member of the Blade knows the man whom he obeys. I have devised it so.

'Each man communicates in code. The codes are elaborate and there is none but understands a mere fraction of them. Let a man ask advice; let him seek authorisation; let him give a command. He will not know who hears. He will not know who answers. He only knows that the Blade has spoken, the Blade has acted.

'For each message is taken by one man and passed to a third, according to the code. The code commands. And none knows who rules him and whom he rules.

'So it is, and ever shall be, that all men – even to the most powerful – pass orders one to the other and believe that they obey the supreme ruler. And they do obey the supreme ruler. He sits in this chair. He is beyond human hurt and his work cannot be undone.

'I am the Blade. Gaze upon me and you look upon life in death.'

Porlock drew the sheet aside impatiently.

'Madness,' he whispered. 'Surely this is madness!'

At this moment the light gave out. Only the moon, gliding among the clouds, offered a pale illumination within the room. Porlock took the next page in trembling hands and carried it to the window, Tom following closely.

'Let enemies of the Blade weep bitter tears,' they read. 'The work cannot be undone. For I have set it in motion and the wheels will turn for ever. They turn slowly, but they will not stop.

212

'I leave this world but I control the city. Is this not admirable? Is it not a thing of wonder? Gaze upon me and you look upon life in death.'

This was all.

'Can this be true?'

Porlock, motionless, let the sheet fall from his fingers. It disintegrated as it touched the floor.

'For how long . . . ?'

The wind fussed at the panes. The moon passed behind a cloud. With a sudden decisiveness Porlock began to gather papers from the top of the desk. Tom saw his dark shadow sweeping them together and lifting them in a fragile bundle. He followed Porlock to the door.

Had one of them touched the chair? As they passed into the corridor the skeleton gave a jerk, slid swiftly downwards and collapsed in a shower of dust and splintered bones.

36　Flight

'For so many years!' Porlock muttered as they hurried along the corridor. He was talking to himself rather than to Tom. 'The leader of the Blade. It's madness, very madness!'

They climbed through the window into the squalling wind and struggled, swaying, up the rope ladder. Fragments of the old documents flaked off and floated away into the darkness. Once on the roof Porlock began to question himself all over again, but in tones so low that Tom could not make out a word.

And then the night erupted. There was a terrible insistent braying sound and the rooftops were suddenly as brilliant as day. It was only as the first radiance dimmed that he was aware of the guttering embers of the flares spiralling down to the ground. The howling sound, which seemed never to cease, prevented him from thinking, from acting. He only felt a disabling fear. New flares shot up into the sky above them, the glare revealing members of the assault party already on their way back across their rope bridge, tiny black spiders on a fragile web.

'Quickly! Off the roof!'

Porlock tugged him to the edge. They swung themselves over, already gasping for breath. There were ropes for hands and feet, but in their haste they rocked crazily from side to side. Their progress was achingly slow. Tom felt something career past his head. They were as good as dead, he knew it. One of the ropes, presumably hit by a missile, simply fell away into the void so that one of his feet dangled in space and only the strength of his arms saved him.

There was such a distance to cross! Porlock, no athlete, concentrated violently on keeping his body vertical and putting one foot in front of the other. Ahead of them one of the party jerked away from the rope. He must have been hit. He floundered in empty air and dropped and dropped away. Tom's despair increased. He and Porlock moved slowly across the trembling, kicking bridge and every moment he expected to be swept away, tossed into the deep blackness. The noise intensified.

They arrived and were hauled up. The dwarf was on the rooftop with the men in dark clothing grouped round him.

'Hurry!'

'Are we betrayed?' demanded Porlock, fastening a quick, stricken look upon the uncomprehending Tom.

'No. The first man across was seen by a sentry. You don't have the individual we wanted.'

It was, in the dwarf's usual manner, an accusation.

'It wasn't possible. It's the devil to explain.'

'As we go.'

Flares burst above them, painful to the eyes. One of the team knelt by the edge of the roof and severed each rope with the swift motion of a sharp knife.

'Groups of three,' the dwarf explained. 'It's pre-arranged. You and the boy with me.'

From a pocket he pulled a length of thick black cloth.

'Tie this around my eyes,' he said. 'If you please.'

'I don't understand.'

'We have to cross the roofs and I can't look.'

'But if you should. . . .'

Porlock evidently found it difficult to express the responsibility he felt.

'Nonsense! The way is not hazardous here. A few buildings and we shall descend. These other fellows will go on further where the way is narrower.'

His judgement of the route was sound. Tom, who had had adventures enough on the rooftops, was relieved to find that the parapets were wide and that, where difficult manoeuvres were necessary, iron hoops had been driven into the walls for support. The two of them helped the dwarf along, Porlock describing what they had found and adding interpretations which, when Tom chanced to overhear them above the noise, were pessimistic in the extreme.

'Nothing but a skeleton, and that ages old . . . documents, written by the Red Blade founder himself . . . there *is* no leader, has been no leader for years without number. . . .'

The dwarf made no reply to any of this, but nodded his head time and again to show that he understood.

' . . . a system so complicated that the organisation continues to function with no one in charge of it. . . . '

They had approached, and the first men had already passed, a door set into the wall when Tom realised with a shock that he recognised it.

'But I've been here before!' he exclaimed. 'When I travelled from the House of the Star to the eastern sector. This is the route by which I went down.'

The dwarf raised his eye bandage and stared at the door for some seconds.

'If that truly is the door,' he said, 'you took more risks than you knew.'

'The steps go down a long way,' Tom explained, 'with uninhabited passages leading from them. Then there is a hidden door and more steps past corridors where I imagined people were sleeping.'

The dwarf shook his head wonderingly.

'That is indeed the place. It is the chief dormitory of the Red Blade. The city guards and some of their most feared assassins live there.'

He replaced the shield over his eyes and indicated that they should proceed.

'At this moment I imagine that it is in ferment.'

'But why the secret door?' Tom asked.

'Many years ago,' the dwarf replied, 'that was the largest hostelry in the eastern sector. As the Blade grew more powerful they seized the important properties for themselves. They needed only the first few floors of that building and sealed the top floors off. Fortunately for us, one of our sympathisers was given the job of fixing that formidable door.'

'And he built in the hidden opening?'

'You can imagine the advantage this will give us when the time is ripe for attack. We have never yet used the door for fear of alerting them.'

His voice hardened.

'You might have ruined everything.'

Tom resisted the temptation to remind the dwarf that his journey would have been unnecessary had he received more help in the first place.

'It was when I emerged from that building that I met the mad archivist from the underground city who took me to the night cafe.'

'The archivist!' Porlock started. 'You met poor Grimbald?'

'He passed old documents to me when he was arrested by the city guards.'

Now Porlock seized him by the shoulder.

'Documents, you say! What documents? Where are they?'

'We have them,' intervened the dwarf. 'And I must tell you, my good friend, that they have been an inspiration to my people.'

'What is in these documents?'

'Prophecies, the construction of the star machine. Nothing that affects your security. But for us they have been as holy writ.'

Porlock released his hold on Tom's shoulder.

'Poor Grimbald. He lost his mind long ago. He could not tolerate our artificial world and we brought him to the surface.'

'But surely,' Tom said, 'he is a danger to you.'

'Not so. He is ignorant of the routes down and speaks with no coherence. Who would believe anything he might say? His family were for generations our archivists, but Grimbald was never fit for the task. I didn't know that he possessed any documents.'

They had travelled beyond the flares and the worst of the din but, looking down to the streets, Tom saw that clusters of lights were moving away from the Citadel in the direction they were taking.

'The archivist had terrible burns,' he remembered.

'I know nothing of that,' Porlock replied. 'I am surprised that he has survived at all.'

With these sombre words they came upon another door, approached by an iron staircase and again it was one that Tom recognised. He had tried it on that perilous journey and had been unable to open it. Now the assault party stopped at the foot of the stairway and the leader tapped the dwarf on the shoulder.

'Your route down, sir.'

The dwarf removed his bandage and took a key from his pocket.

'Gentlemen,' he said in portentous tones. 'You have served our cause with distinction. The fact will be recorded when our imminent victory has been won.'

The men, still with the bemused air of heroes who had prepared to fight a tiger only to find an empty cage, now moved off, leaving Tom and his companions to begin their descent. The way was steep, but there were lights high on the wall every twenty feet or so and these gave a faint and welcome luminescence.

'Died, you understand,' said Porlock, continuing doggedly with his jeremiad, 'before any of us was born. There's been no ruler since he died in that room all those years ago.'

The dwarf seemed hardly to be listening. Tom interpreted his expression and his movements as signifying acute concentration. A fist ground into the palm of the other hand. He took a few steps down at great speed, then paused for a few seconds nodding his head.

'Moreover,' Porlock went on heavily, 'the Blade has functioned very well without him all this time, has it not? It has, it seems, no need of a ruler. And without a leader to defeat, the organisation itself cannot be defeated.'

These mournful words hung in the air for some time. The trio descended in silence. At last the dwarf, who had been leading the way, stopped in his tracks and swung round on Porlock.

'My friend,' he said in superior tones. 'For a man of intelligence and breeding, you are singularly lacking in judgement. What do you suppose the Red Blade guards at the Citadel are doing at this moment. Are they not breaking into the top floor to discover what has become of their leader?'

Porlock shook his head.

'But it is forbidden,' he replied. 'How else should the system work? Look here, at this sheet.'

He held it out and a corner broke off and crumbled into dust.

'Death – "a cruel death" it says – to any man who dares.'

The dwarf cackled derisively.

'Common sense, my man! Comes cheap enough, they say! Will they stand by and allow their leader to be taken? Being discovered out there on the rooftops was the best thing that could have happened to us!'

Porlock, unaccustomed to this rough treatment, puckered his brow painfully.

'Imagine their consternation,' added the dwarf, 'when they find an empty room. Splintered bones, you tell me? Think how many interpretations may be made of those! And you have all the documents – all of them?'

He laughed hoarsely.

'Utter confusion! They must believe we have their leader, dead or alive. They will never be more ripe for attacking!'

He lowered his voice.

'Listen, my friend. What you have witnessed tonight is the beginning of the downfall of the Blade.'

They set off down the steps once more, Tom bringing up the rear.

'Some of your leaders have been captured,' he said. 'The eastern commander. . . .'

'It's true, alas. He was captured and tortured – and eventually killed.'

The dwarf, speaking over his shoulder, could not see the horror in Tom's face.

'A very brave man. He told them nothing. Now we have a new commander. One whom you know yourself, I do believe, from your time at the House of the Star.'

'Who is he?'

'Who is *she* is more to the point.'

'The Sphynx!'

The dwarf inclined his head.

'So she was sometimes called.'

'But she was arrested. I saw it myself. They interrogated her. The night of the fire.'

'A savage fire, Tom. It took hold, you know. Amazing that no one was killed. That beast Clem was badly burned in it and few will be sorry. The old men of the tribunal and their allies fled into the night and the city guard spent all their time fetching water. Our leader escaped.'

'It was she who arranged for me to stay at the House of the Star?'

'Of course. She was our only member there.'

'I think Clem suspected me all along.'

'Quite possible,' the dwarf said airily. 'It was a tricky game to play.'

'And what of the others there – Old Weasel, the musician. . . . '

'Ah, an interesting case. I think he may be of use to us. Nothing definite, mind, but a suggestion that he supports our cause.'

'He wasn't arrested that night?'

'No, indeed! Why should he have been?'

Tom made no reply, happy to think that the great survivor had outfaced disaster once again. He followed his companions down the steps, the air growing warmer by the minute. At last the dwarf signalled them to stop.

'We're almost there,' he said. 'When all is clear I shall leave. Allow some minutes to pass before you go.'

He held out his hand to Porlock.

'The revolution is at hand,' he said. 'I wish that you and your colleagues in the underground city could share it as we have long dreamed.'

Porlock shook the proffered hand.

'I am at this moment,' he said falteringly, as if reluctant to speak, 'engaged upon a mission . . . ' (he hesitated, gazed at Tom, checked the words that first came to his lips) ' . . . a mission which, if it should succeed – though I think it unlikely, almost impossible – would give you greater hope than ever you can have wished for.'

He reached for his spectacles, wiped them tremblingly on a richly-hued silk handkerchief and said no more.

37   Hovels

They were barely in time. Even as they slipped through the door and ran across the street the first lights could be seen rounding a bend not a hundred yards away. The men in front of the mob were running and there was a clamour of raised voices on the night air.

Porlock took him on an exhausting journey. It seemed that he knew every street in the city. They were soon well away from the Citadel and in another sector: they passed through with a curt exchange of passwords and kept pressing westward. It was long past the curfew hour and they several times had to dodge into doorways and alleys to avoid platoons of the city guard.

Tom wondered at his companion's stamina. He never flagged for a moment though they had been walking for all of an hour and had passed through two more sectors of the city. They spoke not a word between them.

At length they came to an area which was poorer than any he had yet seen. There were no large faceless buildings here, but small hovels shoulder to shoulder in tortuous streets. They slowed as they walked on uneven cobbles and Tom marvelled at the ingenuity of the builders, who seemed to have used any materials which had come to hand. One wall alone incorporated a rusted metal inn sign, fitted on its side, the discarded tailboard of a wooden cart and a wild assortment of ill-matching bricks. He assumed that the curfew must be in force here, but this did not prevent small movements on the darkened street.

Porlock led him forward until they could go no further. A long, low building with an unassuming turret at one end lay across the width of the thoroughfare. There were no lights inside, but Porlock did not check his stride. They passed through an arch and into a small courtyard. Steps led down to one side and the pair descended into a narrow corridor which, at last, had a few meagre flickering lamps along its wall. They passed a small, bare room in which Tom thought he saw, though he could not quite believe it, a man kneeling motionless. In another room a single candle burned unattended.

They entered a rather large space, dimly lit and rudely furnished with wooden tables and benches. Porlock sat down and motioned Tom to do the same. There was a smell which he did not know, a kind of austere fragrance. A plaque on the wall beside him was in a language that was strange to him.

'I'm sorry that I doubted you,' Porlock said in a low voice.

'Doubted me?'

'When we crossed from the Citadel. I could not help but wonder. I had planned the exercise as the final test.'

'Test of what?'

'Of you, Tom. Your trustworthiness. If you were treacherous you would surely have betrayed us then.'

Tom could not reply. He was not offended that his honesty should have been in doubt. It was rather that he could not fathom Porlock's deeper meaning. Why should he need to be tested?

'It has been a disturbing evening. Dreadful. I cannot come to terms with what we have learned about the Red Blade. That the leader should. . . .'

His voice tailed away. Tom, who had had time enough to consider the meaning of what they had discovered, found himself speaking eagerly.

'But it's wonderful,' he said. 'Don't you realise that it makes people accountable for the things they do! In the past they have blamed the organisation, blamed the leader of the Blade. They can't do that any more. They must see that it is they themselves who have brought evil to the city.

'It seems to me that people live by dreams. They gain strength from their dreams, rather than from facing the truth. What did we find when we revealed everything to the dwarf? He was angry to find that we had no weapons and could provide no army. He and his friends had invented a false underground city. Because they are good people they had invented a city of goodness, but they were ill-prepared for the complete truth.

'And it's the same with the Red Blade – just the same. The Blade members believe in a supreme, violent, powerful ruler

222

because that's the kind of ruler they wish to have. That is their dream – an evil dream. If they discovered the truth, if they saw those bones in the chair, they would feel cheated.

'Do members of the Blade carry out their vile deeds because they have a vile ruler? No. There is no ruler. That is their excuse. Their dream excuses them. What did that writing say: "Power is with a ghost, because the living wish it so."

'And the good people, who do nothing while they wait for deliverance from underground. Will deliverance come? No. They must provide their own. The dream has prevented them from doing what they should have done. Always blame the dream.

'I long for the day when there are no dreams left!'

He found himself shaking from the intensity of the outburst. He had not planned any of it: the words had seemed to come of their own accord. Porlock had a queer, sleepwalker's expression on his face.

'No dreams,' he echoed, strangely. 'Away with dreams.'

Tom leant forward.

'Are you unwell?'

'No, not unwell. I was recalling a time, years ago, when the very same words were spoken to me.... Let's be done with excuses. Answer for our own actions. No dreams, false dreams. An end to dreams.'

He spoke slowly, as if in a trance.

'Our lives are our own. We make our own decisions. None but ourselves to take the blame. Away with dreams.... I believed it then.'

He closed his eyes and the silence seemed to fall about them. Nobody came. The lights flickered on the walls, weakly.

'I am a rational man.'

Porlock opened his eyes and they had an intensity Tom had not seen before. His voice began to rise.

'Am I then to believe in portents and prophecies? What is this that is demanded of me? Should I now renounce the power of reason?'

Tom, astounded, started back.

'Is the world haunted? Are we ruled by magic, child's play?'

At this moment a figure passed swiftly along the corridor. It was gone in a moment but Tom recognised it, with a panic of incredulity, as the boy with the green scarf. He leapt to his feet.

'Wait!' he cried. 'I know you!'

But Porlock, who had also seen the boy, grabbed Tom by the arm and pulled him down.

'No. Not yet. Not until I have told you.'

'Told me?'

'The whole story. First you must hear me out and then you can decide what you will do.'

38   The Poet of the Wilderness

'Several years ago,' Porlock began, 'a man arrived in the city after a long, exhausting journey. He entered through the east gate and found lodgings in that sector.

'He was a poet. But more than that, he was a man dedicated to the cause of truth and beauty and justice. Soon people began to know of him. They came to visit him, to hear his poems and to hear him talk – for he talked wonderfully – of the world as it was and the world as it might one day become.

'In those times the Red Blade, though powerful, had not yet strangled the city with its network of spies and hired killers. It was a while before news of this man reached the Citadel. Then the message went out to silence him.

'Aware of the threat to his life, he began to move about the city. Wherever he appeared there were many who thronged to hear him and to offer him what protection they could. In return he offered them hope. One notable poem has inspired thousands to keep a grasp of their courage: "Wear me as your spiked heel...."'

Tom, breaking in eagerly, picked up the quotation.

'I will bite into ice for you!'

'You know it?'

'I have read the words more than once. They are on a ruined monument not far from the House of the Star.'

Porlock nodded.

'This man was led to the underground city via the house you know by the east gate. But, although he was gone, the people had been inspired. They rose up. For a time certain parts of the city were seized from the Blade.

'Revenge, when it came, was terrible. Many were killed cruelly, barbarously. The statues and monuments which celebrated

225

freedom were dismantled. The bastion of those who fought for liberty – a large building in the eastern sector – was razed to the ground. Only rubble remains. This was the time when the different sectors were sealed off from one another and the good people began to use the rooftops as the only area safe for them.'

'This man,' Tom asked. 'What did he call himself?'

'He gave no name. He said no man should bear a name until he was free. The people were not free. But his poems he signed with the initials TW. Whether because of this and the fact that he came from far off I am uncertain, but he became known as the Poet of the Wilderness.'

'Those initials,' Tom said, 'are my father's.'

Porlock's face was expressionless.

'They are the initials of many people, my good friend. I am no romantic: no use to build a castle of theory on the sands of coincidence.'

'That is not all. There are things that you do not know.'

With a gesture that seemed more than weariness, almost a token of defeat, Porlock bent his head between his hands.

'Soon after I arrived in the city,' Tom said, 'I met the eastern commander, the man they killed. That was also the time when I first met the dwarf. In a small room which they used as a cell I found a book of maps with a mark against my own part of the country.'

'The wilderness is vast.'

'You don't understand,' Tom persisted. 'My very own village had been circled with ink. A place so small.'

Porlock only nodded.

'In the House of the Star I sang a song from my home village. An old man told me that, years before, the same song had been sung there by a stranger who was known as the Poet of the Wilderness.'

Porlock raised his head and gazed into the gloom, his mind seemingly far away.

'He was a singer of songs,' he said. 'He brought us many of them, wonderful songs. Our evening chorus was one of his gifts to us.'

Tom found himself clutching Porlock by the arm.

'How often,' he cried, 'was that song sung to me by my mother as a child!'

226

One of the lamps guttered and was spent. Porlock took out his handkerchief and dabbed it lightly against his brow.

'I will tell you how it was. When he arrived underground we did not enjoy the harmony which you have witnessed among us. All communities have their times of growth, their times of decay. We were not happy then and this man transformed our lives, revitalised us.

'You saw how the assembly greeted that picture in the debating chamber – the ecstasy! They thought it was the Wilderness Poet, whom they revere as a saint.

'He regenerated our love of beauty – beauty of the eye, beauty of the word, beauty of the way people may live together. He wrote us poems, he taught us songs, he gave us a renewed belief in ourselves. . . . And then he left us.'

'Left you? Where did he go? Why?'

'The last lesson he taught us – those of us who would listen – is that the glory of our underground city is not sufficient. We said, "You would not take a name on the surface where evil reigns supreme. Let us give you a name underground". But he would not accept it. "When the city above is as the city beneath," he would say, "I will be known as who I am".

'He told us that virtue was nothing more than a delightful device unless put to the test – an imitation sunburst in a cavern, he said. We had beauty, but a beauty tamed and protected. A beauty of dreams. You could not care for poor Grimbald underground, he told us, because he was not part of your beautiful dream. He would return to the surface city to discover whether beauty could. . . .'

He paused, calling the words back from the past.

' . . . whether beauty could enter the flames and emerge glowing rich.'

Another lamp died. Although so close, Tom could not clearly make out Porlock's features in the murk.

'I was his disciple, you see. I learned all these things from him. This is why I have tried to bring together the underground city and the good people above. Only . . . ' – he faltered – ' . . . I found that I lacked the strength to do as he did.'

Tom rose to his feet.

'You talk,' he said fiercely, 'but you don't tell me what I need to know. All along you have thwarted me. You have used me and refused to acknowledge that the man you speak of is my father. Deny that if you can!'

'I won't. I can't. Of course I have recognised all along that you might be the son of this man. Of course it is possible. Possible. You came in from the east. You speak with the accent, the man Clutt assured me of that.'

'All those coincidences!'

'Yes, yes. Coincidences. The picture and so forth. I agree. But, you see, I have hoped desperately from the start that the Poet is *not* your father. I have put your credentials and your good faith to the test as often as I could. I have done this partly for your own good, but especially for the city as a whole. It will seem harsh of me to say so, but I sincerely hope that you are disappointed in your quest.'

Tom, dumbfounded, sat down again.

'I don't understand.'

'Allow me to continue with my story. From the first I realised that the Poet was an exceptional man. I owed him everything, even my very life. I shall never repay that debt. But we differed in one respect. I believed in the rule of reason, of logic if you like. He taught the power of mystery, of prophecy, of hidden influences.

'I fear those influences, Tom. I fear that they may be used by evil people as well as good. I am a rational man.'

The repetition of this phrase seemed somehow to mesmerise him. He sat motionless for a while.

'Go on,' Tom said.

'When the Poet returned to the surface city he was a hunted man. He lived a fugitive life. But his very presence in the place inspired the people. They wanted to make him their city lord, in name if not in reality. He said the time was not ripe. He taught that the time of their release would come, according to prophecy.

'He misunderstood the prohpecy.'

'How?'

'There is a double prediction. Perhaps you know it. A boy like a tick entering the wool of the sheep, drinking the blood of the city. Another, following, seeking a father. . . . I told him he was a fool to set store by it.'

'The first boy,' Tom said, 'was the Red Blade founder. Isn't that the story?'

'It was what he believed then. And he believed – why, I don't know – that the second boy would be his own son. "Find him for me", he said. "Swear you will find him". I am a rational man. I counted the prophecy as so much nonsense. I doubted the son would ever arrive from such a distance. I made the vow.'

He paused and the pause extended. His breathing, grown tremulous, sounded deafening in the darkness. When he spoke it was in little more than a whisper.

'Eventually a lad entered the eastern gate looking for his father. I questioned him a little and took him to the Poet. . . . He was not the son. In reality he had not travelled a journey and was not looking for a father. He was an innocent waif, a simpleton if the truth be told, cynically manipulated by the Red Blade. A decoy. Such, you see, is the deviousness of prophecy. They captured the Poet.'

Here he removed his spectacles, tossed them onto the table and pressed his fists against his temples. Tom forced himself to ask the question.

'Killed him?'

'No. Not killed him. Not that.'

'Then what?'

A sound of grief held in Porlock's throat. For a while he could not speak. Then he forced himself into an upright posture and in the process his spectacles were swept to the floor. The glass smashed, tinkling.

'A monumental jest,' he said bitterly. 'The symbol of truth is an ever-open eye and so. . . . '

'They. . . . '

'They deprived . . . they took out his eyes.'

He bent to the floor to gather the pieces of his spectacles, his face hidden. Tom shivered. They had taken out his eyes. It was not warm in the room but he had been unaware of the cold until now. And the darkness. They had taken out his eyes! Minutes passed before Porlock spoke again.

'They released him into the city as an example to others who might oppose the Blade. Fools! Those who live by violence can judge the world only in terms of pain. His influence was undiminished.

'Afterwards he told me that his suffering was pre-ordained.

He meant it as a kindness to me, as if it would lighten the burden. That I should be the tool of prophecy, the destined cause of that agony! Can you wonder that I despise prophecies? Do you understand why I doubt you all I can?'

'But if you really don't believe. . . . '

'Ha! You think the matter is so simple? The strongest of us have weak moments, times when we think the world may indeed be governed by these weird forces. The world has yet to discover the complete sceptic.'

'Where did the Poet go?' Tom asked urgently.

'A sect of poor and humble priests took him in,' Porlock replied. 'A safe place. His only companion is the weak-minded lad who led the Blade's agents to him. He is messenger, watcher, even son to him until his own son shall arrive.'

'The second boy,' Tom said.

'The very nub of the matter. The fulfilment of prophecy. Let's say I'm entirely rational and rule these fancies out. Which I do. They're insane. Nevertheless there are many who do believe them – many who will act upon them and many who fear them.'

'But why should they?'

'Because when that second prophecy is fulfilled – when it *seems* to have been fulfilled with the arrival of his son – the Poet will call on the people to rise up. Your dwarf thinks he has sufficient support, but his forces and the Blade are evenly matched, believe me. The poet speaks and the city is aflame with revolution.'

'A just revolution which you surely support!'

'I support a revolution, but not at any price. There are linked prophecies which may come to pass simply because they seem inevitable. "Like a steel comb he will enter the sheep's wool, rake out the clinging vermin, and" – mark this well, Tom – "mastery shall be restored to the virtuous and the sons of the virtuous and the city will be ruled as in former times."'

'I don't follow this. Surely it foretells a reign of peace and justice.'

'You have said the word yourself: a *reign*. Are we to return to the old ways when one man ruled the city? Do you not see the Poet established as sole city lord?'

'But a good man. You have said so.'

'Are we to return to the control of a dictator, however benign? Hasn't history taught us the danger of that? The power passed down from father to son' – here he gave a tug on Tom's arm – 'and in time abused, turned against the people. Can anyone truly say he knows how he will act with such power at his command. Can *you*?

'I have long sought a liaison between our underground city, which has no dictator, and the people of the rooftops who seek a return to the people's rule of the days before the Red Blade.

'Now you arrive and I am bounden by my vow. But I ask you, in all seriousness, whether it is better to turn now while there is time and go back from whence you came. You have spoken passionately about dreams and responsibility and the myth of leadership. Turn back before you inherit a whole city.'

They heard a sound from within the building. The last two lamps failed at the same moment. Tom thought not only of his father but of Sonia in the underground city.

'I can't return,' he said simply.

'Then wait. I have done my duty.'

He touched Tom lightly on the shoulder and slipped away. The darkness seemed to thicken. It gathered round him. The sound came again: a door. There were footsteps. He was gradually aware of a faint glow from the corridor.

It was a candle. The boy with the green scarf held it high so as better to see him. But his companion, a large man whose beard glinted silver in the dancing light, was not troubled by the gloom. He stepped forward, his arms stretched wide, and Tom leapt towards him, his own eyes blurred with tears.